A
NORTHERN
REBEL

Mary & Tim (handwritten inscription)

A NORTHERN REBEL

SECOND EDITION

I hope you enjoy my novel! (handwritten inscription)

JOHN J SCHAFFER

John J Schaffer (signature)

TATE PUBLISHING
AND ENTERPRISES, LLC

Published by Tate Publishing & Enterprises, LLC
127 E. Trade Center Terrace | Mustang, Oklahoma 73064 USA
1.888.361.9473 | www.tatepublishing.com

Tate Publishing is committed to excellence in the publishing industry. The company reflects the philosophy established by the founders, based on Psalm 68:11,
"The Lord gave the word and great was the company of those who published it."

Book design copyright © 2016 by Tate Publishing, LLC. All rights reserved.
Cover design by Christina Hicks
Interior design by Jomar Ouano
Cover photo of the Orton Plantation painted by Leah [Radel] Weaver and used with the kind permission of her sons, James and Michael.

Published in the United States of America

ISBN: 978-1-68270-877-4
1. Fiction / Historical
2. Fiction / Romance / Historical
15.12.02

This book is dedicated to God for his inspiration and guidance; to Oprah Winfrey, for giving me the courage and conviction to believe I could write a book; to my wife, Diane, for her undying love and support; and lastly to the thousands of Africans, who were unfairly kidnapped and enslaved, during this dark period in our nation's history, who could have used a few Jameson Hartford's in their lives.

"The only thing necessary for evil to triumph
Is for good men to do nothing"

Edmund Burke
British Statesman and Philosopher 1729 -1797

"Develop enough courage so that you can stand up for yourself
And then stand up for somebody else"

Maya Angelou
Poet, Novelist, Actress, Educator, Civil Rights Activist
1928–Present

"There is no greater gift you can give or receive than to honor your calling.
It's why you were born; and how you become most truly alive."

Oprah Winfrey
Talk Show Host, Producer/Actress,
TV Pioneer, Philanthropist, Inspirational Motivator
1954 – Present

CHAPTERS

FOREWORD

The original premise for my story arose in grammar school as I learned about the Civil War and the evils of slavery and tried to understand how a supposedly civilized people could condone the oppression of other people. It was my first exposure to bigotry and racism, and I could not comprehend it. I questioned as to why this was tolerated and was told it was solely for free labor. I disagreed and added that if I had been alive during that time period, and owned a plantation, that I would have freed everyone. I was commended, but told that the other plantation owners and the townspeople would never have allowed it and would have prevented me from doing so at all costs. The fact that I was told I could not do the right thing perplexed me, stayed with me and made me remember that conversation forever. I repeated it years later when I engaged in extensive discussions at several civil rights meetings I attended, while in high school and college in the 70's. The general consensus of those dialogues was that one man could not have made a difference; but I never stopped believing that he could. I then began to think about my beliefs as a story and composed various scenes in my mind, especially when I had trouble falling asleep at night. I fashioned almost the entire manuscript in this manner and kept that story tucked inside me for 30 years. I am glad I could finally put it into words and tell the world that one person can always effect a change. I hope you enjoy the story and take its message of freedom and equality for all, with you, as you journey through life.

Chapter 1

SOUTHBOUND

The train pulled out of Boston bound for Charleston, South Carolina. Jameson Hartford and his wife, Abigail, were on board finding their way back to their native soil. It was only two days ago on April 3, 1861, the telegram that would change their lives forever arrived at their Boston residence on the shores of the St. Charles River. It read:

> We're sorry to inform you of the untimely death of your brother, Josiah. STOP. It is imperative that you return to the town of Willow Hills at once. STOP. As the last surviving son of Jebediah Hartford, you are the sole heir to the Serenity Plantation and all of its contents and possessions. STOP. Please contact this office at your earliest convenience, and apprise us of your intentions with regards to this matter. STOP. We await your reply.
>
> Sincerely,
> Mister Nicholas Mansfield, Esq.
> Attorney-at-law
> Willow Hills, South Carolina

Jameson was stunned by the sad news, but the truth of the matter was that he had not kept in touch with his estranged brother for many years. Still, he was sorry that now he would never be able to make amends. He replied with a return wire, stating that he and his wife would be leaving for Charleston on Tuesday aboard the 6:00 a.m. train and would arrive late afternoon the following day. He would be pleased if someone could meet them and furnish transportation to the plantation. Nicholas Mansfield wired that he would personally be at the station to help them through this trying time. Of course, he was the executor of the will and was getting paid handsomely to expedite the matter.

They had both arisen quite early that day in order to make the first train and were fairly tired. Jameson instinctively let his head fall back on the soft cushion of his seat and began to ponder the events that had led up to this day. Before long he had drifted into an uneasy sleep, and characters and events became as alive as they had been that fateful day many years ago.

Suddenly he was back on the Serenity Plantation in all its majesty with his family and friends, attending the annual summer barbeque hosted by the Hartfords. The yearly event was the place to be, and everyone—from their acquaintances in town to all the people from the neighboring plantations—eagerly accepted the invitation and looked forward to the chance to eat good food and rekindle friendships.

The women were concerned with everyday issues: the price of groceries, the value of education, and the latest fashions from Europe. The men, however, were all assembled in the huge study drinking brandy, smoking cigars, and discussing the important issues of the day. Jameson, his father Jebediah, and his younger brother, Josiah, were all there to thrash out the problems they were having with the Northerners.

Jebediah Hartford was a tall, aristocratic soul in his light-colored waistcoat with matching trousers and hat. He was a stern gentleman who always spoke his mind, and the full mustache he sported made him look even more menacing. His ideals were held by mostly everyone there, including his son, Josiah; only Jameson was of a different breed. In fact, Jameson more closely resembled his mother, while Josiah was the spitting image of his father, ensuring him most favored child status. As usual, Jebediah was the first to speak up.

"Those damn Yankees are driving the prices of cotton and tobacco down in an attempt to bring the South to its knees and let the rich Northern bankers purchase our land at a fraction of its value, in effect stealing it from under us, the rightful owners. We can't let that Yankee scum get away with this. We have to protect what is rightfully ours, no matter what the cost, even if it's war!"

Nicholas Mansfield and all the others agreed wholeheartedly.

"We're ready to fight if it comes to that," said Mister Higgins, the owner of the Moors Plantation. He was a dangerously frightened man of smaller statue.

Worried and extremely upset, he continued with his nervous rant. "Imagine, they're even trying to outlaw slavery. Why, who will plow our fields, plant our crops, and clean our homes?"

"Excuse me, Mister Higgins sir," Jameson interrupted, "but I believe you could hire people to do those jobs, pay them a fair wage, and still make a decent profit."

"And what would I do with my slaves?"

"Free them!"

"Free them! Ha, ha, Jameson, that's a good one."

In unison the entire group of men burst into laughter at the thought of this idea from the brash young man.

"That's enough of that talk, Jameson," his father scolded. "I told you to forget that nonsense and never mention it again, didn't I?"

"Yes, sir, you did, and I don't want to go against your wishes but I really feel that slavery is wrong, and we really could survive without it."

"Stop that ridiculous talk, Jameson, now!"

The crowd was growing visibly upset, Jameson was starting to be labeled a Northern sympathizer, and his father did not take that kind of comparison lightly. He chastised his son even further to ensure his reputation and his son's silence, making a spectacle of the boy in front of all their friends.

Jameson had only dared to voice his opposition to slavery a few times before but solely in the privacy of his own home, being constantly rebuffed by his father and brother. In fact, he would not even refer to them as slaves. He said it was demeaning and instead called them his "workers." But this time was different; he had a captive audience and could not hold his tongue any longer. Something deep down inside of him gave him the courage he required and he became determined to stand up for his beliefs, forcing a debate with his detractors; a debate he had planned on for some time and one he was sure he could win. It was serious now and a war was coming, surely these people would listen to reason, there was so much at stake.

"Daddy, please listen to me, let me explain my stance, you and all these people are mistaken. Slavery is immoral, and we can and should abolish it. You can hire them back as your workers if you desire, but pay them a decent wage so they can survive. They should be free men, not indentured servants."

His father abruptly turned to face his disrespectful son. He grabbed Jameson by his upper arms and pinned him up against the wall.

"I'm telling you this for the last time, boy. Don't bring this topic up ever again. Your brother has no problem with the current state of affairs. Why should you?"

"Please, all I'm asking is that everyone should consider the idea. They are, after all, human beings."

"You're not acting like a son of mine, Jameson. You're showing weakness. Maybe you haven't got the stomach to run this plantation and make it profitable. Maybe I've misjudged you and you really are a Yankee sympathizer at heart."

This led to an outburst of laughter from his brother, the guests, and perhaps most embarrassingly of all, from his wife, Abigail, who had just entered the room. Jameson could not contain his humiliation as he turned beet red. He had to save face and was determined to stand up for what he believed was right. He squeezed out of his father's hands and dared to raise his voice yet again, unable to restrain his repugnance any longer.

"Daddy, please let me speak. I can prove to all of you that you can run the plantation just as effectively using hired workers if you would only listen. I have studied on it and completed some calculations and, if you will allow me, I can show you how you can make just as much money without slavery. Besides, then the northerners will have no quarrel with us and there will be no need to go to war."

One of the guests yelled out, "War, we're not afraid of war with the Yankees, we can beat 'em, can't we gentlemen?"

A rousing, "You bet"… "yes we can"… "no doubt about it," filled the room.

But the guests were growing angry, and Jebediah's loyalty to the South was being questioned.

"That's enough, Jameson!" his father demanded.

"It only takes one man, or boy, to stir up a whole hornets nest of trouble that can spread throughout the South like a boll weevil blight," claimed Mister Higgins.

Jameson, trying to save face, added rather boldly, "When it comes time for me to be in charge of this plantation, I will free those poor people and prove it to all of you."

Jebediah, infuriated that his son would raise his voice and go against his father's orders, bellowed his disapproval. "You think I would leave my plantation to the likes of you? No, you are hereby disinherited! From this day forward I will leave all my possessions to your younger brother, Josiah. What do you think of that? You're not so smart now, are you?"

Jameson looked around, ashamed, and disgraced. His brother was beaming, the crowd was pleased, and his wife was in shock. He wasn't finished, however, and spoke up yet again, this time in a humble almost apologetic tone.

"Daddy you wouldn't do that, would you? Just because of my principles. You simply can't disown me because of my beliefs."

"Don't threaten me boy, I won't stand for such disrespect from a young inexperienced fool."

Jebediah's face turned a blood red while his eyes glared at his rebellious son, then in a fit of extreme uncontrolled anger, he sent a backhanded slap directly to his son's face, knocking him to the ground. He was furious now for being questioned by his insolent son and made to look like a fool in front of his friends. Jebediah would win this altercation at any cost.

"Do I have to treat you like one of my slaves to make you obey me? I can leave my legacy to whomever I please. I provide a good life for you and your wife here, and this is the thanks I get? You apologize to me at once and tell all of these good Southern people you're wrong. Then ask me to forgive you."

Jameson felt ashamed as he lie there on the floor. He was like a whipped puppy and wanted to lash out at the man who had embarrassed him in front of all his neighbors and friends, but his eye suddenly caught the figure of his mother standing in the doorway. Her face was filled with sorrow, for her firstborn son, as she too wanted to act on her boy's behalf, but dare not interfere. This was a man's fight and her intervention would only cause further humiliation for her beleaguered son.

As Jameson gazed upon his mother, his thoughts returned to a time many years ago when he was younger and he accidentally happened to stumble upon her one day in the back of the kitchen. It was the middle of the day and she was standing there with a black woman who was clutching her little child. They were alarmed by his intrusion and terrified that they had been discovered.

"Jameson, what are you doing here?"

"I came in to get a drink, I was thirsty. Mama, who are these people? Are we getting new slaves?"

His mother hesitated for a moment, she looked at the careworn mother and her frail child ready to invent a story that any child would accept as truth then stopped and decided to tell her son the cruel reality.

"Jameson, I am helping these two people to escape and find freedom in the north."

Jameson was puzzled and looked very confused.

"Jameson, my son, slavery is wrong. No person has the right to own another person and force them to toil in the fields. It is an aberration against God and all his commandments. These people are human beings the same as we are, and no human being is better than another, we are all equal. I want you to understand that." She paused for a second gazing at the baffled look on her son's face and then continued, "I have made contacts with other people who feel the same way I do and we are helping these poor unfortunate souls to escape through a connection of safe houses and roads. We call it the underground railroad."

"Does daddy know about this?"

"No son, he would not approve and would try to stop us in our efforts to save these people."

Jameson again looked confused, "Maybe you could explain it to him."

"He would not understand, and does not want to understand. Jameson, what I am doing is against the law, but I feel in my soul that it is the right thing to do and I must follow my conscience. I would ask you not to tell your father or anyone else what you saw here today. Your father would start an argument with me; one that we have had many times before, then he would punish this woman, take her little girl away from her and sell her to another plantation. He would probably never trust me again. I can't tell you what to do but I ask you to search your soul and then follow your conscience. But, know this; I am doing what I believe is right in the eyes of God. We could just as well hire workers, pay them a fair wage and free all our slaves. That is the right thing to do and what I would do if I were in charge of this plantation. I hope you understand and respect all life regardless of color."

Jameson stared at his mother, then at the little girl and her mother and began to question in his mind something he had just accepted as a normal way of life all these years. Suddenly the impressionable youngster experienced an epiphany.

He walked over to his mother, hugged her and said, "I won't tell daddy or anyone. I think you are right mama. In fact I will try to help you, if you want me to."

She hugged him in return and beamed a broad smile as any proud mother would do replying, "Thank you, Jameson, but I don't want you to put yourself in harm's way and get in any trouble with your father. Just your silence is all I need for right now, understand?"

Jameson nodded, smiled at the two black women and said, "Good luck, I hope you make it to the north."

His father was approaching the front door, calling his name and wondering what had happened to his youngest son. The door knob turned as the door slid open. The two slaves and Jameson's mother stood terrified and held their breaths, fearing they had been caught. Jameson looked at the forlorn woman, her raggedy child and his panicked mother; he instantly knew what he must do. Without hesitation, he quickly turned and ran toward the incoming figure. He grabbed his father's hand and lead him back outside and away from the hopeful escapees; forgetting the drink of water that had sent into the house in the first place. Turning, he smiled at the threesome and gave a wink; the women sighed in relief and proceeded with their plans.

The demeanor of the young Jameson changed that day forever. He treated all the slaves with kindness and understanding, always trying to lighten their load and make their lives easier and more bearable, much to the chagrin of his father and brother.

The two slaves never did succeed in their escape. Somehow the plot and the route were compromised and they were recaptured while on the road to freedom. The mother was beaten for trying to escape and, as an added punishment; her daughter was taken from her and sold to another plantation. Sadly, they were never to see each other again. Unfortunately, this was not an uncommon occurrence as the poor workers were at the mercy of the plantation owner; he could do as he pleased, however morally wrong and reprehensible it was.

Jameson had kept the secret all these years and now was voicing his opposition and finding out why his mother had told him to remain silent. She was right. She knew his father, and Jameson had gravely miscalculated the situation. He knew his father wanted to humiliate him in front of everyone and bring to an end his opposition once and for all.

He lifted himself off the floor, brushed off the dirt from his waistcoat and pants, looked at his father and broke the dead silence by calmly replying, "Father, I'm sorry that I am such a disappointment to you, but I don't share your feelings. I can't condone this mistreatment of people of color. I'm sorry, but I must remain true to my beliefs."

Jebediah was now blind with anger that his direct order was being ignored and he screamed, "If that's what you want, get out! You are no longer my son. Remove yourself from my plantation. Try to make it on your own, if you can. Get out today! Go! Now!"

"You can send me away, but I can't live with the guilt and shame of enslaving these poor people. That's not the legacy for which I want to be remembered."

With his head held high, Jameson strode out of the den, taking an unwilling Abigail along with him. Jameson could hear his father continue to curse and rant all the way to his bedroom as he hurriedly prepared to pack his and Abigail's belongings. While the other guests were congratulating Jebediah on doing what was necessary to preserve the Confederacy, Jameson was trembling in fear. There was no turning back now; the incident had progressed way too far for any remorse.

Even his mother could not persuade her stubborn husband to relent and forgive a brash son. The die had been cast and there was no turning back, no room for repentance or regret. Abigail's pleadings also fell on deaf ears; she did not want to leave and tried to persuade Jameson to accept the status quo, as all the other Southern plantation owners had, but she was his wife and was obligated to follow her husband, wherever life would lead them.

Jameson awoke startled, bathed in sweat from the all too real nightmare. The recurrent dream took its toll, however, leaving him visibly shaken.

Abigail asked him, "What's wrong, Jameson? What happened?"

Jameson shrugged it off. "I just had a bad dream, nothing to worry about."

He did not believe that for a second and knew that all that bigotry still existed, and it may even be worse than before.

Upon his exile from Serenity, Jameson set his sights northward where he felt the people held beliefs similar to his own. He settled in Boston, Massachusetts, and started a new life.

Jameson Hartford was a rather tall, blue-eyed, handsome figure of a man; he possessed all the attributes of a Southern gentleman. He was strong yet polite, outgoing yet refined in his nature. He had lost most of his Southern accent during his ten years in Boston, yet all the Northern aristocrats could still detect some of that "drawl."

Abigail, on the other hand, was fair, brunette, and brown-eyed. Her hair was always neatly coiffed, swept up upon her head. She pretended to be frail, like her mother, so others would feel guilty and be inclined to take care of her. She was always complaining on one thing or another. It was too hot, too cold, she had a headache, nothing was ever right. She was the daughter of Beau Lansing of Tall Oaks, a neighboring plantation, and she enjoyed all the benefits of being a privileged lady of a Southern household. Truth be told, Abigail kind of liked being waited on and doted upon by the indentured servants. She could not understand her husband's obsession with abolishing it and tried unsuccessfully many times to change his mind. Yet being a loyal and obedient wife meant she had to depart along with him when he was driven out by his father.

Jameson had acquired a job at the First Bank of Boston as a teller and worked his way up to the vice president position. He purchased a nice home overlooking the St. Charles River and was able to employ two people to clean and cook, permitting Abigail a lot of leisure time to enjoy some of the finer things in the life of a family in the 1850s. She attended afternoon tea parties, sat on a few women's suffragette councils, and rubbed elbows with the local social dignitaries. She relished it. They almost had it all.

The one thing that they both desperately desired was children. For some reason, Abigail could not conceive a child. They were both young and healthy and were checked out by the area's finest physicians; yet for some reason, children eluded them. The doctors prescribed rest and relaxation. Perhaps they were both too active—him at work, her with all her pet projects. Yet they pursued their lifestyles eagerly, seeming to think they had all the time in the world.

When the telegram came, Jameson asked for a leave of absence from his job in order to return to South Carolina and tend to his family's affairs. Abigail saw it as a chance to rekindle a dying romance and perhaps, at long last, they would be able to have children. Besides, she couldn't wait to see her parents again and the life she so loved on the plantation but was forced to leave because of Jameson.

Now they were on their way back to Serenity for the first time in ten years. Jameson did not even return when his parents died in the flu epidemic of 1850. In fact, his brother, Josiah, did not bother to contact him, lest he try to wrest control of the plantation from his younger brother. Even when he found out after the fact, he made no effort to return.

During all his time of exile, Jameson had only received one letter from his mother, wishing him well and informing him that his father had discovered their secret, helping slaves escape to the north. She wrote how upset he was with her and forbid her to continue in her ways. He wanted to know who else was involved and she refused to answer. When she declined to give up her other contacts, he made sure she was never alone again and hired a guardian so no other temptations would arise. She was in effect under house arrest and constantly watched.

Jameson immediately sat down and crafted a carefully worded reply, but no other letters or telegrams were forthcoming, no doubt intercepted by his father before they could reach the intended recipient. He wished he could have returned to help her, and now perhaps his time had arrived.

The train thundered on, and again Jameson began to speak of old, troublesome dreams. He would now finally get the chance to prove to the rest of Willow Hills how he could run a successful plantation without the need for slavery.

"It won't be long until I free them," boasted Jameson." I will free all of them, and the town will see that slavery is an unnecessary evil."

Abigail let him have his moment but feared for him. The tight little community would never allow him to fulfill his dream. The town would eliminate the cause—Jameson—before his freedom disease could spread and cause an epidemic. He was expendable; there was no doubt about it. They had all heard the tales of others who had tried to do the same thing and met a dastardly fate. Abigail was scared that her husband would meet the same end.

The train was bringing both of them to a confrontation neither of them anticipated. She stared out at the nameless towns and countless changes of scenery that whizzed by her window, and she was scared. The hypnotic sound of the steel wheels on the rails was somehow strangely comforting and seemed to bring peace to both of them, if only for the moment.

The locomotive finally pulled into Charleston, South Carolina, a sizable city with cobblestone roads and large complexes, housing various businesses and shops. It was bustling with people and carriages, all hurrying to one place and another. It was loud and lamp-lit, but it did not compare to Boston in size and stature. Still, it was something to behold, a welcoming sight after such a long rail trip.

Jameson and Abigail disembarked and retrieved their luggage from amongst the other valises and chests.

"Jameson, Jameson Hartford," a voice cried out.

They turned around to find Nicholas Mansfield, the attorney. He was there waiting for them as he had promised in his wire. He was a man of below-average height, though rather stout, with a large stovepipe hat upon his head, no doubt to make him feel taller than the stature life had bestowed upon him.

"How was your trip?" he asked.

"Long and uncomfortable," Abigail piped in.

Nicholas replied, "That's too bad. I'm afraid you're in for a little more unhappiness. I have a horse and carriage waiting to take you to Serenity. I hope it meets with your approval. It's the only manner of transportation available to get you to the plantation from the rail station."

"Oh great." Abigail sighed.

"That's fine," said Jameson. "It's been a long trip. I can't wait to see the place again. How does it look?"

"It's the same, sir. Nothing much changes down here," said Nicholas. He turned and called to his servant, "Sammy, pick up these bags and take them to the carriage. Then help these nice folks into their seats. Come on. Hurry it up." He turned to Jameson. "You have to push them, or they move at a snail's pace."

"I'll carry my own bags and Abigail's also," said Jameson, "no need to trouble him."

"It's no trouble. That's what he's here for," said Nicholas. "It's his job. Now come on. We have to hurry so we can get there before nightfall."

Off to the side, Jameson noticed a lot of commotion.

"What's going on over there?" he queried.

"Oh that, that's just a slave auction. Nothing to concern you, sir," said Nicholas as he tried to persuade the two visitors to keep moving along.

But Jameson stood there and watched as the black men and women in chains and tattered clothes were being sold to the highest bidder. They were scared and confused. They did not understand what was happening to them. One by one, they were forced up onto the platform by a husky, bearded man with a patch over one eye and a tri-corn hat pressed tightly upon his head. He wore a naval captain's uniform that seemed out of place. Aiding and abetting him was his protégé, who appeared to be a black man.

The poor blacks were put on exhibition and exchanged for cash. As they were sold, they were loaded onto a buckboard, taken on a ride to a strange place, and pressed into labor for the rest of their lives. Jameson shook his head in disgust, vowing to himself to help these poor forlorn people.

"Who is that?" Jameson asked, pointing at the uniformed man.

"That's Mordechai LeBrute. He used to command a slave ship to Africa before it was outlawed. He still fancies himself a captain, though now he just manages the slave auction."

"You mean he used to kidnap the poor Negroes from their homeland, shanghai them, if you will, and bring them here?"

"Oh, Mister Hartford, you make it sound so horrible."

"It is horrible, sir. Men have no right to do this to other men. And what, may I ask, happens to the people who do not get sold?"

"I don't know. I suppose someone will buy them. If not, well… I'm not sure. I never thought about it. They don't return them to Africa. I am sure of that," Nicholas said, laughing.

Jameson, stunned, snapped back, "I find no humor in this situation. In fact, I find it appalling."

He stared in bewilderment and disbelief at all the so-called upstanding citizens bidding feverishly to purchase other human beings. He wondered if one person would be able to change the mindset of so many. He was up to the challenge, however, and would certainly try his best.

Nicholas Mansfield tapped him on the shoulder and said, "We have to leave now, sir."

At the coach, Sammy provided the booster step for them to climb inside. The coach was made of polished wood and completely encased the passengers. Surprisingly, it accommodated the three of them quite comfortably. Sammy the driver sat apart from them up in front, totally exposed to the elements. The ride on the unpaved road was bumpy but not all together unpleasant. They were jostled and occasionally jolted, as one of the coach wheels would hit a deep rut.

"Be careful up there, Sammy," Nicholas ordered.

"Sorry, sir," Sammy responded.

The scent of honeysuckle filled the warm, humid spring air that seemed to engulf them and hold on tight. The climate was a sudden change from the colder, rainy weather that they had just left in Boston, and neither guest was properly dressed for the unexpected heat, making the trip even more unbearable.

Jameson asked Nicholas how his brother had died.

Nicholas said, "It was a terrible accident. He was out hunting, fell off his horse, and broke his neck. It was very unfortunate. Let me expresses my deepest sorrow." He paused, and then he added, "If I may be so bold, sir, can I ask you what your intentions are for the plantation? Do you plan to sell it? I may know an interested party."

Jameson said, "I might stay for a while and run the plantation but not with indentured workers. I plan to free them and hire workers, pay them a weekly stipend, and prove that you can be a successful landowner without slavery."

"My dear sir," Nicholas said, "you can't mean that. Why, that would upset the whole balance of things. Your neighbors, in fact the whole town would be up in arms about that news. Besides, these people can't read or write. What would they do if you freed them? They have no skills except what they're taught to do."

Jameson interrupted, "I intend to educate them and then offer them the opportunity to decide what area they would like to pursue in life. Men do not have the right to enslave another group of people simply because they are a different color. In fact, let me expand on that. All men are created equal and endowed with the right to life, liberty, and the pursuit of happiness, regardless of race, creed, or color. It states that quite clearly in our constitution, does it not?"

Nicholas shook his head, avoiding the question. He added, "Don't be foolish, my boy. Think before you act. You haven't been here for a while. You forgot how things are done down here. Didn't you get the news up in Boston of that awful John Brown raid at Harper's Ferry? They were trying to incite a slave insurrection. I tell you it has left a lot of folks nervous down here.

Are you aware that the South Carolina legislature voted to secede from the union a few months ago? Tempers are flaring. There could be a war coming. These are unsettled and dangerous times down here in the South. You don't want to stir up more trouble than you can handle, now do you, my boy? Don't you remember the story of Silas O'Shay? He tried to free his slaves and mysteriously disappeared, never to be heard from again."

"I heard that story," Jameson remarked suspiciously. "I thought it was told to frighten people into submission. I figured he just moved back up North to be with family."

"If that were true, why was his neglected and abandoned plantation sold at auction and the proceeds donated to charity? If he simply moved, wouldn't he have sold his property and kept the money? No, I tell you, he was purposely silenced, and so will you if you persist in this silly idea of yours."

Jameson said, "Nevertheless, I fully intend to free these poor, wretched souls, and I want you to draw up the necessary papers so I can give each person I own his freedom."

Nicholas argued, and Jameson fired back again and again in a verbal exchange of heated emotions. Abigail pleaded with both of them for silence. They quieted down for a few seconds then started the debate again, louder than before.

Finally Abigail shrieked. "Enough! Stop this now, or I will start screaming and I won't stop until we get to the plantation."

They reluctantly agreed to disagree.

The coach rambled on toward Serenity in an uneasy peace. Sammy sat quietly up front driving the horses. He had a wide smile on his face that he could not contain.

The horses' hooves hitting the hard roadbed and the squeaks of the springs on the carriage filled the dead silence. The ride seemed to be longer than Nicholas Mansfield had stated. It was hot and humid, further compounding the uneasy peace Abigail had secured. She was visibly uncomfortable and also at the breaking point. Neither man wanted to upset her any further, so the peace was secure. The dust being kicked up made Abigail cough, and she quickly reached for and covered her face with a large lace handkerchief.

She disgustingly stated, "Will this ride never end?"

Jameson and Nicholas felt the same way but for different reasons.

Chapter 2

SERENITY

It was nearing dusk as the coach finally approached the plantation. Turning off the main road, the horse drawn carriage proceeded under the wooden arches, revealing the large white sign: "Welcome to Serenity. Peace to all who enter here."

Jameson supposed that peace was dependent upon your color and status and hoped he could change that. They heard the crack of a whip and the pleas of someone in pain begging for mercy as the coach approached the worker's living space—Slave Row, as it was known. He saw a black man tied to a tree and a white man preparing to whip him while the other unfortunate souls were made to stand and watch in horror.

Jameson jumped out of the carriage, ran up to the two men, and demanded, "Stop this! Stop this at once!"

The white man said, "Who do you think you are to tell me what to do?"

Jameson replied, "I am the new owner of this plantation, Jameson Hartford, and there will be no more of that kind of inhumane treatment here ever again. Do you understand me, sir?"

"If that is your wish, sir, then I will gladly comply. Allow me to introduce myself. I'm Abner Slycott, the overseer. My job is to get these slaves to produce. This one here tried to escape. You have to let them know who the boss is, or they'll all try to run."

"Nonsense!" said Jameson. "Cut him free at once and never whip him or anyone of them ever again. Do you understand?"

"I do, sir, but you'll regret that decision. As the overseer, I know how to get a good day's work out of a bunch of lazy darkies. Just let me have a free hand like your brother did."

"I'll discuss this with you later, Mister Slycott, but be forewarned," yelled Jameson.

Abner Slycott was a big, burly fellow. He was unshaven; his clothes were unkempt and dusty. He spoke in a harsh voice and had a look of hate in his eyes. He was duly suited to his profession.

The poor man was cut down and tended to by the other workers. Jameson looked at them and their abominable living conditions, shook his head in disgust, and told them he would return to speak with them shortly. They did not look up from the ground, as it was forbidden for them to look directly at the master of the plantation. He vowed to himself to start changing things shortly, but for now he climbed back into the coach and proceeded to the plantation house. Mansfield and Abigail just stared at him in disbelief.

The first structure that came into view was the old, large barn where he and his brother used to play as children. They would tumble into the haystacks after jumping from the loft. It was large enough to accommodate eight horses, two buckboards, a carriage, and assorted farming tools. In the fall, it was used for storing the cotton and curing the tobacco leaves prior to selling them. New boards could be seen amongst the old, weathered ones, replaced as soon as rot was detected in an effort to preserve the all-important structure. Chicken coops abounded, as well as some cows and pigs. It could be described as a small farm, but the real value was in the large cotton and tobacco crops that spread over several hundred acres.

The plantation house loomed directly in front of them. It was just as he had remembered it, maybe more beautiful than his memory had allowed. It was large and twice as elegant. The tall, majestic columns were reaching up to the clouds, supporting the freshly whitewashed mansion and its many dark, shuttered windows. The stairs lead up to the large, shaded porch where he spent many hot afternoons and nights sipping an ice-cold lemonade or iced tea. Beyond were the twin front doors, beckoning to all, provided you were invited. It was beautiful, a masterpiece of architecture. The doors swung open, and out came Nanny and Uncky, the house servants.

Nanny was a term of affection for the woman who cooked, cleaned, and tended to all the household duties. She took care of Jameson and his brother, Josiah, from their youngest years onward. She fed them, bandaged their wounds, and cared for them when they were ill. She wasn't a servant to them, more like a nanny. A cheerful sort with large, smiling eyes, she always wore a kerchief around her head tied in a huge, ornamental bow and an apron cinched around her ample waist. A wise old soul if there ever was one.

Uncky was also a term of endearment for the kindly old gentleman who taught the two boys how to ride a horse, fish, whittle, and fix just about anything around the plantation. He even taught them how to load a rifle for when they went hunting with their father. He relished telling them interesting bits of folklore and sometimes ghost stories on dark, moonless nights. A tall, thin man with a timeworn face, he always wore a jacket with tails and a derby hat. They never thought of him as a servant either, more of an uncle. Nevertheless, he and Nanny were both slaves, bought and paid for.

Jameson ran up to them and said, "You're both still here! I can't believe it! It's good to see you again."

"It's good to see you again, Mista Jameson, sir," said Uncky, "We missed you, sir, oh, and you too, Miss Abigail."

The two men shook hands repeatedly and patted each other on the arm.

Nanny and Jameson embraced. He kissed her on the cheek and she returned the affection. They both looked at each other, laughed, and hugged once again, as if they were long lost relatives finally reunited after far too many years.

"I missed you, Nanny."

"Oh, Mista Jameson, I'm so happy you're back. It's been a long, long, long time. I worried so about you after you left," said Nanny. "Come on in. I'll fix you somethin' to eat. You must be hungry." The greeting for Abigail was polite but a lot colder.

Jameson yelled to Nicholas Mansfield, "Have those papers drawn up! You know the ones we talked about. I'll be in town tomorrow to pick them up and to sign any legal documents I need to take ownership of the plantation; oh, and thank you for the ride."

Nicholas only shook his head as the coach pulled out.

Once inside, Jameson remembered the high ceilings, the large chandelier, and the massive, winding staircase leading up to the second-story bedrooms. As he entered, the kitchen was off to the left, and next to it was the large dining area. It consisted of an oversized, hand-polished wooden table with chairs enough to satisfy the whole family. Beautiful china cups and dishes, along with personalized silverware and candlesticks, and a silk tablecloth and napkins adorned the table. The dining area was always at the ready for family or unexpected guests, though now it was seldom used. The kitchen had all the latest conveniences of the 1860s: a wood-burning stove, large pump in the marble sink, shiny pots and pans, sharp cutlery, and, in the corner, a smaller dining table for Nanny and Uncky. The kitchen was ruled by Nanny. It was her domain, and she let everyone know that she was the boss.

The study was a large room off to the right with bookshelves lining the whole wall. Jameson wondered whether anybody had the time to read or would ever have the time to read all those books. A fireplace was on the corner wall; huge windows along the front brought abundant light into the room. A large wooden desk, made of imported Norwegian wood, sat near the window. Two plush twin sofas faced each other in front of the fireplace. It was both an inviting and foreboding room. Jameson smiled as the memories he had suppressed came flooding back into his consciousness.

There were three bedrooms upstairs with a large marble bathroom. Each room had huge featherbeds with goose down comforters on them. Vanities, chests of drawers, and full-view mirrors decorated each room. Large closets to neatly arrange the many outfits of the Hartfords' were a mainstay.

"Where is Bethany Sue?" he inquired.

She was the wife of Josiah, his deceased brother.

"She's upstairs in her room. She don't come out much since Mista Josiah died," said Nanny.

"Come on, Abigail. Let us pay our respects to her," he said as he took her hand and led her up the grand staircase.

"I'll bring your bags up, sir," said Uncky.

"I'll get the food on," said Nanny. "It'll be so good to have that man back again."

Jameson and Abigail approached Bethany Sue's room and knocked on the door, but there was no answer. He knocked again and called her name. No answer.

Jameson opened the door and said, "Bethany Sue, its Jameson and Abigail. Are you all right?"

"I know it's you. I saw you drive up," said Bethany Sue. "What do you want me to do, pack up and leave immediately?"

"Don't be ridiculous," said Jameson. "I'm taking over, but you are welcome to stay here as long as you like, forever, if it pleases you. You are my brother's wife and always welcome here."

"That's most kind of you, Jameson, but I...I..." Bethany Sue fell on the bed and began weeping.

The untimely death of her husband was still too hard for her to bear. She was frail and much too thin and pale. Her hair was unkempt, and she was always in her night clothes, seldom, if ever, going out of the house since her husband's demise.

"I'll talk to her," said Abigail.

Josiah and Bethany Sue had one son they named Jebediah, after Jameson's and Josiah's father. It was rumored that the boy was conceived prior to their wedding, a real scandal that rocked the small community. In fact, to protect the family name, the exact birth date of the child was a secret. Bethany Sue was only tended to by Nanny, acting as a midwife. No doctor was present. The official announcement of the birth was delayed to nine months from the date of the marriage.

The child was spoiled. He had little respect for anyone or anything. He was so unmanageable that he was sent away to school. He was attending classes when the news of his father's death reached him. He returned for the funeral then quickly fled back to school. Jeb had his sights set on greatness and had no desire to run a plantation. Jameson and Abigail had not seen Jeb since they lived on the plantation. Neither side tried to keep in touch. To be honest, they were a bit envious of Josiah and Bethany Sue. After all, Jameson was the eldest and could not manage to produce any offspring or even a single heir to the family name. Jealousy was a cruel feeling.

Bethany Sue was always looking for affection from her son and husband. Jeb had no time for her; his own ambitions took priority over his family. Josiah was busy running the plantation and entertaining friends. He did not really love Bethany Sue but was trapped into marrying her because of the pregnancy. It was rumored he found a release for his affections elsewhere. She was lonely, a feeling that was only compounded when her husband died suddenly. Abigail felt sorry for her and tried to comfort her.

Jameson left Bethany Sue's room. He flew down the stairs, past the kitchen, yelling to Nanny, "Keep the food warm. I'll be right back."

He proceeded outside and had all intentions of heading straight to slave row, but something caught his attention and mesmerized him. He stood there for a moment and then began to fondly remember all the entertaining his family did on the large, sunlit porch—Saturday socials and dancing with the beautiful southern belles in their fancy gowns and powder-white complexions. He recalled the many romances, first kisses, and too much indulgence in the demon whiskey. This is where he met and courted Abigail, tasted his first mint Julep, and sparred with his brother for the attention of the prettiest girls. It seemed like only yesterday. Then, unexpectedly, the pleasant memories turned to sadness as he remembered the many arguments he had had with his father over slavery.

His younger brother, Josiah, was no better, always competing with him for family dominance. Josiah even tried to steal Abigail away from Jameson, not because he loved her but just to prove he could best his older brother. There was a rumor that Abigail even considered it but was skeptical of Josiah's real intentions and decided to remain with the sure bet, Jameson. Josiah was always trying to please their father and coerce the birthright away from Jameson. Apparently it worked, as the whole plantation passed to the younger brother when his parents passed on; only now had the wrong been righted, but at such a cost. Jameson mused on how money and riches could divide a family and cause such unnecessary hatred.

He was snapped back to reality as he heard Abigail complaining from inside the house. "I forgot how hot and uncomfortable it is here. What I wouldn't give for the cool breezes of Boston. Jameson, are you out there? Do you hear me? Jameson?"

He wasn't in the mood to listen to more complaining, so he decided to quickly leave the porch and go and check on the workers. He couldn't wait to tell them of his plans for their freedom.

He stopped briefly at the family graveyard and meandered over to the headstones where his mother, father, and brother were buried. There was a lack of compassion on his part, even as an eerie cold descended upon him and enveloped him. He stood there as haunting remembrances caused chills to run down his spine as if the dead were trying to warn him. The ominous presence seemed to hover over him. Voices from beyond were trying to reach out and vindicate themselves from their earthly transgressions. He shook off the peculiar feelings and continued on his way, determined to right the wrongs of his previous generations.

Chapter 3

SLAVE ROW

Slave row was nothing more than spare wooden boards nailed together to form hastily made shelters for the poor workers. It was one long building with cots lined up in a row from one end to the other. Beds were nothing more than old sheets stuffed with hay and covered with discarded blankets that had holes in them. A structure to be used as an outhouse was set off to one side in the woods. Privacy and ample space for simply surviving was nonexistent. There were fires burning outside to provide warmth and a cooking area that was cluttered with old pots and cracked plates. It was not a fit place for humans to live.

As he approached, he heard again the sound of a cracking whip. He saw Abner Slycott threatening a black man; he was sure it was the same man as earlier, tied to the same tree.

"I told you to stop that!" Jameson screamed as he ran to the poor man's aid. "I told you I never wanted you to whip these people again. What part of my order did you fail to understand?"

Slycott said, "You don't understand, Mister Hartford. This slave was trying to instigate the others in a revolt against you. I overheard him and wanted to teach him a lesson."

"That's not true, master," a young black girl cried out. "He wasn't saying any such thing, master, honest. Mista Slycott, he don't like Amos, so he uses any excuse to beat him."

"Why you little scum!" screamed Slycott. "I'll teach you to lie to the master," he said as he raised his whip.

Jameson raised his hand and grabbed the whip before it was able to reach its mark. "Enough!" he asserted. "That will be enough. I told you never to whip these poor people again!"

Slycott replied, "Sir, they won't work unless you put the fear of God into them."

"God would not want these people treated like this, and he certainly would not condone slavery. You deliberately disobeyed my order. Your services are no longer required, Mister Slycott."

Slycott was in complete disbelief at what he was hearing and boldly shot back, "You callin' me a liar? You take the word of a slave over mine?"

"You can finish out the week. Then I want you out of here, and I mean off my property. Also, you will not inflict any physical or verbal punishment on these people for the remainder of your employment. Is that clear?"

Slycott questioned, "How am I supposed to get them to work if I can't threaten them or even yell at them?"

"Use your natural-born charm," Jameson sarcastically replied.

Slycott was outraged at being made to look like a fool in front of the indentured servants and gave a halfhearted, "Yes, sir." Then he noticed the workers giggling under their breaths, and he could not contain his anger. "You won't get away with this. I heard about your slave lovin' ways. This ain't over."

"Hold your tongue!" yelled Jameson.

Slycott steamed off, muttering under his breath something about revenge.

Jameson looked at the poor group of men and women in tattered clothes. They all stood there with their heads down, wondering what was happening.

He said, "I'm sorry about this. It won't happen again. I promise you. Please look at me. I want to see your faces and get to know each and every one of you."

They slowly raised their heads and gazed at the new master.

"That's better," he said. Then he turned to address the young girl who spoke out. "You're a very brave girl. What's your name?"

"I'm Lilah, Master Jameson, sir," she said meekly. "Really my name is Delilah, but everybody just calls me Lilah."

She was a strikingly beautiful woman. Her hair was cropped quite short, but her large, sad eyes and perfect facial features complimented the short hair.

"Hello, Lilah," Jameson said. "I'm happy to meet you. Are these all of the workers belonging to Serenity?"

"They are, master," Delilah said. "Mista Josiah always said he was meanin' to buy more so we wouldn't have to work so hard, but he never did."

"Well, Lilah, please introduce me to the rest of these folks, if you would be so kind."

No one had ever spoken so nice to her before, and she didn't know how to react, but she had to obey her master, so she proceeded to introduce the other people.

"This is Amos, but you already know him. You saved him from two beatings."

Amos said, "Thank you, master, thank you."

Jameson smiled and nodded his head.

She continued, "This is Zeke. His real name is Ezekiel. This is Nate. His whole name is Nathanial. This is Daniel. That's not short for anything, just Daniel. This is Jonas. This is Alex or Alexander. This is Becky. Her whole name is Rebecca, and her child Lizzie, short for Elizabeth. This is Sarah and her son Ozzie. I'm not sure what that's short for. And this is Eli. His given name is Eli... Eli..."

"Elijah?" said Jameson.

"Yes sir, that's it," replied Delilah. "Elijah."

"Do you have any children?" Jameson queried.

Delilah did not respond, but a sad look came over her face, and she looked down toward the ground.

"That's nothing to be ashamed of," Jameson said, "My wife and I don't have any children either." Then he remarked, "You all seem to have biblical names."

Delilah explained, "Mista Josiah said that he named us all from the good book in the hope that it would save us. I don't think it saved us from much, so I guess it didn't work."

Jameson only saw the irony in it, but now, perhaps, he could save them.

"Are any of these people your family, Lilah?"

She again grew sad and answered, "No, sir."

"Do you know where any of your family members are?"

"I can't say, sir."

"If you have an idea, I wish you would tell me. Maybe I can help locate them."

She finally spoke out, "Sir, I was taken from my mother and sold to Mista Josiah and brought here."

Jameson was saddened by the news and told her he was very sorry.

Figuring he had caused enough heartache for the poor girl, he turned to the rest of the servants and addressed them, "Hello, everyone. I'm Jameson Hartford. I'm the new owner of this plantation. I want to offer you a proposition."

They all looked confused, so he reworded it.

"I plan to free all of you and hire people to tend the cotton and tobacco crops and pay them a daily wage to prove to the rest of the community that you can run a profitable business without slaves. I will go into Willow Hills in the morning and secure your freedom. I want to be sure it is done legally so no one can dispute the matter. I will return with your freedom papers, and you can all move on."

"Where do we go, master?" asked Daniel. "We don't know anything but this."

"Don't worry," said Jameson. "You can still work here if you desire, but you will no longer be property but free men earning a daily wage…money that you can use to buy things, like clothes and food. It is a much better way to live, believe me. I'll help you get an education so you can read, write, and learn a trade."

He could see they were still confused or untrusting of him or maybe a little of both.

"Well, you discuss it amongst yourselves, and I'll answer any questions you have tomorrow. Okay?"

He bid them a goodnight, glanced over at Delilah, and smiled. She smiled back. He felt an instant connection with her and hoped he could help her, as well as the rest of them embark on a new life. He started back up to the house. They stood motionless, full of doubt and unsure of their fate.

After Jameson had gone, Amos spoke up, "I don't trust him. He's just another white liar."

Delilah scolded him, saying, "He just saved you from two beatings and fired that evil overseer because of it, and you don't trust him? Well, I do, and I think he will free us."

"If he does, the first thing I'm gonna do is run for it," said Amos. "I'm headin' north as fast as I can go."

"You're a fool, you are," intoned Delilah. "You can't read, can't write, can't do anything but pick cotton and tobacco. You probably don't even know which direction north is, and you think you're gonna be a big black man in a white man's world. You're a fool."

Amos just shook his head and murmured. "Bah!"

Jameson went back to the mansion and asked Nanny to gather together all the extra blankets, pillows, linens, and available food. He had Uncky harness a horse to a wagon. Together they loaded the supplies, and he delivered them to the needy souls at slave row. Their living conditions were appalling, and he was determined to right this wrong immediately.

Jameson called for Delilah, and she obediently emerged from her shack. He handed her all the items and told her to distribute them to the others. She suspiciously accepted and called the others to come forward. One by one the poor souls filed out of their hovels, curiosity abounding. They were astounded by the gifts bestowed on them by the new stranger. Each in turn politely thanked him and graciously accepted the new items. They would eat and sleep better today than ever before.

Jameson smiled and winked at Delilah. "Things will get better, I promise you."

She smiled a perplexed smile, not sure of his motives but hoping for the best.

They looked at each other longer than they should have, and it was noticed by an ever-lurking Slycott. He was especially filled with anger and jealously at this latest outrage but was afraid to say or do anything, at least for the moment.

Jameson wished Delilah a good night.

She said, "Thank you," paused for a few seconds, and then added, "Good night to you too, Mista Jameson, sir."

He climbed up into the wagon and headed back to the mansion.

Abigail was waiting to have dinner with Jameson and was growing impatient. When he finally arrived, she sternly said, "I've been waiting for you. What took you so long? Where did you run off to? Never mind, I don't want to know. Just sit down and let's eat."

So Jameson and Abigail sat down to a silent dinner. Bethany Sue took her food in her room as had become the norm. The food was as delicious as he had remembered, and he ate every last morsel. He thanked Nanny for the meal. Abigail said nothing. Jameson told Nanny to be sure the workers received enough food and whatever other essentials they required. He wanted to relieve their suffering as much as he could right away and then concentrate on giving them their freedom. Abigail gave out a loud sigh.

As they were finishing their iced teas, Jameson heard a noise outside in the yard and went to the door to investigate. He witnessed a coach with a long, flat wagon attached to it parked in his yard. He noticed two undernourished, sickly looking Negroes chained in that wagon. As he approached, the black driver, wearing a sailors outfit, got down and opened the door of the coach. Out stepped a big, burly, muscular man with a full beard and a patch over one eye. He was clad in a naval captain's outfit, but he looked a lot like a pirate. Jameson recognized him as the slaver trader from Charleston.

"What do you want here?" Jameson asked.

"Are you the owner of this fine-looking plantation, sir?"

"I am. Again, what do you want here?"

"Allow me to introduce myself. I am Captain Mordechai Le Brute. I have a couple of fine slaves here I can sell you today at very reasonable prices, six hundred dollars for the lot of them."

"Couldn't sell them in town, huh?" Jameson taunted.

"I see you were there, so you know I sell quality merchandise."

"They're not merchandise. They're human beings."

"Take a look at them, sir. Petey, me lad, get them out of there so the man can see them. Look alive there, you swabs."

They were both shaking, scared, and obviously emaciated, yet obeyed immediately for fear of retribution. Petey, was a black man himself, yet somehow he felt no remorse aiding and abetting his white boss and mistreating his own people.

"Look here," Mordechai continued, "a mother and daughter, good team. They can please you too, if you know what I mean. I can personally vouch for the mother. I taught her all she knows during our long sea voyage together. I call her Azure, because I first laid me eyes and body on her while on the deep blue ocean." He laughed. "But you can name them anything you want. You buy 'em. You name 'em.

Jameson was horrified at what he was hearing, but he felt compassion for the two women and wanted to help them. "Don't they already have names?" he asked.

Mordechai continued, "They have some funny sounding African names. All they need are some good Christian names, you know, names we can all pronounce. Then just let your overseer break them in, teach them who's boss, learn their place. They'll catch on fast enough."

Jameson replied, "What's wrong with treating them with kindness, helping them to adjust?"

Mordechi laughed. "You'll never get this plantation to produce if you treat them like that. If you like, Petey here can break them in for you. He's good at it, right, Petey old man?"

"Yes, sir, I can do that right enough," Petey replied.

Jameson looked at Petey. "You ought to be ashamed of yourself, treating your own people like that. Have you no pride?"

"I'm doing my job. It's better than being a slave, isn't it?" Petey replied.

"Is it?" Jameson retorted. "And as for you, Le Brute—"

"That's Captain LeBrute, sir," Mordechai boasted.

Jameson continued, "What you have chosen as your life's work is reprehensible. It is an abomination. You repulse me, sir, but I do want to buy these two unfortunate souls so I can set them free along with the rest of my workers."

"You're beliefs are of no concern to me," Mordechai replied angrily. "I provide a service. If I didn't do it, someone else would. Maybe you can get it abolished." He laughed.

Jameson, not wanting to continue the debate lest he lose his chance to save the two needy souls, reached into his pocket and counted his cash. He realized he did not possess enough money to complete the transaction.

"I am presently unable to meet your sale price, sir, but I am going into Willow Hills tomorrow, and I will procure the required amount at that time. If you can bring them back here tomorrow afternoon, I will purchase them from you."

"You have some strange notions, you do, but, I don't care what you do with them after I get me cash," Mordechai responded.

"I suppose I can return, if I don't sell them in the meantime, that is. It costs me time and money to keep them for an extra day, you know. I have to feed them and provide sleeping accommodations."

"You can leave them here. I'll assume those responsibilities, and you can simply return tomorrow for the cash," Jameson offered.

Mordechai hesitated. "No offense, sir, but, I have a strictly cash business, no credit, especially to a stranger with odd ideas."

Jameson answered, "All right, bring them back here tomorrow, and I'll give you six hundred and twenty dollars. That should cover your expenses."

Mordechai agreed. "It's a deal, sir. Nice doing business with you."

Jameson added, "For heaven's sake, please feed them. I don't need them to be ill."

"I'll scrounge something up for them, sir. Don't you worry about that."

"Wait!" Jameson yelled. "Nanny, come out here, please."

Nanny burst through the door. "What's wrong, Mista Jameson?"

"Nanny, please get these people something to eat."

"Yes, sir, right away." Nanny disappeared back into the house.

"That's generous of you, sir," Mordechai said.

Jameson stood there patiently waiting. Silence abounded.

Nanny reappeared with plates full of chicken, grits, cornbread, and collard greens. Petey lunged forward to get first choice.

Jameson yelled, "That's not for you. It's all for them." He pointed at the poor mother and daughter. "You can have what's left if there is anything, that is."

Petey looked at Jameson then at Captain Le Brute, who nodded his approval of Jameson's caveat. The two lost souls were reluctant to indulge until Mordechai gave them the go ahead. Then they dove into the food with a veracity that Jameson and Nanny had not seen before. Evidently, they were severely undernourished and could not eat fast enough, fearing the feast would be taken away from them at any moment. It was all devoured within minutes. Nanny got them some glasses of water to wash it all down. They gratefully looked at Jameson and Nanny but were afraid to utter a word.

Jameson said, "Sorry, Petey, it appears there's nothing left. Perhaps if you took better care of your own people in the first place you would have been rewarded in return."

Petey gave Jameson a look that could kill as Mordechai yelled, "Get them back in the wagon, Petey! We're out of here. See you tomorrow, sir, have the seven hundred dollars ready."

Jameson said, "I thought we agreed on six hundred and twenty dollars."

"We did, but the other eighty dollars is for insulting me first mate, Petey, unless you'd like to forget the whole deal."

Mordechai knew Jameson wanted the two women and would pay whatever exorbitant amount he wanted to charge him. After all, trading was his business. He took advantage of the situation and used the two captives as a bargaining tool.

Jameson sighed. "No, I'll pay the seven hundred dollars, but be sure they're not harmed in any way."

"Hear that, Petey me lad, no harm." He laughed as the small caravan pulled out.

Jameson and Nanny sadly looked at each other. He hoped the pair could survive for twenty-four hours until he would be able to help them. They turned and retreated into the house.

Delilah was hiding behind the barn, watching the whole drama unfold. She was amazed and astonished, observing all that occurred, and she was becoming infatuated with the new master. She smiled to herself as she was sure he would indeed help her people, and they might actually live to see freedom.

Abigail had already gone to bed. She didn't care what was happening outside. It didn't concern or interest her.

Jameson said goodnight to Nanny and climbed the stairs to the bedroom. She was already asleep, or pretending to be, so he just undressed and slipped beneath the covers. It was not long before he too fell asleep in the comfortable feather bed, drifting off with pleasant thoughts of freedom and compassion.

It was a long and arduous day with even harder days to come. He and Abigail had spoken nary a word between them since arriving at Serenity. They were both afraid to stir up topics that they hoped the other had forgotten.

Chapter 4

VISITORS

The morning was heralded with the crowing of roosters. Jameson and Abigail rose from their long, restful sleep, washed, dressed, and went down to breakfast, again being careful not to say the wrong thing and start an argument. While they were still having breakfast, they heard the sound of a horse and buggy coming up the road. It stopped at the front of the house.

"Hello in there!" the cry came from outside.

It was Beau Lansing, owner of the neighboring plantation Tall Oaks and Abigail's father. Tagging along for the ride was Annabelle, Abigail's younger, more attractive sister and her only other sibling. Annabelle was an exquisite blonde, blue-eyed Southern belle. She also had eyes for Jameson and had attempted many times to steal him from her older sister. Although Jameson may have preferred Annabelle, the protocol of the day was that the eldest daughter was to be married first, which he reluctantly obeyed, especially since he had compromised her virginity. She most certainly would have been disgraced had he reneged on his promise, and that was just not an acceptable alternative, even if his heart was someplace else.

Beau Lansing was a loud, boastful sort of person. He always spoke his mind regardless of the consequences. He had a perfectly chiseled face, square jaw, and piercing eyes. Full of confidence, he sat tall in the saddle and looked dapper as usual, the quintessential Southern gentleman. He was good at intimidation and used this tactic on everyone, including the girls and their mother, who were a little afraid and in awe of him. Tall Oaks was a much smaller plantation than Serenity, measuring only a few hundred acres and sustaining one crop—cotton. Beau was always looking for a way to expand his holdings and had his ears open for any available opportunities.

"I came to see my daughter and son-in-law!" yelled Beau.

They ran out to meet him. Abigail embraced him, and Jameson shook his hand repeatedly.

"How are you doing, darling?"

"I'm fine, Daddy," said Abigail. "It's so good to see you. How are you and Momma?"

"She's feeling poorly today. You'll have to come over to see her, girl. She misses you terribly."

"I'll be there, Daddy, just as soon as I can, this afternoon, if possible."

"Hello Jameyson," Annabelle said in her sing-song, flirtatious voice. "I missed you. Did you miss me?"

She was dressed in the finest silk and lace pink gown with matching bonnet and parasol. She appeared to be trying to impress someone or perhaps seduce him.

"Hello, Annabelle. It's nice to see you again. You haven't changed much," Jameson replied.

Abigail added, "Except she still dresses like a hussy."

"Mind your manners, Abby," Annabelle said. "You're talking like a Northerner."

"Don't you call me a Yankee, you…you hussy you."

"How dare you call me a hussy! I should slap your face unless, a certain Southern gentleman were to defend my honor." She gazed at Jameson and fluttered her long eyelashes.

"That's enough, you two." Beau intervened. "You haven't seen each other in years, and the first thing you do is start arguing again."

"Well, she started it."

"I did not. How dare you accuse me?"

"Well, you accused me first."

"Stop it… now!" Beau ordered.

There was immediate silence as their daddy's voice indicated he meant business.

"Abby, here's a little welcome home present I bought for you," he said as he handed her a large box.

"Oh, thank you, Daddy." She beamed as she took the box and ran inside to open it and try it on.

"You go in with her, Belle, and let me have a man-to-man talk here with my son-in-law."

"Oh, do I have to?" Annabelle said as she gave Jameson a shy little look.

"Get inside," Beau ordered.

She jumped, yelling, "See you later, Jameyson."

Beau took Jameson by the arm and led him down the path away from the house. "How are you doing, my boy?"

"I'm fine, sir," he replied.

"No, maybe I should ask you, *what* are you doing?"

"What do you mean?"

"Look, Nicholas Mansfield stopped at my place on his way back to town yesterday and told me you had intentions of freeing your slaves. Is that so?"

Jameson said, "What if it is? It's my business."

"If only that were true, son, you don't understand our situation down here. You've been up North too long. Look, we need the slaves for cheap labor to pick the crops, do jobs you can't get anyone else here to do. Why there's not even enough folks down here to do all that planting and harvesting if we didn't use the blacks. And if we could hire outsiders, the salaries we would have to pay them would eat into any profits we could make. The prices we get for our cotton and tobacco are not very high, and you need to save money where you can. Do you understand, my boy?"

"I don't, sir. I checked the figures, and you can make a profit, granted not as much as with the servants, but a decent profit, nonetheless. Besides, forcing people to work this way is very wrong."

"Son," continued Beau, "you will make a lot of enemies if you pursue this silly venture of yours. If you free your slaves, that news will spread, and all the other slaves will want their freedom. There are quite a few blacks down here. People will fear an uprising. You will be igniting a fire that will spread rapidly, ravaging the countryside and ruining our way of life forever. Don't do it, my boy. At least give it some serious thought."

"I will sir," said Jameson, wishing to be respectful and not continue the conversation.

Abigail came running out of the house wearing her new bonnet, followed by Annabelle. "I love it, Father! I love it!"

"Wear it in good health, my child," Beau said with a large smile, as he felt he'd gotten through to Jameson and put an end to this nonsense of freedom. "I have to leave now," Beau cried. "Someone has to keep my plantation running. Don't forget to come see your mother, child."

"I won't, Daddy."

Beau Lansing mounted the coach and called to Annabelle to get on.

She looked at Jameson and said, "Help me get in, Jameyson?"

He obliged as Beau rolled his eyes. "Don't forget to come and see me too," Annabelle, said, touching Jameson's cheek.

The coach pulled out, and the two visitors were gone.

Jameson and Abigail watched as they galloped away. Abigail was thrilled. Jameson was wary. He told her he had business to attend to and proceeded to the barn. She sighed and shook her head then cheered up as she thought of her plans to visit her mother.

Jameson hitched the horse to the buckboard and drove down the path to slave row, where he was surprised to see Abner Slycott.

"Are you still here?" he said.

"I'm glad to see you, sir. I wanted to speak to you about my job. I misspoke yesterday, lost my temper. I didn't mean to insult you, sir. I regret all that happened," Abner stated.

"Not now, Mister Slycott. I'm here to see Delilah."

"I believe she is out in the fields already, sir. I'll get her for you."

"No, don't bother. I'll get her myself."

Jameson was about to depart when Delilah emerged from her shack.

"Oh, there you are," Jameson said. "Climb up here. I want to take you someplace."

She was afraid she had been too outspoken the day before and sadly asked, "Are you gonna sell me, Mista Hartford, sir?"

"No, no, nothing like that. I want you to accompany me on a little…search-and-rescue mission."

Delilah looked confused but politely obeyed and proceeded to climb onto the back of the flat wagon.

"No, no, Delilah, come ride up here alongside me, not in the back."

Slycott spoke out, "Mister Hartford, it's proper for the slave to ride in the back, not up front with the master."

"I don't care about protocol, Mister Slycott. I want her up here with me."

Slycott mumbled something under his breath as Jameson applied the foot brake and jumped off the wagon. He took Delilah's hand and helped her up the step and into the seat. She looked terrified but did not say anything.

Slycott watched suspiciously as Jameson led the wagon down the road. He was not at all pleased to see Jameson undermining his authority with the slaves particularly that slave. Slycott had his eye on her for a while but was hesitant to make a move without the owner's approval. Now he wanted his job back, so he would just have to bide his time.

Maybe I can turn this in my favor, he thought as he yelled at the slaves to get back to work. He decided to pay a visit to Abigail at the mansion and start a little trouble for the new master.

Jameson and Delilah were leisurely travelling down the road when he noticed how frightened she was. He asked, "Why are you so nervous, Lilah? I'm not going to sell you, honest! I don't bite either, you know." She was reluctant to reply, so he asked again, "Seriously, Lilah, what's the matter?"

Delilah finally responded, "I don't know what you want from me, Mista Hartford, sir."

"I don't want anything. I'm going to take you back to the plantation you came from to see if we can find your mother. I have a little cash with me, and I'm hoping if we find her, I'll have enough that I can buy her and free her along with you and the rest of my workers."

Delilah looked quizzically at Jameson and said, "Why would you do that for me? What do you want me to do?"

It was Jameson's turn to look puzzled, and then he realized that no one had ever done anything nice for her or any of the other workers without requiring something in return.

He said, "Lilah, I just want to help you and the others. I have no ulterior motive. I mean, I don't want anything, except maybe to see you smile, that's all. I promise."

She raised her head, looked directly at him, and smiled. It was only a half smile, but he felt he was gaining her trust.

"Now do you remember what plantation you came from?"

"Yes, sir, it was the Moors Plantation. A Mista Higgins owned it."

"Ah, yes, I know it well. We can be there in five minutes."

"Yes, sir, master," she replied.

"Please don't call me master, Lilah. I'm nobody's master. Mister Jameson will do just fine, okay?"

"Yes, mas—I mean, Mista Jameson."

Delilah was sitting as far away as possible from Jameson. The wheel of the carriage hit a rather large rut in the road, almost knocking her to the ground. Jameson instinctively reached over, grabbed her, and pulled her in close to him.

He put his arm around her and said, "That was close. Sorry, I didn't see that hole. You better stay close so I don't lose you."

Delilah was wary, but the half smile returned as she enjoyed the rest of the ride.

It was a cloudy day, and it certainly felt like rain as Jameson led the horses down the path to the Moors plantation, telling his story of freedom to a welcome ear. He stopped in the fields as the overseer approached.

"What can I do for you, sir?" the overseer asked.

"My name is Jameson Hartford, sir, from the Serenity Plantation, and I'm looking for a female worker I believe is working here. Her name is, um, what is her name, Delilah?"

"It's Leah, Mista Jameson, but everyone called her Lee."

"Her name is Leah, sir, or maybe just Lee. May I speak with her for a moment?"

Delilah was visibly excited at the possibility of reconnecting with her mother when the overseer said, "We have no slave with that name on this plantation, sir."

"Are you sure?"

"Yes, I know all the slaves we have."

"How long have you been employed here, sir?"

"Five years now, and we never had a slave by that name since I've been here."

"Do you mind if we look?"

"No, sir, go right ahead, but I'm telling you the truth."

"I'm sure you are, but sometimes names change, you know how that is."

"Yes, sir, I do."

Jameson helped Delilah down from the coach, much to the concern of the overseer, and told her to go into the fields and see if she could find her mother. She eagerly left, running with anticipation and hope.

The overseer eyed Jameson and asked, "Do you mind if I ask why you're looking for this slave?"

Jameson replied, "Leah would be the mother of this girl I brought with me. I'm trying to reunite them."

"Why, sir?"

"Would you want to be separated from your mother and not know what happened to her?"

"She's a slave, sir. It doesn't matter."

Jameson raised his voice, "It matters to me, and it should matter to any self-respecting human being. She is a living person not an inanimate object."

The rest of the time was spent in awkward silence until Jameson apologized for the outburst.

Delilah returned, looking very sad.

Jameson said, "You didn't find her, did you?"

"No, sir, she's not here, and no one will say anything, whether they knew her or not."

"I'm sorry, Lilah." Jameson turned toward the overseer and asked, "Can you get them to tell you if they know where Leah or Lee might be?"

"I can't do that without Mister Higgins approval, sir."

"Okay, I'll ask him. Is he up at the house?"

"No, sir, he and the missus are away. They went on a trip to Europe. They won't be back for a while."

Jameson sighed. "Thank you anyway, sir. You've been more than accommodating."

The overseer nodded and went back to his duties. Jameson helped Delilah back into the wagon, and they departed.

Delilah was softly sobbing as her hope dwindled to despair. Jameson was distraught. He thought he was doing a good deed, and it turned into a very sad occasion.

He said, "I'm sorry, Lilah. I'll come back when Higgins returns from Europe and ask him again. In the meantime, let's visit a couple more nearby plantations and ask them, okay?"

Her outlook brightened a bit as she nodded and smiled, but it was a very sad smile. "Thank you for trying, Mista Jameson. I really 'preciate it."

It was beginning to thunder and lightning, signaling a storm was approaching. They hurriedly stopped at two more plantations, but no one knew or heard of Delilah's mother. The third plantation had a female named Leah, and once again Delilah's excitement grew, but it was quickly dashed as the woman turned out to be someone else entirely. Delilah was very depressed and dejected as they headed back to Serenity.

To make matters worse, it began to rain. Delilah was clothed in only a short-sleeved and knee-high cotton garment. She was drenched and shivering. Jameson took his coat off and draped it around her to keep her warm; then he placed his arm around her and held her close, trying to console her. She did not know how to react but nestled in close and felt strangely safe. He also enjoyed holding her next to him, perhaps a little too much.

The lightning flashed and the thunder roared as the two unlikely souls held onto each other in a newfound friendship. The horse uneasily trotted homeward.

Abner Slycott knocked on the door of the Serenity mansion.

Nanny answered. "What do you want?"

"That's no way to talk to your boss."

"You ain't my boss. Mista Jameson, he's my boss. Now what do you want?"

"I want to see Missus Hartford."

"What fer?"

"That's none of your business."

"Everything that happens in this house is my business."

"Just get her. Now!"

Nanny reluctantly obeyed. "Wait here," she demanded as she happily slammed the door in Slycott's face.

A few minutes later, Abigail appeared. "Mister Hartford is not home, Mister Slycott."

"I know, ma'am. I hate to bother you, but do you know where Mister Hartford and Delilah went and when they'll be back? I have some work for the young girl to do."

"Who is this Delilah?" Abigail queried.

"Why she's a young, attractive slave that Mister Hartford took away in a wagon with him earlier this morning. I thought you knew."

Abigail replied, "He took her in a wagon?"

"Yes, ma'am, they've been gone quite a while now. He is coming back with her, isn't he?" Slycott asked in a snide manner.

"I'm sure he will return. I'll tell him you need to speak with him," Abigail replied.

Slycott thanked her and walked away with a grin filling his face. Abigail looked a little worried as she shut the door.

Bethany Sue appeared from the shadows and mysteriously spoke, "And so it begins."

"What do you mean?" said Abigail.

Bethany Sue pulled her into the den and closed the door. Nanny could only speculate on the trouble that was about to be unleashed.

The coach carrying Jameson and Delilah pulled into slave row. Jameson took Delilah's hand and helped her down from her seat. They were both drenched. He tenderly smiled at her and expressed his sorrow at not being able to find her mother.

He still had a hold of her hand as he said, "Don't give up hope. We'll find her."

Delilah finally gave him the smile he was waiting for and said, "Thank you for bein' so nice to me. I'll keep hopin'."

Slycott was nearby and heard the conversation. He came forward, forcing Jameson to finally let go of Delilah's hand. "Your wife is worried about you, sir," he lied. Then he ordered Delilah, "Get back to work."

Jameson told him Delilah was to be left alone and did not have to work for the rest of the day. She gave Slycott a smug look as if to say, "You can't hurt me anymore."

Slycott said, "Sir, I want to speak with you about my job."

"Not now, Mister Slycott. I have to get home. You told me my wife is looking for me."

And with that Jameson climbed back into the buckboard, winked at Delilah, and quickly headed home. Delilah stood there watching him then realized she was still wearing his jacket.

Slycott already noticed and made a comment. "What did you have to do to get that, huh? Was it worth it?"

Delilah did not respond, simply turned her back on him and ran into her shack, clutching the jacket. His scent still permeated the fabric, and it made her feel safe, if only for an afternoon.

Abigail was waiting as Jameson entered the house. She pulled him into the den and closed the door.

"Where did you go with that slave girl?" Abigail demanded.

Jameson was taken aback but answered, "I took her to the Moors Plantation to try and find her mother."

"Is that all?"

"What are you talking about, Abby?"

"I heard what happens between masters and pretty slave girls."

"Are you crazy, Abby? Nothing like that happened. Where would you get an idea like that?"

"Never mind, I just know. Where is your coat, Jameson?"

He looked at himself then realized he was in trouble.

"Where is your coat?" she asked him again.

He reluctantly replied, "I put it around Delilah. It was raining, and she was shivering, and I didn't want her to get sick."

"Where is it now, Jameson?"

"I forgot to take it back. I'll get it later."

"You'll get it now, and you'll get rid of that…Delilah. Sell her and get her off this plantation."

"I will not. Nothing happened. I did nothing wrong."

"Jameson, you will do as I say and sell her immediately, or there will be a problem, a big problem."

Abigail stormed out of the den, up the stairs, and into their bedroom, slamming the door. Jameson stood there with Nanny and Bethany Sue staring at him.

He walked out onto the porch followed by Nanny, who whispered to him, "That no-good overseer came up here while you were gone and told Miss Abigail all about you and Delilah, trying to stir up trouble. Then Miss Bethany Sue pulled Miss Abigail into the den, and God knows what those two were cookin' up."

"Thanks, Nanny, you always look out for me."

"You can be sure of that, Mista Jameson."

All the pieces fell into place and it all made sense now. He ran down to slave row to even the score.

He found Slycott lurking about and yelled, "You dare interfere in my private life! Get out of here now. Get off my property at once before I forget I'm a gentleman. You're employment is terminated as of this moment. If you're here when I return, I'll shoot you for trespassing. Do you understand?"

Slycott only shook his head yes and quickly mounted his horse, as there was no reasoning with a man who he had such hatred in his eyes. Abner Slycott realized he may have gone too far, but he also knew he had not yet played all his cards.

Jameson was all fired up and decided to do something noble this day. He went back to the barn and began to saddle a horse then stopped and realized he had not ridden a horse in many a year, so he opted to take the buckboard again, as that would be the safer choice. He then headed for the house to tell Abigail where he was going. He went through the front door, up the stairs, and into their bedroom. Nanny was just watching, hoping for a happy ending.

He approached Abigail and said, "I don't want to fight with you anymore."

She was silent.

He shrugged his shoulders and added, "Are you giving me the silent treatment now?"

Again, there was no reply.

"Well then, I'm going into town to attend to some legal business."

"You're not going to pursue that silly freedom idea, are you?"

He just stared at her.

"We have it good here. I like being waited on, not having to cook or clean. What's wrong with that?"

"It's not good for them, is it?" countered Jameson.

"Why not? They have food, clothing, a place to sleep, and it's all free for them. All they have to do is what you tell them to do."

"Would you be happy if it was reversed and they owned you?" Jameson shot back.

Abigail ignored his question and added, "You can be nice to them. You don't have to overwork them or punish them. You can give them time off; treat them like they're almost the same as us." Suddenly Abigail realized what she said. "I mean…well, you know what I mean."

Sadly, he did. She felt that the Negroes were not as good as the whites that they were really beneath her.

Jameson looked pathetically at her and said, "I thought I knew you, Abigail. I thought deep down inside that you felt as I did, that these poor people were being exploited and needed our help. I'm sorry to find out that you and I see things so differently."

She glared at him and yelled back as he left the room, "Don't forget to sell that Delilah while you're there. I want her gone by day's end. Do you hear me? By day's end!" she screamed, following him down the stairs.

Ignoring her, he went out the door and onto the wagon. He could not drive away fast enough.

Jameson stopped to check on his workers and be sure Slycott was gone. Eli told him the overseer had indeed left and in quite a hurry. They were all visibly happy and relieved. He asked them to continue working the fields, and he would start paying them as of today. They gladly obliged. He found Delilah and told her he was going into town to get the freedom papers and would return soon.

"Are you going all by yourself, Mista Jameson?" she asked him.

"I have to do this alone," he said, "There may be trouble. Not everyone thinks this is a good idea, you know."

"I 'spect not," she said, "but we'll prove them wrong, won't we?"

"You bet we will, Lilah," he said as he smiled at her again.

"I'm not afraid of them, sir," she stated.

"I know you're not, but I'm afraid for you, so I want you to be safe and stay right here, okay?"

"Yes, sir," she replied.

He saw something in that girl, a clever determination that he admired a lot.

Before he could leave, she said, "Mista Jameson, I have your jacket in my shack. I'll get it for you."

"Why don't you keep it? I hope it will keep you warm and safe and remind you that I'm not a bad man."

"I already know that, Mista Jameson," she said as she gave him a large smile.

"That's the smile I've been waiting for, Lilah. I hope you will always continue to be able to smile like that," he said as he hit the reins to the horse and sped off down the road.

She watched him disappear into the distance, smiling all the while.

Abigail was in the house sobbing when she heard a voice.

"He's making a big mistake."

Abigail turned to find Bethany Sue on the stairs.

"This will be his downfall and the end of Serenity if you don't stop him."

Abigail brushed past her and ran up the stairs to the bedroom. Deep inside she felt Bethany Sue was probably right; she needed to stop her husband from ruining her life. Jameson was about to confront bigotry face to face and learn the horrifying truth about his friends and neighbors.

Chapter 5

WILLOW HILLS

It was late morning as Jameson arrived in the town of Willow Hills and noticed how much it had prospered and grown since he had last visited ten years ago. Various shops and stores lined each side of the road, which stretched before him for about quarter of a mile. *It must be thriving*, he thought to himself and smiled.

As he drove down the main street, he wondered if any of the people he knew were still in business. Was it his imagination, or was everyone staring at him as he passed? He smiled at the people, but no one smiled back. Some were even spitting. Were they spitting at him? This certainly wasn't the friendly little town he remembered. Wait, was that the overseer Abner Slycott he spied? Whoever it was quickly disappeared into a shop.

Jameson drove past the blacksmith, the general store, the sheriff's office, the gunsmith, and then stopped as he came upon the saloon. He remembered how he and his friends would sneak into town in the evening and watch the men of Willow Hills file into Taffeta Jones Gentleman's Entertainment Emporium for a libation and wind up going into the back room to gamble their money away or worse yet, be coaxed into going upstairs with one of Taffy Jones's mistresses. Those wonderful painted ladies who supplied intoxicated gentlemen with evenings of debauchery and, dare he say it, sex.

He wondered if he could recall their names. Let's see, there was Lulu, Candy, Cherry, and oh, yes, Jezebel. They were all very voluptuous, and every young boy dreamt of the day when he would be old enough to pass through those swinging doors and see for himself what excitement awaited him on the inside. He smiled as he remembered the night the boys saw their own fathers going inside, and they wondered if their mothers were aware of what was going on. Of course they did not or there would have been hell to pay for the poor fellows. In fact, the women wanted the saloon closed, because they considered it a palace of sin, sending their husband's home drunk and reeking of cheap perfume. But with a town run solely by men, there was little chance of that ever happening. Besides, Taffy Jones contributed heavily to various charities and causes, which benefited the town and surrounding areas. She knew how to grease the wheel.

Jameson remembered watching all the ladies parading down the street. They were all something to behold, dressed in beautiful, low-cut dresses with thigh-high slits he and his friends would hope for a strong breeze to blow open and reveal those long legs and lacy unmentionables. Parasols kept the sun from spoiling their perfectly pure, creamy complexions. Each woman had a different and distinct hair color. Candy was blonde as the bright sun. Cherry was red as a southern sunset. Lulu was orange as a ripe carrot, and Jezebel was jet black as a moonless night. The boys would wonder if the colors were natural, knowing the only sure way to find out was to take them upstairs and check in those illegal areas. Jameson wanted to go in, but he had more important business to attend to, and he began to move on.

"Hey, Jamey boy," someone shouted.

Jameson turned around to see his two old friends, Travis McGhee from the Heather Hills Plantation and Bobby Wilkins from Providence.

"I can't believe it. How are you, boys?" Jameson said as he jumped off the buckboard to embrace his old compadres.

Bobby looked the same—clean-shaven and dressed in a gentleman's outfit complete with vest and bola tie. He was the handsomer of the two. Travis still had his long moustache, which he liked to twirl, and was much more casually dressed, just a shirt, trousers, and scuffed-leather boots. He was the bawdier one and the troublemaker of the trio.

"It's good to see you both!" Jameson bellowed.

"Let's go into Taffy's and get a snoot full!" exclaimed Bobby.

"How did you boys know I was back in South Carolina?

Travis spit on the ground and said, "Everybody knows your back. Old man Mansfield spilled the news. It spread like wildfire."

"Are you still chewing tobacco?"

"Yep," said Travis as he spit the juice out again. "You oughta try it. It's good!"

"It's a disgusting habit," said Bobby. "He just won't quit."

"I agree." Jameson nodded.

"Hey we got a lot of catching up to do, Jamey boy, let's go into Taffy's, for old time sake. What do you say?"

"I can't right now. I have something I have to take care of first," Jameson asserted, "but how about tomorrow or the next day?"

"You ain't really thinking of freeing your slaves, are you?" Travis said, again spewing out a stream of tobacco juice.

"As a matter of fact, I am. I guess I don't have to wonder who told you that," Jameson replied.

"Jamey boy, Jamey boy, you can't really be serious. You've been talking about doing that since we've known you. Didn't you outgrow that foolish idea of yours yet?" Bobby said.

"It's not a foolish idea, and I fully intend to do just that," Jameson stated.

"You're making a big mistake and making a lot of enemies. Take my advice, forget the slaves, and let's go have a beer, a little fun and, well…whatever else comes up," Travis urged.

"It's on me, my old friend. C'mon," Bobby pleaded.

"I'd love nothing more than to spend time reminiscing with you two, but I can't today. I gave my word," Jameson said apologetically.

"Gave your word to who? A bunch of darkies? You put them above your old buddies? What happened to you up North, huh, boy? Are you a Yankee now?" Travis yelled as he spit yet again, this time narrowly missing Jameson's shoes.

Jameson only looked at him and then added, "I guess I've grown and changed. There's nothing wrong with wanting to help a group of people who have been wrongly enslaved. Now if you'll excuse me."

Jameson tried to leave. Travis put his hand on Jameson's shoulder, preventing him from moving.

"You ain't gonna do this to us, Jamey boy."

"Let him go, Travis. He's changed. He's not one of us anymore."

"Yeah, I guess you're right," Travis agreed as he spat one last time, this one landing right on Jameson's shoe.

Jameson pushed his arm away and said, "I'll forget that because we're friends, but don't ever do that again."

"Don't do me any favors, Jamey boy," Travis taunted. "If you think you're man enough, let's go!"

"No, Travis," Bobby said, stopping the confrontation. "Let him go. This is not the place or the time."

"Yeah, you're right. Good-bye, friend," Travis sarcastically yelled as Jameson got on his buckboard and rode away.

The whole occurrence saddened Jameson as he realized that even his best friends from childhood did not understand what he was trying to do. They would rather fight him than allow him to do the right thing and free his workers. He became more determined than ever.

He drove down the street and stopped in front of the bank. He went in to meet with Thaddeus Bordeau, the manager and father of Bethany Sue. Thaddeus was the wealthiest man in town and looked the part. He was always dressed in a well-tailored suit, stood tall, and commanded respect wherever he went. People were afraid of him as his wealth brought him immense power. He could easily foreclose on any number of loans, putting people out of business, or just as easily loan money to start or expand existing businesses. Everyone knew him and catered to him. Jameson asked to speak with him and was ushered into his office.

"I'm Jameson Hartford," he said.

"I know who you are," said Thaddeus.

"I'd like to know how much money is in the Serenity account, if you please."

"I'll work it up and have it for you tomorrow. I'm very busy right now. Good day."

"Mister Bordeau, I need some cash today. Right now!"

"Yes, yes, how much do you require?"

"I need at least five thousand dollars."

"That's a tidy sum. May I inquire as to your immediate need?"

Jameson wanted to tell him it was none of his business but thought twice about another confrontation and said, "I intend to buy two women from that pirate Mordechai Le Brute."

"Five thousand dollars for two slaves, you're being hoodwinked, sir."

"No, no, the two women are only seven hundred dollars, and I know he's cheating me, but I really want to help those two unfortunate souls."

"Going to try to free them as well, are you?"

"How did you hear about that?"

"Everyone knows about you, Hartford," Bordeau disgustingly replied. He handed Jameson the cash and added, "Here, sign this, and then be on your way."

Jameson put his signature to the note and then said, "Sir, I think you should come out and see your daughter. She needs help."

"I'll thank you to keep your views to yourself and stay out of my family's affairs, now, good day again!"

"Thank you," said Jameson as he was quickly and unceremoniously ushered out of the office.

That was certainly not a friendly encounter, Jameson thought.

He rode the buckboard to the front of Nicholas Mansfield's office, disembarked, and entered. He greeted Nicholas as one of his assistants pushed past him and ran out, obviously for some sort of an emergency.

"Do you have all my legal documents and freedom papers drawn up, Mister Mansfield?" he asked.

"Not yet, Mister Hartford," he replied.

"Well, I guess I'll just remain here until you can get around to it."

"I'd rather you gave me another day. Perhaps I can bring them out to you tomorrow?"

"I don't want to inconvenience you any further. I'll wait."

Mansfield sighed and shook his head.

Within a few seconds, the front door opened, and in sauntered old Doctor Robert Pritchard along with Sheriff Shelby Mathison. Doc was an old-time Southerner with a kind face and reassuring smile. He was the only doctor in the vicinity and administered to all the townspeople. In fact, he delivered most of the children who were now adults and having babies of their own. He genuinely cared for these folks and Willow Hills.

The sheriff, on the other hand, was a relative newcomer. He was a tall, menacing figure with a nasty glare on his face that was supposed to frighten people, and it did. He was determined to impose his will according to the law as he interpreted it. He would do anything to keep his job and please the residents, even if it was not legal.

"Hello, Doc, it's me, Jameson Hartford. Don't you remember me?"

Doc grunted. "Hello." He looked troubled about something.

Sheriff Mathison said, "Forget the pleasantries. We need to talk, Hartford. You can't free your slaves."

Jameson looked at Mansfield. "Someone has a big mouth," he said. Then he turned back to the sheriff.

"Why not?" queried Jameson. "They're mine. Are they not?"

"Look here," continued the sheriff.

"Wait. Let me speak to him," said Doc Pritchard. "I've known you a long time. I brought you into this world, and I'm only looking out for you now, son."

He then proceeded to spout the same speech that was given to him earlier by Beau Lansing, almost verbatim.

"Don't worry. I know what I'm doing. It'll be okay, really," Jameson said.

"You can't do this. I'm warning you," said the sheriff. "Don't come down here and think you can be one of them lousy, filthy son of a bitch Yankee trouble makin' scum. You'll regret it."

"Are you asking me or telling me?" said Jameson. He turned to Nicholas. "I want those papers now, Mansfield. Now!" he demanded.

Mansfield reached into his desk drawer and pulled the papers out. It appeared he had had them ready all the time. Jameson grabbed the documents and freedom papers, checked them out, then placed them into his pocket. He wished them all a good day, pushed past the sheriff and Doc Pritchard, got into his buckboard, and proceeded to leave town.

The sheriff turned to Mansfield and told him, "We need to get the other men together. We've had enough talk. It's time for action."

"Are you sure this is the only way?" asked Doc. "There has to be an alternative."

"We discussed it last night," the sheriff said angrily, "and we all agreed. Jameson Hartford has to be stopped!"

"But—" Doc said.

"No buts. You're either in or out," demanded the sheriff.

"Well then, I'm out," Doc said.

The men waited for Jameson's buckboard to leave town then sprang into action in the sheriff's office.

Jameson, having finished his business, began his long ride home, passing the same shops and stores, getting the same nasty looks and reactions. This time he understood the reason for the venom and shrugged it off as something that they would all have to accept and hoped they would eventually follow suit. He passed the last store and headed down the deserted dirt road back to the plantation.

He was just on the outskirts of town when he heard horses galloping up from behind him. He stopped the wagon to see what was going on. He turned to spy five or six horses with riders, rapidly approaching. Suddenly, he realized the riders were all covered in white sheets. They all wore pillowcase hoods with eyes and mouth holes cut out of them.

The riders stopped at his wagon, pulled out their guns, and pointed them directly at him as one of the masked men spoke. "Jameson Hartford, you are guilty of crimes against your community."

"What? What are you talking about? Who are you men?" Jameson nervously asked.

One of the hooded riders demanded, "Get a hold of him. Tie him up. Get the rope. C'mon, let's get this thing goin'."

Four other men grabbed him, dragged him out of the wagon, bound his hands, and forced him to stand up in the back of his buckboard. He was trying to put up a fight and free himself but was severely outnumbered. These men knew what they were doing and this crime had been rehearsed in advance many times before being executed here today. They fastened a noose from a rope they had brought and put it around his neck. The other end was secured around a nearby sturdy oak tree limb. They were planning to hang him on the spot, no trial and no witnesses.

Jameson screamed, "What are you doing? What is the meaning of this? What crime have I committed? You can't do this!"

"Shut up," shouted one man, spitting a wad of tobacco juice on the ground.

Jameson's horse was getting excited and started to buck and whinny. One of the hooded men grabbed the reins to hold the nervous steed in place lest they lose their precious captive too quickly.

Jameson was screaming, "No, no, stop it! Please stop it!"

"Shut up, just shut up and listen. You will be hanged right here and now unless you agree to keep your slaves and not free them."

Jameson in a panic said, "What difference does it make?"

"It makes a big difference to us, and you will do as we say."

"Why? You can run your plantations without using these poor people. Let me prove it to you," Jameson pleaded, trying to reason with them.

"We don't want to hear your ridiculous ideas, Hartford."

The rope was tight around his neck, and his legs were getting wobbly as overwhelming fear began to set in.

"You lousy, filthy son of a bitch Yankee trouble makin' scum," someone shouted.

"Let's get this over with," another shouted. "Slap the horse!"

"No, no, I beg you!" Jameson shouted. "What do you want me to do? I'll do what you want. I'll do anything. Don't hang me, please."

"Say it," the hooded man demanded. "Say, I won't free the slaves."

Jameson, paralyzed with fear, reluctantly gave in and screamed, "I won't free them!"

"Call them what they are, Hartford. Say, I won't free my slaves. Say it!"

Jameson sobbed. "I won't free my…slaves." He almost choked on the words but had little choice in the matter.

"And you'll rehire Abner Slycott as your overseer and won't interfere with the way he handles your slaves."

"Yes, yes, anything." Jameson wailed. "Anything you want."

The hooded man said, "And Hartford, don't tell anyone about this. Do you understand?"

"Yes, yes, I understand," cried Jameson.

"Should we take the freedom papers?" one rider asked, expelling a stream of brown juice to the ground.

"No, let him keep them as a reminder of today, but God help you, Hartford, if you give them to those slaves of yours, you understand?"

"Yes, yes. I won't, I won't." Jameson cried.

The lead rider then ordered, "Cut his hands free and untie the rope. Remember Hartford, if you renege on your promise, we will come again, and next time you will hang! Don't think of crossing us. Do you understand?"

"Yes, yes, I understand completely. I'll do whatever you say," Jameson grudgingly said as the rope fell free of the tree and collected at his feet.

With that they rode off. Jameson, trembling, collapsed into the buckboard; his heart was pounding, and he was gasping for breath. Struggling, he removed the noose from around his neck and threw it to the ground. He climbed into the driver's seat and watched as the riders faded into the distance and the dust cloud vanished. Paralyzed with fear, he remained there for a while, breathing heavily and continually wiping the sweat from his face.

It was a long, painful journey home. He kept turning around and checking the horizon for fear the hooded riders would return. There was no reason to hurry, for he had no idea what he would do or what he would even say when he finally arrived back at Serenity. He was ashamed of himself for being such a coward. Perhaps the vigilantes were just bluffing and would not have fulfilled their threat, but he was too frightened to take that chance.

Who were these men, and why were they so afraid of him freeing his slaves? Would they try to make him disappear as they did to Silas O'Shay and anyone else who dared to challenge their views? So many questions and fears filled his mind, and now he had to return to the plantation and tell those poor souls that he could not free them, because he valued his life more than their welfare. It was late afternoon, and the sun was beginning to go down. He shook the reins to jostle the horses into a small gallop. He desperately needed to reach the safety and security of Serenity before the night enveloped him. For the first time since he was a child, he was afraid of the dark.

Chapter 6

SERENITY UNDONE

It was already dusk as Jameson approached the Serenity Plantation. He had been gone a good part of the day, and as he turned into the gates, he was hoping to avoid any human contact. As luck would have it, the workers were coming in from the fields.

"Nice to be back again, sir."

Jameson turned and was startled to see Abner Slycott leading the line of exhausted men and women. "Don't you worry, sir, I'll make them work," he said sarcastically, "Just like you want me to, after all, you're the boss," he said as he broke into hysterical laughter.

Jameson was shocked and speechless as his eye caught Delilah's. She was looking quizzically at him. He could not face her and slapped the horse with the reins, quickly making a hasty retreat up to the house.

Amos whispered to Delilah, "I told you. He was just another white liar."

Delilah wanted to run after him and ask what had happened, but she dare not step out of line. Fear mixed with sorrow filled her soul as tears ran down her face.

As Jameson pulled closer to the plantation house, Uncky came up to him and said, "We were worried about you, Mista Jameson. Are you okay?"

Jameson said nothing and ran up the porch stairs past Nanny and straight into the study. He slammed the door and started pounding the desk, throwing books, vases, and lamps. He found a bottle of whiskey and began to drink. Then he fell down on the couch and broke into tears.

The front door of the house opened. It was Abigail, returning home from visiting her mother at Tall Oaks.

Nanny spoke, "Oh, Miss Abigail, I'm glad you're home. Somethin' is wrong with Mista Jameson. He came home and went straight into the study, locked the door, and things are crashin' and breakin'. I'm scared for him."

"I'll see what happened, Nanny," Abigail said as she walked to the door. She could not open it, so she banged on the door and said, "Jameson, is everything okay? Open up, darling. I need to see that you're all right."

There was a few seconds of silence; then the door was unlocked.

Abigail walked in. "Jameson, what happened? What's wrong? Tell me."

He looked at her; still visibly shaken, and said, "I don't think I can tell you just now."

She said, "Well as long as I can see you're all right and not hurt, let me tell you about my day. I'm just back from visiting my mother at Tall Oaks. She's fine, but you really should go see her. She was concerned for your welfare. Anyway, I'm late because I wanted to wait for my father to come home. He was out on some sort of business. He wouldn't tell me what it was, but he gave Margie, you know, our house slave, a large, old dirty bundle of sheets and pillowcases. They looked like they were in very poor condition as some had round holes cut into them. I don't really understand the business side at all, but why would he need sheets, especially damaged ones? Anyway, my mother really missed me and…"

Jameson stopped her. "What did you say? He had dirty sheets with him?"

"Yes, darling, I don't know what that has to do with cotton—"

"Listen to me, Abigail. I have something very important to tell you." Then Jameson related the entire sordid story to her, every detail.

"You don't mean to imply that my father was part of that mob, do you?"

"Yes," said Jameson, "it all makes sense. He comes here to warn me. All the people in town already know why I was there. That's why they were so distant. The sheriff gives me one last warning. Wait! What the sheriff said to me about being a lousy, filthy son of a bitch Yankee trouble makin' scum , the hooded man used those same words. That was the sheriff, he was in on it! The man spitting tobacco juice on the ground, could that have been my old friend Travis? Oh my God! They had it all planned. They knew I would give in."

"Jameson, such language in front of a lady, I can't believe this," Abigail said. "You're accusing my father and the sheriff of committing a crime. This is preposterous, Jameson. I won't stand here and listen to this." She started to leave then turned around and said, "For your own safety stop this nonsense about freeing the slaves and act like the master of this house. Just do what the town expects of you and everyone will be happy. Act like their friend instead of their enemy, and they'll treat you like their friend. In time, you'll get used to the idea."

"I will not!" Jameson shouted. "Now that I know it is a plot by my so-called friends and family, I will not be intimidated!"

Abigail shouted back, "I married a Southern gentleman. Now I find out you are nothing more than a Yankee rebel rouser, bent on destroying your life and mine. I won't let you do that!"

She stormed out of the room, slamming the door behind her.

Nanny was patiently waiting. "Is there anything I can do, Miss Abigail?"

"Yes, get my husband some common sense and a backbone," she shouted back so Jameson could hear her. Then she ran up the stairs to their bedroom.

Nanny was confused but dare not question the mistress. She walked over to the door of the study and knocked carefully upon it. "Mista Jameson, you okay in there?"

He replied, "Please leave me alone, Nanny. I need to think."

"Yes, Mista Jameson. If you need me, just yell. I'm here for you, like always."

Jameson stood in silence. He was bewildered by what he had just heard. This was not the woman he had married either. Clearly they had grown apart. Jameson wondered if she had even instigated the whole matter. Could he trust her anymore? Could he trust anyone?

He sat back down on the couch, took a large gulp from the liquor bottle, then another, and still another, until he could no longer hold his head erect and simply slumped over and passed out. There he remained for the rest of the night.

During the next few days, Jameson kept a very low profile, remaining in the mansion as much as possible, refraining from human contact at all costs. He wanted no confrontations with Slycott and certainly didn't want to see his workers. What could he say to them? Better to just ignore the whole situation and remain safe. Leave everything status quo, that was the easy solution to a most difficult problem.

He slept every night in the study with a bottle of whiskey clutched in his hand. There was no consoling him, though Nanny and Uncky both tried. He even avoided Abigail viewing her as the enemy, not his wife. He was scared and ashamed, fearful and humiliated, all caused by his so called friends, neighbors, family, and his ever suffering conscience.

One particularly hot day, the doors and windows were all open to allow whatever breeze there was to cascade through the house and cool down the rooms. Jameson was sitting at the kitchen table as Nanny was trying to coerce him to eat a little something. She was concerned for his health and well-being.

"You're gonna waste away to nothin' and kill yourself if you don't come to your senses. Here I made you some toast and put a little strawberry jam on it for y'all. Eat something please, Mista Jameson, I hate to see you like this."

Jameson tried to get some of the food into his stomach, partially because he liked and respected Nanny and partially because he knew she was right. As he raised the toast to his lips, in the distance he heard the crack of the whip and the scream of one of his workers. He was startled.

"Shut that door!" he demanded, "I don't want to hear that."

Nanny started to obey, then stopped and turned toward the cowering Jameson.

"Just cause you don't hear it doesn't mean it ain't happening," Nanny responded in a stern voice.

He looked at her, stunned that she would address him in such a manner. Another crack of the whip and another scream changed his look to sadness, as he got up from the table, covered his ears and hurriedly entered the study, grabbing his trusty friend, the whiskey bottle.

"That ain't gonna help you. It's only gonna make things worse," Nanny screamed after him as he ran like a scared rabbit into his wooden refuge.

He slammed the door and looked helplessly around the room. He knew she was right but he did not think he possessed the courage to do what was needed to be done. He fell onto the sofa, cracked open the bottle and debated with himself on his next move. Things could not go on this way. Either he gives in to the pressure of his peers or he fights them….or maybe he should just leave and return to Boston. He wrestled with the choices in his mind, over and over, then he did something he hadn't done in a while; he glanced upward and prayed to God for guidance.

"Please help me. I don't know what to do. Give me a sign, anything, just so I do the right thing."

He took another swig and then another until an idea suddenly occurred to him. He stumbled over to the desk, grabbed a piece of paper and a quill pen, dipped the point into the inkwell, shook off the excess ink, and began to write.

> I, Jameson Hartford, being of sound mind and body, hereby add this codicil to my last will and testament. I willingly free all the workers that I own, and I leave the Serenity Plantation and all its belongings and holdings to the three Negroes known as Nanny, Uncky, and Delilah. They are to sell the property and divide the proceeds up equally among all the freed workers. Then they are all to be escorted North to Canada, never again to be enslaved. That is my final wish. I have written this of my own free will and deem it to be so done according to my word.
>
> Signed, Jameson Hartford 8th, April, 1861

Jameson felt proud of himself, momentarily thinking he had outwitted the whole community. He had beaten them, one way or another. He took the note, grabbed his bottle of courage, and managed to walk over to the couch, whereupon he drank and drank until nothing made sense; then he just fell over and passed out on the couch. The forgotten codicil was left on the table by the couch, in full view for any prying eye to find.

Chapter 7

SHADES OF BROWN

It was late when Jameson awoke from the liquor-induced sleep. He knew he had had a little too much of the whiskey, but he also knew what he must do. He left the house and walked unsteadily down to slave row.

He entered Delilah's shack, grabbed her by the arm, and said, "I have to talk with you privately."

His alcoholic breath filled the still, windless night air, and she was frightened but had to obey the master. The other servants looked on in dread, but no one dared interfere.

He led her away to the barn, looked directly into her eyes, and said, "I owe you and the others an explanation."

He proceeded to tell her what had happened. He was both embarrassed and ashamed. The fear, anger, and cowardice welled up inside of him, causing tears to fill his eyes and roll down his cheeks. He told her how sorry he was that he could not free them. Delilah now understood his broken promise and why the horrible overseer was back.

"I'm a coward," he said. "I let you down. I let you all down."

She touched his face, wiped away the tear, and said, "I understand. It's not your fault. You didn't want to die. Nobody does. I forgive you. We all forgive you. At least you tried. That's more than anybody else ever did for us."

He gazed at her, bewildered by her kindness and understanding toward what he'd done. How could she have forgiven him so easily?

Delilah boldly asked, "Sir, could you please tell me why these people hate us so much? What did we do to them? They came to our land, took us against our will, and put us in chains in the bottom of a ship. They brought us here to their homes and treat us like dogs. They make us work sun up to sun down and give us rags to wear, scraps to eat, and shacks to live in while they enjoy all the best of everything. Why, sir? Why do they do this to us?"

Jameson felt remorse for her and shame for his own kind but felt compelled to find out more about this lovely young woman, so he queried, "Are you from Africa?"

"No, sir, I was born here, but my mama was African."

"Who is your father?"

"I'm the child of a plantation master who raped my mama one night. I don't know who my father is. My mama said it would be better if I didn't know. When I was old enough, I was sold to Mista Josiah, and they took me from my mother. I always figured she was still at the Moors Plantation, but now I don't even know where she is or if she's dead or alive. All I remember is just how much I cried when they took me away and brought me here."

"Don't give up hope. We may still find her," Jameson said as he took her hand. This time it was his turn to wipe her tears away.

Delilah looked up at him with helpless abandon and pleaded, "Mista Jameson, I need to know. Please, tell me. Why do they hate us so much?"

Jameson looked at the beautiful black woman and knew he needed to answer her question. He paused for a moment to try to collect his thoughts and then said, "I wish I knew. I've tried many times to answer that question. I believe they wanted inexpensive labor to tend the crops, and you and your people fulfilled that requirement. As the number of slaves increased at each plantation, you actually outnumbered the owners, and they became afraid of uprisings. You know they are more afraid of all of you than they will admit. I think they actually view slavery as a necessary evil, and in some strange way they convince themselves it is acceptable. It's all very curious when you consider we live in a country where we are governed by a constitution that states all men are created equal and believe in a God that created all men in his own image and likeness. The whole concept is just so wrong. I wish I could do something to change it. Black or white, we're all God's children."

Delilah looked confused and said, "But we are not black, and you are not white, sir. Look." She picked up a piece of paper off the ground and held it next to Jameson's arm. "The paper is white. Y'all not that color. Y'all tan." Then she looked around and found a piece of coal. She held it up to her arm and said, "See, I not black, like this piece of coal. I'm brown. Y'all are light brown, and I am a darker brown, but we are both of the same color. We're not black and white opposites, only darker and lighter shades of brown. We are not so different after all, are we? Besides, shouldn't we judge a person by what's in their heart? Isn't it more important to be a good, kind, lovin', carin' person? Isn't that what really matters, not a person's skin color?"

Jameson smiled and said, "You are a very intelligent woman. You deserve better than this, and I will try to give it to you." With that his courage returned, and he reached into his pocket and produced the freedom papers. "Come with me," he said and grabbed her hand.

He led her up and into the great house. She obediently followed.

She had never been allowed inside the grand house before and was amazed by all she saw. It was so clean and large, filled with so much furniture; it was overwhelming! She stood in awe at all the wondrous things her eyes beheld. She just couldn't comprehend it. They had so much, and her people had so little. He led her into the den, grabbed a pen, and proceeded to sign all the freedom papers, asking her again the names of all the workers so he could fill them out correctly. He handed the papers to her and told her to give them out to all the people, but tell them to keep everything a secret for now—put them in their pockets and tell no one, act as if nothing happened, and wait until he could initiate a plan to get them all out safely.

"What about you?" Delilah said. "What about your safety?"

"Don't worry about me. I'll be all right...but thank you for caring. You're more concerned about me than my own wife."

He reached over, pulled her close, and kissed her on the cheek.

"Thank you for opening my eyes and giving me courage. You are the answer to my prayers."

Delilah was stunned and a little concerned, no white man had ever treated her so kindly, let alone kiss her.

Jameson hesitated. "Can you read the names I've written, Lilah?"

"Yes, I can read and write some, enough to get by."

"How? Who taught you?" Jameson queried.

She hesitated, not wanting to get anyone in trouble. It was a crime to teach a slave to read and write.

"It's okay," he said. "I wouldn't punish anyone for teaching you. In fact, I would commend them."

She instinctively trusted the new white master and told him it was Nanny. Nanny had to learn to read and write so she could order groceries and supplies and communicate with dressmakers, travelling salesmen, and the doctor. The lady of the house, Bethany Sue, did not want to be bothered with such things and left it all up to Nanny to keep the house running smoothly. Delilah, in turn, tried to teach the other workers, but it was hard. They had no interest after toiling all day in the fields. The little children, Lizzie and Ozzie, were quick studies, though, and caught on very fast.

As Delilah reached for the papers, her hand touched Jameson's hand. They both stopped and looked at each other. He noticed how beautiful she was with her bright brown eyes that seemed to penetrate his very soul. She noticed the kindness in his handsome face and felt a definite kinship with him. A kind of electricity passed through them, and they were temporarily transfixed on each other. Neither one could fully explain it, but they both felt it. Being a little frightened, she pulled away, thanked him, and left for slave row. Jameson watched her leave. He didn't even realize he was smiling, but a figure at the top of the stairs did. She saw and heard it all.

Delilah returned to slave row where all the others wanted to know what the new master had done to her. She recounted her story and produced the signed freedom papers. They were all shocked and surprised at the announcement. Some of the women wept with joy, while some of the men jumped up and down, unable to contain their happiness.

Amos said, "Let's leave now. We can get far away before the sun comes up."

Delilah scolded him, saying, "No, Amos, we can't leave until Mista Jameson says it's safe. I gave him my word that we would all act like nothin' had happened."

"Why should we?" Amos griped.

"He's puttin' his life at risk for us," Delilah pleaded. "The least we can do is wait, like he asked us to."

They all agreed, though Amos was not so sure. The levity died down, but their spirits were buoyed. They could easily endure a few more days, knowing freedom was within their reach.

Delilah touched her hand where it had brushed against Jameson's. She could still feel the tingling and wondered what it meant. She looked up toward the mansion and smiled. She knew she dare not think such thoughts, but somehow could not help it.

Chapter 8

FALSE FRIENDS

The next morning Jameson ate his breakfast alone. Neither Abigail nor Bethany Sue joined him. Bethany Sue probably needed professional help, but no one dared to mention it. Jameson had tried, but her father would not hear of it. Nanny could do nothing more than to sigh and shake her head. Abigail, on the other hand, was upset with her husband and was determined to teach him a lesson by refusing to have anything to do with him, including depriving him of any sexual intentions.

Jameson saddled the horse to the buckboard. He was heading into town for supplies. As he passed slave row, he saw Slycott readying the whip to punish some poor male yet again.

"I told you that was no longer permitted on this plantation, Mister Slycott."

Slycott scornfully looked at Jameson and said, "I thought I was in complete charge of the slaves, Jameson?"

"It's Mister Hartford to you, sir, and I am in charge of this plantation and all that happens on it. There will be no more physical discipline to these people. Do you understand?"

"Look, I'm the overseer, and my job—"

"You're job," interrupted Jameson, "is to do what I tell you to do. I'm going into town, and when I return, if I find out you hurt any of these people, I will take that whip to you myself and see how you like it. Do I make myself clear?"

Slycott, astonished, mumbled a yes but was embarrassed that he was chastised in front of the workers, who were all secretly smiling. Jameson winked at Delilah, pulled her aside, and told her to let him know of any misdeeds.

"You're my eyes and ears, Lilah. Together we can win, don't you agree?"

A broad smile came to her face as she proudly replied, "Yes, sir, Mista Jameson."

Jameson rode off. Delilah watched him until his shadow disappeared over the horizon.

Abner Slycott was also watching, wondering what had just happened and what it all meant. He slithered off into the shadows to ponder these disturbing developments.

Jameson arrived in town in about an hour. This time people were smiling at him, wishing him a good day. *What hypocrites*, he thought. *I guess what they don't know won't hurt me.*

It was a sunny, warm day, and the town was full of people busily hurrying along. As he passed the general store, he spotted an older Negro gentleman loading groceries into a coach for a customer. He was being taunted by two children. They were calling him names, and one of them picked up a handful of dirt from the street and threw it at the poor man. He simply brushed the soot off of his clothes and continued loading the supplies. Jameson stopped his wagon and chastised the children.

"Hey, there, don't do that. Leave this man alone."

The young boy replied, "Why? He's only a slave."

"He's a human being. How would you like it if I threw dirt at you?"

"I'd tell my mommy and daddy on you."

The boy bent down to get another handful as Jameson climbed down from his buckboard. The children got frightened and ran back into the store.

Jameson turned to the poor black man and said, "I'm sorry for that."

The man replied, "It's okay, sir. You get used to it, but thank you all the same."

"You shouldn't have to put up with such bad behavior and blatant disregard for human decency."

As Jameson was speaking, the children, with their mother and the storekeeper, emerged from the shop.

The woman asked her child, "Is this the man who yelled at you?"

The child nodded yes.

She addressed Jameson, "What is the meaning of this?"

Jameson tried to tell her what had transpired but was surprised at her reaction. She not only defended her children but gave Jameson a dressing down for interfering.

Jameson, undaunted quickly retorted, "Madam, this is a human being, and he should be treated with the same respect you would give to any other person. You're teaching your children hatred. You know children aren't born with prejudice. It's something they learn from narrowminded, hateful parents such as yourself."

"Well, I never was so insulted."

"You and your children didn't think anything about insulting this poor man, did you?"

"Get into the coach, children. We're leaving." The children obeyed and climbed aboard as the coach beat a hasty retreat.

The shopkeeper then caught Jameson's attention. "Why don't you mind your own business and get away from my store. You're bad for business. I'll lose customers on account of you."

He pushed the black gentleman back into the store and slammed the door. Jameson proceeded on his way, wondering if he had made matters better or worse. At least he spoke up for people who had no other voice than his. He hated bullying perhaps because he had been the victim of such behavior in his youth, both from his father and his younger brother, and now from the town, his friends, and even his own wife. He wished he could help them all, but he knew he would be lucky if he could manage to secure freedom for his own workers.

He pulled up in front of the bank and entered. "Good morning, Mister Bordeau," he said.

"Why, Jameson Hartford, what a nice surprise. How are you, sir?"

"Fine today," Jameson continued. "I wonder if you had a chance to look up my account and find the balance."

"Of course, just a second, my friend," Thaddeus said. "Ah, here it is. You have all of $20,516 dollars, quite a tidy sum."

"I'll take it all," said Jameson.

"All of it?" countered Thaddeus. "Why would you need such a large sum?"

"I'm going to fix up the plantation. Buy another one of those cotton gins. Get new horses, mules, plows, and farm animals. I want to fix up the barn, and oh, yes, the slaves' quarters need to be rebuilt, can't have them getting ill. They don't work when they're sick."

Jameson was lying. He needed the money to help his workers get to freedom. That last lie was an especially nice touch, indicating how he had supposedly come around to their way of thinking.

"Besides, I will be bringing in the crops soon, and that will replenish my account. Also, I'll be transferring money from my bank in Boston down here to you just as soon as I can get to the Western Union office."

"No problem. I'll have it for you immediately," said Thaddeus. "By the way, how is my daughter, Bethany Sue?"

"She's still very depressed. She might need professional help."

"Nonsense," Thaddeus responded. "She'll be fine. She just needs time."

The real reason Thaddeus did not want anyone to think his daughter was not of sound mind was that it might reflect on him, and the bank might also be thought to be unstable, causing people to start withdrawing their funds.

"Here it is, Jameson. Spend it wisely, my boy. Good to do business with you. Good day."

"Good day to you, Mister Bordeau."

He then proceeded to the lawyer Nicholas Mansfield to drop off the signed deed and inheritance documents, giving him sole ownership to Serenity. Everyone was so friendly. It was just too obvious what was going on. As long as he towed the line, they were all his friends, but should he deviate from the accepted norm, they would become his worst enemies; if they only knew of his plans.

On his exit he met the sheriff and Doc Pritchard.

Doc asked him, "Are you feeling okay today?"

"Yes, why shouldn't I?" replied Jameson.

"No reason, just asking," Doc said.

Jameson realized Doc must have known about the hooded riders attack on him yesterday but was sure he was too old to have been a part of it.

Shelby Mathison exclaimed, "Of course he's okay! Just look at how healthy he looks. He's got the face of a man who knows what's best for him. Isn't that so, Hartford?"

Jameson would have liked to wipe that smug grin right off the sheriff's face, but he knew he had to play the game.

"I certainly do know what's best, and I intend to do just that," Jameson retorted. The sheriff looked a bit confused as Jameson added, "Excuse me, gentlemen, I have to get back to my plantation and make sure everything is going as planned. Good day!"

"Good day," they replied.

The next stop was the gunsmith. Jameson went in and purchased five rifles and three pistols with enough ammunition to start a small war. He told them he liked to hunt, and he also heard that there were Yankee spies about, and he needed to protect his property and loved ones. No one suspected a thing. The town was confident their indoctrination was successful. He loaded a pistol and kept it close by, just in case, but there would be no hooded riders after him this time. He proceeded home, confident that his charade had worked. He looked up to heaven and thanked God for answering his prayers. This time the ride home was pleasant and uneventful.

Jameson decided to stop at a remote section of his plantation and try his new firearms. He needed to know if he had to reacquaint himself with how they worked. He also might need to improve his aim should he be required to use his guns for self-defense. He filled the barrel with gunpowder, dropped in a pellet, tapped it down with the plunger, pulled back the hammer, raised the rifle, aimed at a knot hole in a tree about eight yards away, and fired. To his surprise he hit the knot hole square in the center. He surmised that once he had learned how to shoot, he never forgot.

He next readied a pistol, performing the same routine, then aimed at the same tree and was suddenly shocked when he heard a voice say, "Don't shoot! I give up. Please don't shoot me."

Out from behind the tree stepped a black man, visibly scared, dressed in tattered clothes. He was shaking and begging for mercy.

Jameson asked, "Who are you?"

"I'm called Willy, sir."

"What are you doing on my plantation, Willy?"

"I'm sorry for trespassing, sir. You see I'm...well, I'm..."

"You're a runaway slave, aren't you?"

"Yes, sir, but please don't shoot me. I give up. You can send me back."

Jameson quickly responded, "I wouldn't think of sending you back. Maybe I can help you. Come hide on my plantation, and I'll try to find a way to get you north to freedom."

"Why would you do that for me, sir?"

"I'm against slavery, Willy, and I intend to free my own workers. You can join us if you would like."

The conversation was stopped as they both heard approaching horses, and Willy, in a panic, ran off into the trees and brush before Jameson could stop him. At least he was headed in the right direction—north.

Two men appeared and identified themselves as slave catchers. Introducing themselves as Marty and Bobby Ray, they asked Jameson if he had seen a man whose description perfectly matched Willy. They said he was a runaway from the Moors Plantation, and they were hired to bring him back, dead or alive, preferably alive. Jameson said he did indeed see a man run off in that direction—pointing west—about ten minutes ago, and if they hurried, they would surely catch him. They thanked him, made a snide remark about the black fool not even knowing which way was north, and rode off toward the west.

Jameson searched for Willy but could not find him. He hesitated to shout as it might bring the two slave catchers back. Instead, he said a prayer for Willy to find a safe passage and hoped he would find his way to freedom in the north.

He again raised the loaded pistol, aimed at an old tree stump, and pressed the trigger. The gunpowder exploded, sending the pellet flying. It reached its target and lodged itself in the dried-up bark. Jameson happily concluded that he could still fire his newly acquired weapons and would indeed be able to defend himself should the need arise. He mounted his wagon and turned the horses for home, remarking to himself that he would be home earlier than anticipated.

Jameson arrived back at the plantation to find an unfamiliar coach parked outside in the yard. It was nicely adorned with gold appliqués shining against a spotless, gleaming black veneer.

Jameson couldn't help but admire the coach and took a closer look inside. The seats were leather with silver and gold ornamentation. There were even tufted pillows on the seats to make the ride smoother, he supposed. The driver up in the front paid no mind to the prying eyes of Jameson; he just stared forward, holding the reins as someone ready to leave at a moment's notice. It must belong to someone of importance, Jameson deduced, and quickly ran inside the mansion.

Nanny looked shocked to see him back so early but said nothing. She just looked at him and then looked up the stairs toward the bedrooms. Jameson understood and quietly climbed up the stairs and paused outside the door to his bedroom. He could detect whispers but could not make out any of the words. He reached for the doorknob, turned it, and pushed. The door did not move. It was locked from the inside. He could hear rustling and louder murmurings, so without further hesitation, he lifted his leg and boldly kicked at the door. It flew open to reveal Abigail and another man. They were clothed, but not all the buttons and bows were neatly fastened or tied.

Abigail exclaimed, "Jameson! You're home early."

He just looked at her then at the strange man, who was visibly shaken.

Abigail continued, "This is Ned Barrows. He's the mayor of Willow Hills. He stopped by to say hello. Isn't that nice of him?"

Jameson gave the stranger the once over, eyeing him up and down. He was of medium height, had a pencil-thin mustache, and was dressed in a finest of fabrics with a vest that was unbuttoned.

"Hello, Mister Hartford," he said nervously as he extended his hand in friendship, "It's nice to meet you."

Jameson just stared.

Abigail said, "Jameson, don't be rude. Greet our esteemed guest."

"What's going on here, Abigail? Are you having an affair?"

"Jameson, I'm shocked and appalled at your accusation. Where are your manners?"

He repeated his question, "Abigail, are you having an affair?"

She again elusively evaded the question, "Jameson, what a ridiculous notion that is."

Ned tried to add, "Let me assure you, Mister Hartford sir, that—"

Jameson interrupted, "So let me understand. I'm supposed to believe that you just happened to stop by while I was out and not expected back for a few hours, and you're entertaining my wife, in our bedroom with the door closed and locked...and nothing happened?"

Abigail said, "Jameson, you're making yourself look ridiculous."

Jameson looked at Ned and yelled, "Get out!"

"Jameson, stop this now!"

"Shut up, Abby. Mister Barrows, get out now before I forget that I am a gentleman."

"Don't speak to me in that manner, Jameson, and he does not have to leave. Perhaps you should leave until you calm down and begin acting civilized again."

Jameson grabbed Ned by the collar and the seat of his pants and pushed him out of the bedroom, down the hall, and finally shoved him down the stairs. Ned stumbled, step after step, only regaining his equilibrium as he reached the bottom. He quickly ran for the door and left.

Abigail said, "That was very rude, Jameson."

"Are you cheating on me, Abby?" he asked again.

Abigail stood there for a moment then boldly retorted, "You cheated on me with that slave girl, and you have the audacity to accuse me of the same thing."

"I did not cheat on you, Abby."

"Well then, tell me, what is the meaning of this?" Abigail said as she produced the handwritten codicil Jameson had drawn up the day before. "You insist you are innocent, yet you leave an entire plantation to a woman you claim you are not involved with, that's hard for me to believe."

Jameson tried to defend himself. "I never said I didn't care about her. I do care about her and all the workers. I wanted them to have a chance at freedom in case something happened to me."

Abigail yelled, "You wanted to take care of them! What about me? You would rather leave everything to the slaves than to your own wife? And you expect me to believe nothing else is going on? Come now, Jameson. I'm not that gullible."

"Abby, you have to believe me. Nothing happened. Besides, you would still inherit all our belongings in Boston."

Abigail said, "So I'm worth at least half of your estate, and a little whore you just met is worth the other half, and you're insisting that you're innocent. Leave me alone, Jameson. I have a lot of thinking to do."

Abigail tried to shove him out of the room, but Jameson grabbed her arm and said, "You still didn't tell me if you cheated on me or not."

Abigail looked Jameson straight in the eye and said, "I already told you. If you don't believe me, what else can I do?" She pulled her arm free and ordered him to get out. "Leave me now. I need to be alone."

He walked out of the room and slammed the door behind him. He went down the stairs, passing Bethany Sue, who had a peculiar grin on her face, and went straight into the study to look for a bottle of whiskey. He needed to drown his doubts and sorrows in order to make the lies seem more believable. He searched in vain, but someone apparently hid all the liquor.

He sat down at the desk and placed his head in his hands. Everything was becoming so complex. Nothing was going according to plan. He felt as if he was not in control of his fate. He cursed himself for not hiding the codicil then rebuked himself for feeling guilty. Next, he assured himself that he did nothing wrong, and he did not want to believe Abigail would cheat on him, but he had to admit, he was attracted to Delilah. Suddenly his thoughts turned toward her and the rest of the workers. He had better check on them. He left them alone far too long, and Slycott was not to be trusted.

Chapter 9

FAMILY SECRETS

Jameson left the house and once again boarded his wagon. He drove out into the fields to find Slycott and be reassured that he had not harmed any of the workers. He saw them laboring in the hot sun, but no Slycott. He stopped and asked one of them where the overseer was. Alex told him Slycott had gotten drunk after Jameson had left this morning, and they did not know where he was. Jameson asked him where Delilah was. He said she was over on the other side of the barn near the slave's graveyard.

They were all very grateful for receiving their freedom papers and swarmed around Jameson to thank him for his kindness. Worried that Slycott or another outsider might be watching or listening, Jameson held his finger up to his lips and motioned for them to be quiet. He whispered to them they would all be leaving as soon as he could ensure their safety. The workers all understood and went back to their grind, but with smiles on their faces.

Jameson drove the buckboard up to the house, got out, and proceeded to walk around to where all the workers were buried. As he approached, he heard a drunken Slycott forcing himself on Delilah.

"You tried to turn Hartford against me. You owe me something, girl."

He tried to kiss her, but she pulled away.

"What's the matter? Abner's not good enough for you? I ain't rich enough? I don't own a plantation like those Hartfords?"

Delilah was trying desperately to get away from him, begging for mercy. She was wearing the jacket Jameson had given her, and it angered the inebriated overseer even further.

He grabbed her arm and yelled, "Hartford didn't give you this for nothing. Do you think he'd still want you if he knew that you had a baby with his brother? Do you? Well, I doubt it. You want me to keep quiet; all you have to do is please me."

He pulled her close and tried to kiss her. She squirmed and wriggled her arm free from the jacket sleeve as Slycott yanked at it to keep her from escaping. The jacket tore then ripped and finally split in two right down the seam as the overseer's anger raged.

"Get away from me, Mista Slycott. Please leave me alone," pleaded Delilah.

He managed to grab her again. "No slave says no to Abner Slycott. You'll do as I say or else."

"No, she won't," Jameson said sternly. "Get away from her."

Delilah pulled herself free and ran behind Jameson for protection.

Slycott said, "Is she your whore now, Jameson?"

"Don't call her that. Don't ever call her that."

"I'll show you who the real boss is," Slycott boasted as he came at Jameson.

The first punch was deflected by Jameson. The second punch was thrown by Jameson, and it hit Sylcott right on the jaw. The big man was stunned but quickly regained his composure and came at Jameson again. This time he connected with a right cross, which sent Jameson to the ground. Slycott kicked him repeatedly then got down on his knees and proceeded to pummel the dazed Jameson with punch after punch.

"I'm going to kill you, Yankee." He snorted.

Suddenly, there was a loud thud, and Slycott fell to the ground. Delilah stood over him holding a bloodied two by four.

"Are you okay, Mista Jameson?" she asked. Bending down, she gently picked up his head, held it in her arms, and wiped the blood off his face.

"I'm okay," he said. "Thank you for that. You're very resourceful."

"Thank you for savin' me," she said. "He's an evil man."

Slycott moaned. "Oh, my head, what hit me?"

"Get out! You're fired, Slycott!" Jameson yelled.

"You can't fire me. You know what will happen to you," Slycott reminded him.

"You just try it, Slycott. You'll be the first one I kill. Now, get out!"

Slycott stumbled away, holding an egg-sized bump on his head, but added, "You'll be sorry. You'll see." He could barely stay on his feet and had to use the barn for support as he staggered to his horse and rode away.

"I'm worried for you," said Delilah.

He was deeply touched that she cared for his well-being and said, "Don't worry. I'll be ready this time." He was trying to reassure her and himself.

She tore off a piece of her dress and tenderly cleaned the blood from his wounded face, and using her fingers, pushed his hair back into place. "There, you're as good as new," she boasted.

He smiled and said, "Thank you. You're very sweet."

They stared at each other, yearning for something more. That strange feeling once again manifested itself as they both kept looking at each other, and then Jameson broke the uneasy silence.

"Why are you out here in this graveyard, Lilah?"

She looked to the side but said nothing. He turned to notice a small unmarked grave with flowers on it, removed from all the others.

"Who is buried here?" he asked.

She hesitated, not sure of what to do. Then desperately needing to unburden herself of the grief, she said, "My little baby girl."

"Your baby girl? What? How did she die? What happened to her?"

Delilah did not want to answer.

"Who was the father? Was it my brother, like Slycott said?"

She looked at him, her face filled with shame, and said, "Yes."

He asked, "Why, did you want to have a baby with my brother?"

"Mista Jameson," she interrupted, "I didn't have a choice whether I wanted to or not. When the master says to do somethin', you don't say no, 'cause if you do, you get punished. You just obey, that's all."

"Did you love him?" asked Jameson.

"No, I didn't love him. I didn't even like him. You have to do as you're ordered. The first time I said no and tried to fight him off. He beat me bad. It took two or three weeks for the bruises to heal and go away. When he came again for me, I couldn't say no. He held me down by my hair and said if I tried to stop him he'd rip it out of my head. He came many more times for me, and after a while I just became numb."

Reliving the past was too much for her, and she started to weep and shake uncontrollably. Jameson took her gently into his arms and tried to console her.

He held her close, stroked her head, and said, "It's okay. Everything will be all right. I'm so sorry for you. I apologize for my brother's actions. That should never have happened, and it won't happen ever again now that I'm here."

She responded to his caressing and seemed to calm down.

"Are you feeling better?" he asked.

"Yes, thank you, Mista Jameson. I'm sorry," she apologized and instinctively pulled away.

"Can I ask you how your child died?"

"Yes, sir, I'll tell you if you want to know, but you won't like it."

He tenderly touched her arm and said, "If you think you are able to tell me, please go on. I need to know."

Delilah reluctantly related her story. "Her name was Eve. Your brother named her that because she was his firstborn girl, like the first woman in the Bible. He didn't have no interest in Miss Bethany Sue anymore, so he turned to other women, including the slaves. When Miss Bethany Sue found out, she got real mad. She yelled and yelled. She hated him and me too, although I had no choice.

"She came down to slave row one night and dragged me off by my hair into the barn. Mista Slycott was there. He was ordered to hold me down while she chopped off all my hair, and then she told him to shave my head bald. When it was done, she looked at me, laughed, and said, 'Now Josiah won't think you're so pretty any more. He won't bother with you again.'"

"I can't believe this," said Jameson.

Delilah hesitated, wondering if she was too outspoken with the new master. "Maybe I shouldn't be tellin' you these things," she said.

"No, no, please continue," Jameson pleaded. "I should know the truth."

She wanted desperately to tell someone of the injustices that were perpetrated upon her, and Jameson's insistence made her feel somewhat secure, so she continued. "Well, you know how they say Mista Josiah fell off his horse and died?"

Jameson nodded. "He didn't?"

"Well, Nate was the one who found him, and he said the cinch on the horse saddle was cut. That was the same horse Mista Josiah rode into town every night after supper. The rumor was he was seeing someone in town. Uncky saw Miss Bethany Sue messing around by the horse before he rode off. We think she cut the cinch so he would fall and get hurt, to punish him. We don't think she meant to kill him, but that's what happened.

"After that, she went mad. She came down to slave row and told me to give her the baby. She was going to get rid of her. I begged her, 'Please don't do that. Don't take my baby.' She grabbed her, and I wouldn't let go, so she called Mista Slycott to help her. He grabbed the child from my arms and pushed me backward. I tripped and couldn't hold on to her. She slipped out of my hands and his hands and fell to the ground. She hit her head on a rock, and…she died."

Delilah paused and began to cry again. Jameson held her again and asked her if she wished to stop telling him the story.

She said, "No, Mista Jameson, I really need to tell someone." She continued, "When my baby died, I was screamin' and cryin'. Miss Bethany Sue slapped me again and again until I stopped. Then she told me to get rid of the child and bury the baby in the slaves' graveyard. 'But don't you dare mark the grave,' she threatened. Then she just up and walked away."

"I'm so sorry," Jameson said. "Didn't anyone call the sheriff?"

"It's no crime to kill a slave," Delilah said.

"Well, what about Josiah? Surely the cut saddle cinch would prove it was attempted murder."

"Miss Bethany Sue is the daughter of the richest man in town, Mista Bordeau. Nobody wants to go against him. Besides, they would probably have blamed me and hung me."

Jameson now understood why she was so afraid of him when he took her on their search for her mother.

"Delilah, I'm so sorry for what happened to you. I feel like it is partly my fault. I should never have left this place. I should not have confronted my father. If I had just been the good quiet son, I would have inherited this plantation and been able to put an end to this injustice and perhaps spared you the horrors you had to endure. I will make it up to you somehow, I swear I will. I promise you things will get better, I swear to God they will."

He pulled Delilah close to him and gently kissed her head. This time she did not pull away from the new master. She felt safe and secure for the first time in her life. He continued to hold her until she calmed down. Once she had regained her composure he tried, in his own amateurish way, to cheer her up.

"You know, I kind of like your hair this way. You look beautiful in short hair, Lilah, really beautiful."

"Thank you, Mista Jameson. You're very kind to me," she replied, as the hint of a smile crossed her tear-stained face.

He found a piece of discarded wood and whittled a small cross with his knife then carved the name Eve on it. He handed it to her and told her to place it on her baby's grave. A tear rolled down her cheek as she thanked him and tenderly placed it on the mound of soil. He kissed her head again and gazed lovingly into her soulful eyes. Time seemed to stand still as they became mesmerized by the same feelings they felt that night in the house. He pulled her closer to him and she gladly obliged. They did not have to utter a sound, all the words they needed were spoken in their hearts. Sparks flew between them as if someone had lit a fire. They could not take their eyes off of one another, it all seemed so right, like it was their destiny. They could not stop what was happening and neither one wanted to.

A clatter from the chickens outside suspended the magic, and the two souls returned to reality. They parted—she back to slave row, he up to the main house. They thought they were alone but there were two figures in the window watching them. It was Bethany Sue and Abigail.

Jameson stopped and turned. He couldn't help but watch Delilah as she walked away. Then he slowly strolled back to the mansion. Upon entering the house, he was feeling a little guilty and thought he might try to make amends with his wife. He proceeded up the stairs and straight into his bedroom, where he found Abigail packing a suitcase.

"What is the meaning of this?" he inquired.

"I'm leaving you, Jameson. You are not the man I married. You are ruining everything—our home, our life, our future, all for those slaves. I believe you care for them more than you do for me, especially that little slut. What's her name? Delilah. Yes, I know all about you two. Bethany Sue showed me the two of you out there holding each other. If I had any doubts before, I certainly am convinced now. I will not let you touch me after you've been intimate with that…woman. We have a little misunderstanding, and you can't wait to take up with someone else, even a slave. Now I know why you left this plantation to her. How could you do this to me?"

"Abby," he pleaded, "nothing happened. I swear."

Then he turned to Bethany Sue and asked, "How could you do something like that?"

Bethany Sue answered with only a wry smile.

He turned back to Abigail and repeated, "You have to believe me. She's lying to you for some reason."

Abigail said indignantly, "Why would she lie to me, Jameson? And if you don't care about her, then why didn't you sell her like I told you to do? It's because you secretly want her, don't you? You…you're a cad!" She slapped him across the face. "Good-bye, Jameson. I'll be living at Tall Oaks from now on."

"Abby, wait," Jameson pleaded. "Nothing happened. We were just talking. She told me what happened to my brother and how horrible she was treated. I swear nothing else happened."

"I don't believe you anymore, Jameson, good-bye."

And with that Abigail proceeded out of the room and down the stairs. She ordered Uncky to get her bags and drive her to her father's plantation. Uncky had no choice but to obey.

Jameson stood there in amazement. She was right. He had put the needs of the workers above all else, but they needed him. They had nowhere else to turn. No one cared about them but him. He wanted to go after her, but his heart and mind were somewhere else.

"I'm glad she's gone."

Turning around, he was startled by the figure of Bethany Sue in the doorway.

She continued, "Now all we have to do is get rid of that no good shameless hussy Delilah woman, and you and I can be together again, Josiah, as if nothing had ever happened."

She moved toward him, arms outstretched.

Jameson, shocked, pushed her away and said, "What's the matter with you? I'm not Josiah. I'm Jameson. Josiah's dead."

"Don't push me away, Josiah. I love you," she pleaded as she came forward again.

He shoved her back out of the room and slammed and locked the door. He stood there for a second in total disbelief of what had just occurred. He was both physically and mentally exhausted and could not deal with any more problems. He just walked over to the bed, fell across it, and lie shattered, pondering all the day's events. He could not believe what was happening to his life. He grabbed a pillow, wrapped it around his head and tried to drown out all the sounds swirling around in his mind.

He could still hear her on the other side of the door, turning the knob, trying to enter his room, and wailing, "Josiah, I'm here. I love you. Open the door. Please let me in, my dear husband. I'll wait for you, my darling. I forgive you."

He twisted and turned praying silently, *what should I do? What should I do?* Exhaustion took its toll and he was finally able to fall into blessed sleep.

Bethany Sue lay there in the hallway, weeping and mumbling about her Josiah. Unexpectedly her fantasy took on a new life, and she quickly rose and ran down the stairs. She stopped in the kitchen where she grabbed a long, sharp knife then proceeded out the front door and, in a frenzy, headed straight for slave row.

She arrived and started screaming, "Josiah, where are you? Are you with that whore again? Come out here at once."

Sarah emerged from her shelter and politely stated, "Miss Bethany Sue, Mista Josiah ain't here. He's dead."

"Don't lie to me. I know he's down here with that Delilah woman. I'm going to kill her for seducing my Josiah."

"Calm down, Miss Bethany. Let me make you some nice hot tea, okay?"

Sarah was stalling for time as she motioned to the others to get Delilah out of the area to safety. Everyone realized the severity of the situation and summarily ushered Delilah out of the door at the far end of the shack. Once free, she quickly ran off to hide by the barn until it was safe to return. Sarah continued to try to calm down the rather psychotic behavior of the unexpected visitor.

"Miss Bethany, Delilah ain't here. There ain't nobody here that you're looking for, I promise you."

"I want that harlot," she screamed as she shoved Sarah aside and ran into the shelter, wielding the knife.

Once inside, she searched frantically, looking for her imaginary enemy. She overturned some cots, threw pots and pans and blankets, disrupting everything, and then finally emerged from the structure. Jealousy filled her eyes as she ran from one slave to the next, questioning them as to her husband's whereabouts, all the time threatening them with the sharp blade in her hand. The workers only stood there, not knowing what to say or do.

"I'll kill her for taking my Josiah away from me. Where is she? Where is she? I just want my husband back. I just want him back alive, alive, alive," Bethany Sue pleaded as she began to break down in tears, then turning the knife toward herself.

"I, I want my husband back. If I can't have him here, then I shall go to him."

She raised the knife as if ready to plunge it into herself, Sarah shouted, "Don't Miss Bethany Sue, stop!"

Bethany Sue hesitated and then screamed loudly, "I can't do it, I want to, but I can't. I'm so sorry Josiah, so very, very sorry."

She collapsed to the ground and released her grip on the sharp blade which fell out of her hand.

Sarah cautiously approached her, helped her up, and walked her back to the mansion. She turned her over to Nanny, who patiently helped her inside and up to her bedroom. Bethany Sue kept murmuring something about Josiah and how sorry she was for something or other. Nanny couldn't quite make sense of her ramblings and just told her to try and get some sleep as she tucked her into bed. Bethany Sue cried herself to sleep as she had done for so many nights since that fateful day.

Chapter 10

ENCOUNTERS

Jameson tossed and turned until the wee small hours of the morning, unable to fall asleep. His thoughts were filled with the events of the day: Abigail, Bethany Sue, and especially Delilah. He felt guilty about Abigail and shocked by Bethany Sue but couldn't get Delilah out of his mind. She suffered so much at the hands of unscrupulous men. He decided to rise, get dressed, and go down to slave row to be sure she was all right. He carefully opened the bedroom door, and being reassured that Bethany Sue was not there, he crept along the wall and down the stairs, finally reaching the main door. He turned the knob and pulled the door open, letting the hot, moist air engulf him.

He started down the path then suddenly stopped, wondering what he would say to her. Would she think he was coming to take advantage of her, to hurt her like his brother did? He decided this was not such a good idea and it would be in his best interest to go back to the house. He turned to retreat but was stopped by a voice.

"Mista Jameson?"

He turned around to see Delilah standing there; looking absolutely beautiful bathed in the pale moonlight.

Startled, he began to ramble. "Lilah, I couldn't sleep. I was concerned, I mean, worried about you. I wanted to be sure you were all right. You were so sad. I wanted to say again how sorry I was."

She walked toward him.

He kept on speaking. "Abigail left me. She thought you and I... Well, uh, I mean, she's gone back to her mother."

Delilah said softly, "I know. I saw her leave."

He continued nervously, "I want you to know that you never have to fear me. I would never hurt you or force you to do anything you didn't want to do."

Delilah looked seductively into his eyes and whispered, "You wouldn't be forcing me."

Jameson, confused for a second, did not know what to make of this beautiful brown woman. He stuttered. "Are you saying, I mean, that you... and I, that is, you would—"

She softly spoke. "You're the first white man who ever talked nice to me or even treated me with any kindness. You saved me from that horrible Mista Slycott, and you care enough about me and my people to give us our freedom, even though it puts your life in danger. You're the most wonderful person I ever met."

She leaned in close to him and pressed her moist, soft lips firmly yet gently on his. He did not hesitate and kissed her in return. She tasted so different yet so delicious. They looked deep into each other's souls; she could see the desire in his eyes, he could read the need in hers. They would never forget this moment for the rest of their lives.

Delilah joined her hand into his and slowly led him into the barn. They crawled onto a pile of hay and began to kiss each other passionately. She started to unbutton his shirt. He, in turn, removed her dress. They fell into each other's arms and gave into the temptation and the lust. They wanted each other badly.

He ran his hands up and down across her young body, touching her first with his fingers and then with his lips. She returned the affection with eager anticipation, exciting him more and more with every touch—caressing, hugging, and kissing so deeply as they united their two bodies in love. It was a love neither one of them understood, but that didn't seem to matter, as his lighter tan skin and her darker brown skin blended together into a beautiful shade of brown. Their state of ecstasy grew stronger and stronger, finally releasing all the pent up fear and anxiety in the beauty of the moment.

Then they lay exhausted yet content in each other's arms, enjoying the forbidden love each one felt for the other. They were lost in the moment and did not care about the time until they heard the rooster crow. Reality was calling them back. They hastily got dressed. He couldn't resist a last kiss before letting her leave, hoping this was not the end. They made no promises to each other, for they both knew the risks and perils of their tryst. However, he just couldn't erase the big grin he had on his face as he made his way back to the house. They couldn't help turning around, looking back at each other and smiling one more time, wishing the moment did not have to end. He could still taste her sweet scent in his mouth and vowed to himself to preserve the memory for as long as possible until he could taste her once again.

Delilah was also smiling and dreaming of a love she knew could not be. She slowly sauntered back to slave row only to find the other slaves in turmoil.

"Oh, Lilah!" Becky cried. "Amos has run off. We told him to wait like you and Mista Jameson said to, but he said he got his freedom papers and he's leavin'."

"Didn't you try to stop him?" screamed Delilah.

"Oh, yes," said Eli, "but he pushed us out of the way and ran."

"The fool, the big fool," complained Delilah. "I have to go tell Mista Jameson." She ran back up to the main house.

She pounded on the door.

Nanny opened it. "What's wrong, child?" she asked.

"I must talk to Mista Jameson right now. It's very important."

"He's up to his room. I can't disturb him now, child."

"But I must see him."

Suddenly the door opened wider, and there stood Bethany Sue. Delilah gasped in fear but was determined to tell Jameson what had happened.

"You get out of here, you little whore!" Bethany Sue screamed. "Haven't you caused enough trouble?"

"Please, Miss Bethany Sue, I have to see Mista Jameson," Delilah pleaded.

Bethany Sue slapped her across the face and threatened her. "Get out of here now! I will not let you corrupt Josiah again with your wiles, you little tramp. If I see you near Josiah again, I'll kill you, I swear. Now get out!" She slammed the door.

Delilah, stunned and scared, turned and slowly walked away. Nanny stared at Bethany Sue, and now fully realized something was dreadfully wrong.

Amos was running through the woods when he heard the sound of horse's hooves from behind. He turned to see two slave catchers quickly gaining on him. He tried to dodge them, but they were skilled in their trade.

They chased him, yelling, "You better run for your life, boy."

Throwing a net on him, they were finally able to bring him down.

"I ain't done nothin' wrong," Amos said.

"A black man by himself running through the woods, now that's mighty suspicious to me. Don't you think so, Marty?"

"I surely do, Bobby Ray."

"I'm not a runaway," said Amos. "Look, look here. I got freedom papers." He reached into his pocket and pulled out the crumpled note.

"Let me see that," Marty said as he grabbed the paper. He opened it, read it, and looked at Amos. "This ain't no freedom paper. Why it says right here that this is a runaway slave, and if found, return him to Jameson Hartford for a big reward."

"No, no, it can't say that," claimed Amos.

"You callin' me a liar, boy? We're gonna have to teach you a lesson for that. Bring me my butcher knife, Bobby Ray."

Amos began to plead for his life.

"We ain't gonna kill you, boy, just cut off something you ain't gonna need to use any more like a finger, a toe, or maybe… something else, if you get my meaning."

Bobby Ray shouted, "You're gonna regret trying to escape."

Marty started toward the terrified Amos, the knife glistening in the moonlight. Amos instinctively retreated but fell backward against a fallen tree limb and began screaming. His hand found a large rock in the debris and, being a strong man; he grabbed it and swung his hand up, hitting Marty in the head.

Marty fell over. Amos grabbed for the knife as Bobby Ray came at him. The knife plunged itself deep into Bobby Ray's stomach, and he fell on top of the panic-stricken Amos. Amos pushed him to the side, got up, looked with horror at all the blood on his hands and clothes, and headed straight into the forest.

Amos ran and ran until he could scarcely catch his breath. Then he suddenly realized he left his freedom paper back with the slave catchers. He must return and retrieve his only hope for survival. Panting heavily with sweat dripping out of every pore, he started back, cautiously canvassing the landscape for the two slave catchers or any other unwelcome guests. When he arrived, the men and their horses were gone. He looked around for the paper, hoping they dropped it somewhere, but he could not find it. There was a lot of blood on the spot where they tried to attack him. He must get out of there, but without his freedom paper he did not stand a chance. They would surely come looking for him. He would get caught and probably hung for the murder of a white man. Amos had no alternative but to return to Serenity. He quickly started back.

Chapter 11

UNWELCOME GUESTS

Jameson returned from the bedroom and entered the kitchen. He sat down at the table to enjoy a hearty breakfast, pretending he had been asleep and nothing had happened.

He told Nanny and Uncky, "Go into town this morning and bring back Doc Pritchard for Bethany Sue. She needs help."

Nanny and Uncky both agreed and said it was about time. Nanny told Jameson that Delilah had come by earlier, saying she needed to see him. He acted nonchalant, not wishing to arouse any suspicions, and said he would go see her as soon as he finished breakfast. Then he reached into his pocket and produced the last two freedom papers. He filled in their names and handed them over.

"You're free now," he told them.

"What are we gonna do with this, Mista Jameson?" Nanny said. "We don't know how to do anything but what we do here. You take them back."

He was puzzled. "Don't you want to be free?"

"We were always free in our minds, Mista Jameson. They can own our bodies, but they don't own our minds. If we think we're free, then we are free."

Jameson convinced them to hold on to the papers should they ever need them. Trouble was coming, and he did not know if he would survive. He asked them to leave immediately for the doctor. They would be safer in pairs than alone. Nanny said again that Delilah seemed real upset when she came by earlier, and Miss Bethany Sue had slapped her. Jameson could no longer hide his concern. Wiping his napkin across his lips, he said he was finished eating and quickly rose from the table.

Jameson left the house and hurried down to slave row. He smiled when he saw Delilah, realizing she was safe. She, on the other hand, had a concerned, worried look on her face.

He took her in his arms and asked, "What's wrong, Lilah?"

She told him of Amos's flight. As she was relating the story, Amos emerged from the fields.

Jameson chastised him. "You fool. I told you to wait until I could devise a plan that would allow us all to leave in a group to assure our safety."

Amos apologized. "I'm sorry, Mista Jameson. I really am."

Then he reluctantly began to relate his story, telling them how he lost his papers and that he might have killed someone.

"This is bad," Jameson said. "Trouble will follow and follow quickly. I have to change my plans. We have to get everyone out of here immediately. You," he said, indicating Amos, "will have to stay here with me to ensure the others' safety. They will be coming for you and me. They might let the others pass without incident."

Jameson told the free workers to hurry up and load the wagons with supplies, clothes, and all their belongings and to leave immediately. They wanted to stay and help, but Jameson was adamant that they go and enjoy their new freedom. He assured them he would be fine, although he severely doubted it. They reluctantly obeyed, and the one-time slaves quickly stowed their meager belongings then boarded the two wagons in the hopes of finding a better life.

"Do any of you know how to handle a gun?" Jameson asked.

"I do, Mista Jameson," said Eli. "Mista Josiah used to take me huntin' with him."

Jameson gave him a loaded pistol and extra ammunition. "Keep this out of sight, but don't hesitate to use it if you have to. Head north. Keep the morning sun on your right and the afternoon sun on your left. Remember moss grows on the north side of the tree trunks, so you'll always know in which direction you are going. If we can, Amos and I will join you later."

Delilah said, "I'm not going. I'm staying here with you, Mista Jameson."

Jameson argued, saying, "Lilah, I can't promise that I can protect you from what is about to happen."

She would not be dissuaded.

"Don't make me leave you, Mista Jameson. I'm not afraid. Please let me stay and help you and Amos."

"You're free, Lilah. Go and start a new life."

"I don't want to go without you, Mista Jameson," she pleaded.

He was stunned and strangely pleased by her assertion. He really didn't want her to go but feared for her safety.

"I might be killed, Lilah," he countered.

She immediately answered, "If you die, then I die with you."

He knew what was happening between them, but he could not sort it all out just now. Realizing he could not change her mind, he allowed her to remain. The wagons pulled out.

Jameson now turned his thoughts toward saving himself, Delilah, and Amos. "We have to find a place from which we can make our stand," he said. "The house has too many windows and points of entry. They could get us from all directions. I believe the best place is the barn. It has one entrance and only a few small windows. They have to come directly at us."

He gathered the rifles and ammunition into the barn and asked either of them if they ever fired a gun, neither had. It was too late to teach them, but he would show them how to load a gun.

The muskets only fired one shot at a time then had to be reloaded. You had to pour gunpowder down the barrel, add a pellet, and use the plunger to tamp it tightly into the chamber. Then you pulled back the hammer, aimed, pulled the trigger and bang! The gun went off.

He told Delilah to try and reload the gun. She was a quick learn but a bit slow and awkward. She would improve. She would have to if they were to survive. They practiced, planned, and paced nervously. Amos kept apologizing, though it was too little, too late.

Jameson wondered how long they would have to wait for the masked vigilantes. He did not have to speculate long. Within the hour there came the sound of horse hooves, many horse hooves. They could be heard rapidly approaching the plantation. Jameson pushed Delilah and Amos into the barn, grabbed a rifle, took a deep breath, and waited.

The hooded riders came ten strong up the road armed with rifles, swords, torches, and ropes.

Jameson called out, "That's far enough. You're trespassing on private property. Leave now, or I have the legal right to defend myself."

He knew he did not stand a chance, one against so many, but he had to try to bluff them. They, on the other hand, assumed Jameson would crumble under the fear, as he had done before, so they took their time to let the anxiety swell within him.

"We have come for two reasons," the man in the front said. "One is to hang that slave who killed Bobby Ray, the slave catcher."

"There are no slaves here," Jameson stated, "only a free man who defended himself against an unwarranted attack. Come out here, Amos, and tell them."

Amos appeared.

"That's the other reason, Hartford," the rider said. "You broke the agreement you made with us."

"That agreement was made under duress," Jameson claimed. "You can't hold me to that. It's not legal, and you know that, sheriff. Yes, I know it's you, Shelby Mathison, and I presume Slycott is there as well as Thaddeus Bordeau, Beau Lansing, and yes, even my dear old friend, Travis McGhee, oh, and all the other so-called upstanding and law-abiding citizens of Willow Hills."

The riders were startled, but did not waiver.

"We're not ashamed. Take off your hoods, men," Slycott ordered.

He removed his shroud, and one by one the others followed suit. Jameson recognized some of them as the people he had named. Others were from town, and three in particular were the Wrabble Brothers from the neighboring Spanish Moss Plantation. They were trouble makers and were referred to as white trash.

"Where are the rest of your slaves, Hartford?" demanded the sheriff. "We didn't see them as we rode in. Don't tell me you freed them. I don't want to have to waste my time trying to round them up."

"That's none of your concern," Jameson said, hoping to give his workers time to get safely away. "Let's stick to the matter at hand. You're trespassing. Now get out, or I'll shoot."

"That's the one who tried to cut me, Mista Jameson," Amos said, pointing at Marty.

Marty glared at Amos and said, "We're not leaving without that murdering slave."

"Then you'll have to go through me," Jameson said and raised his rifle.

"You only got one bullet in there," Slycott quipped. "You can't get all of us. You can't reload fast enough. Let's go, men!"

"I'll shoot," retorted Jameson.

Slycott and Marty started to ride toward him, wielding swords as rifles were inaccurate and hard to aim while galloping on a horse. Besides, they all expected Jameson to turn coward as he had done during their first encounter. Marty charged forward into the lead, wanting to kill Amos as revenge for his friend's death. Jameson stood his ground, aimed, and fired, hitting Marty squarely in the chest. He fell to the ground.

"Now I got you, Hartford!" Slycott screamed and galloped toward him.

Jameson threw the used rifle to Delilah in the barn. She, in turn, threw a loaded one out to him. He cocked the hammer. Slycott was almost upon him, cackling and waiving the sword back and forth like a sickle cutting through the brush. There was no time to aim. Jameson placed the rifle on his hip, raised the barrel, and fired. A loud bang ensued, and Slycott fell off the saddle into the dirt, his white sheet turning blood red.

Amos panicked. "There's too many of them. They're gonna get me," he said as he left the security of the barn and started to run.

Two of the Wrabble Brothers took off after him.

"No, come back!" Jameson yelled.

He dropped the empty rifle. Delilah threw him another loaded one. The riders swung their swords. Jameson raised his rifle and fired, hitting one, but there was no time to stop the second rider. He reached out his sword and slashed Amos across the neck. Amos fell to the ground.

"That's pretty resourceful, Jameson!" yelled the sheriff. "How many more guns have you got hidden in there?"

"Just keep coming and I'll show you," Jameson said.

Delilah was feverishly trying to reload the empty rifles but was clumsily spilling powder all over the barn floor in her haste. The riders were beginning to have second thoughts, fearing they had underestimated an ever-resourceful Jameson Hartford.

"Now give yourself up, Jameson, and we'll make sure you get a fair trial," yelled the sheriff.

"A fair trial for what?" exclaimed Jameson. "I did nothing wrong. I'm defending myself against trespassers who are threatening to kill me."

As the war of words continued, the carriage from town arrived carrying Doc Pritchard, Nanny, and Uncky.

"What's going on here?" demanded Doc. "Are you civilized men or a bunch of animals?"

Suddenly the plantation door opened, and Bethany Sue came running out, screaming, "I heard gun fire. Josiah, are you all right?"

"Stay there, Bethany Sue!" yelled Jameson. "Don't come any closer."

She started to run toward him. At the same time, the Wrabble brother who had slain Amos came charging back from behind toward an unsuspecting Jameson. He was going to avenge his brother.

"Look out, Mista Jameson!" cried Delilah.

She threw another loaded rifle to him. He caught it but only had time to hold it up to deflect the swinging sword. Jameson fell to the ground as the sword knocked the rifle from his hand. The gun fired upon impact with the ground.

The frightened horse reared up on his hind legs as Bethany Sue ran in front of it, crying, "Josiah, Josiah."

The horse's hooves collided with the confused Bethany Sue, causing her to fall backward to the hard ground. The rider was also thrown from the saddle and fell head first to the firm earth, temporarily knocking him unconscious. Doc and Thaddeus ran to Bethany Sue.

She was hurt and murmuring, "Daddy, don't hurt Josiah. I love him. He's my husband."

Jameson said, "Have we had enough death yet, Bordeau? Are you more interested in getting rid of me than you are in taking care of your own daughter? Is money more important than her welfare? And what of you, sheriff? Does persecuting me ensure your re-election? And you, Lansing, is cheap labor so important to you and the rest of the town that you don't care what you do to preserve it?"

As he was tending to Bethany Sue, Doc said, "Thaddeus, she needs medical attention, both physically and mentally, or you might lose her forever."

Thaddeus looked at his daughter. "Forgive me, my child. Forgive me." Then he turned toward the sheriff and said, "I'm leaving, Sheriff. I want no more of this."

They placed Bethany Sue on the buckboard and started to leave.

"I'm going too," said Beau Lansing. "I'll deal with my slaves in my own way."

"We got the murdering slave. The hell with Hartford!" someone shouted.

"I won't forget!" yelled a Wrabble brother. "You and I still have a score to settle, Hartford. You killed my brother."

"Shut up, Dawson," said the sheriff. "Get going." Then he had a second thought and whispered to Dawson Wrabble, "You and your brother find out where Hartford's slaves are. We can't afford to let them escape."

Dawson replied with a wicked smile. "We'll find 'em. Don't worry, Sheriff."

One by one all the riders turned and left, taking the dead and wounded with them.

"See you later, Hartford!" yelled Dawson Wrabble as he and his brother draped the dead body of their kin across his horse and rode out.

Jameson grabbed Delilah, and the two of them ran to the fallen Amos. Unfortunately, it was too late; he had already succumb to the deadly wound. All they could do was dig a grave and bury him, placing a cross above it inscribed with his name. He was finally a free man.

Jameson took Delilah by the hand and led her into the house. She did not question him, just dutifully followed his lead. She would spend her first night with him inside the once-forbidden mansion. Nanny and Uncky were happy to see Jameson and Delilah had survived the battle and were unharmed.

"Thank God you two are safe," said Nanny.

"Is it all over, Mista Jameson?" Delilah asked.

He shook his head. "It'll never be over as long as men hate men simply because of the color of their skin."

For tonight, however, it was over, and they could find peace in each other's arms in crisp-white sheets on a soft, clean feather bed. And they did just that. There would be no bales of hay for them this time. They fell exhausted onto the welcoming mattress and cuddled close to each other.

He whispered softly to her, "You were great out there, Delilah. I couldn't have done it without you. You are a very special woman, brave and caring. The kind of woman a man really needs." He glanced at her beautiful face and noticed she was already asleep.

Too tired for anything else, he also fell asleep and enjoyed a moment of peace, free from the hatred of the outside world. Smiles covered both their faces.

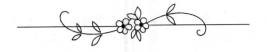

Chapter 12

A BRIEF RESPITE

The morning sun came through the window and crept up the bed, reaching Delilah's eyes. She awoke, unsure of where she was. Then realizing she was in Jameson's bed, she turned toward him.

"Wake up, Mista Jameson," she urged. "It's morning!"

He stirred and finally managed to open his sleepy eyes, and there, to his great delight, he saw Delilah's bright, smiling eyes gazing in disbelief at him.

He said, "You know you're a free woman now. You don't have to call me Mister Jameson any longer. Why not just call me Jameson?"

She gave him a coy smile and said, "I'll think I'll call you James. Yes, you need a shorter name like mine, and you certainly look like a James, if that's okay with you."

He grinned and said, "That's fine with me."

He grabbed her, pulled her close, they looked deep into each other's eyes and they kissed. They were both aroused and excited at being so close to one another again. He remembered how sweet she tasted and longed to sample her many gifts again. They gave into temptation, and for the second time, as he rolled on top of her, they joined their two souls in love. A deep satisfying love that signified a new life was beginning between them. They became one as their bodies' united, hot flesh pressing against hot flesh. They drew deeper and deeper breaths as the fire of love raged in their bodies, moaning, gyrating and finally exploding in a burst of ecstasy, reaching pleasurable heights, that neither one had ever known or experienced before, culminating in a loud cry of relief.

When it was over, they continually kissed each other, not wanting the moment to end; they couldn't help smiling and just looking at each other.

Nanny was calling from downstairs. "Breakfast is ready. It's not gonna stay hot all day."

"We're coming, Nanny," Jameson called.

He told Delilah they had to get dressed. Looking closely at her, he remarked that she was about the same size as Bethany Sue. He took her into Bethany Sue's room and told her to pick out an outfit to wear on their trip.

"I couldn't, James. It wouldn't be right."

"You can't wear those old rags of yours," he stated. "Now that you're free you have to look the part. If it makes you feel better, I'll leave some cash for it, so it won't be stealing."

She agreed.

He went back to his room to get dressed and gather up a few more items to take with him.

A few minutes later, Delilah appeared in the doorway in an elegant outfit complete with a large sun bonnet. It was a light-tan color with lacey frills and a large bow around the waist. Jameson stopped, looked adoringly at her, and thought to himself, *in another time she would have been accepted as the lady of the house.*

"You look beautiful," he said.

"Thank you, James. For the first time in my life I feel pretty."

He took her hand and led her down the stairs to breakfast. He pulled the chair out for Delilah to sit down at the table as a true gentleman would, and the both of them were ready to partake of a delicious meal. Nanny was stunned but asked no questions. The look on her face said it all.

"Everything is delicious, Nanny," he said. "Thank you."

Delilah never saw so much food and did not know where to start. She had a little of everything and then a little more of everything, eating a little too much.

"Slow down, child. You'll get sick," said Nanny.

"Do you still have to go, Mista Jameson?" Nanny asked.

"I do," answered Jameson. "I have to catch up to the others and help them reach freedom up North. Then I will return and decide what to do with Serenity. Maybe I'll still try to hire people to work her and prove that slavery is an unnecessary evil. But my first duty is to be sure my former workers attain their freedom. I don't trust the people around here to leave them alone on their journey. You and Uncky are still welcome to join us."

"Thank you, Mista Jameson, but we talked it over, and we decided we will stay here. It's what we know. But it's good to know we're free to make our own choice."

He arose, walked over to her, and kissed her cheek. "I don't know if I ever told you, but I love you, Nanny. You've never been a servant to me. You've always been more like a second mother, always watching out for me, taking care of me, and just being there whenever I needed you."

Nanny wiped the tears from her face and said, "Oh, Mista Jameson."

They hugged for quite a period of time. Nanny asked him how long he would be gone. He said he didn't know for sure but thought he would return within a month, long before the harvest was to begin.

A knock on the door interrupted the delicious breakfast. Nanny went to open the door.

"Hello, Nanny, is Jameson home?"

"Why yes, Miss Annabelle. I'll go get him. Please come in."

"Thank you so much."

Nanny went back into the dining area, whispering, "Mista Jameson, you ain't gonna believe who's here to see you."

Jameson looked perplexed.

"It's Miss Annabelle."

Jameson's look changed to one of dismay.

"That girl is trouble. Mark my words. You best stay away from the likes of her."

"I guess I have to see what she wants," he muttered as he rose from the table and proceeded into the hall.

"Hello, Jameyson," Annabelle said in her usual sing-song, temptress voice.

She looked stunning, as usual, in an elegant pink satin dress with a matching bonnet and shoes.

"Hello, Belle. What can I do for you?"

"I wanted to express my sorrow upon hearing that my sister has moved out and left you," she said as she put her arms around him.

He took hold of her arms and held her at bay, answering, "It's all right. I'm fine."

"Don't you need some consoling? I'm very good at consoling," she playfully added.

"No, I'm fine, really Belle, I am."

"Abby said you took up with a slave girl, but I said, 'Not my Jameyson. You're wrong. He just needs a real woman, that's all.'"

She kept trying to hug him, moving closer and closer as he kept trying to restrain her, retreating backward, step by step.

"Now, Belle, behave yourself."

"Oh, Jameyson, why should I? You know you always wanted me, and I always wanted you."

"No, no, you're mistaken. I'm not that man any longer."

"I can make you that man again, Jamey, if you'll just let me."

He could swear she had as many arms as an octopus, constantly grabbing at him. He would try to push one arm away, and it seemed like two more were wrapping themselves around him.

Jameson at last had backed all the way up to the dining area, and Annabelle spotted Delilah sitting at the table, watching her.

"Who is that, Jameson?" The tone in her voice suddenly changed to one of jealousy and seriousness.

Before Jameson could answer, she continued, "Don't tell me that Abigail was right and you have taken up with a slave? Answer me!"

Jameson said, "This is Delilah, and I do care for her."

"You what? Jameson, what is wrong with you? Tell her to get out of your house and back to the fields where she belongs," Annabelle demanded.

"No, I won't do that," Jameson responded.

The anger in Annabelle's voice was apparent as it grew louder and louder. Her whole demeanor became altered as she now stood akimbo, directly in front of Jameson, staring him down face to face. "You would prefer a slave to me? Tell me that isn't true, Jameson, and tell me now!"

Jameson calmly replied, "She is staying. I would prefer that you leave. Please go now."

"Oh my goodness, what has happened to you? Did my sister do this to you? Keeping sex from a man is a powerful weapon for a wife to use just to get her way, but to have it turn out like this? Well, I never."

"Belle, Abby had nothing to do with this. Now please leave."

"You've insulted me and my womanhood. I demand satisfaction."

"Oh, Annabelle, don't be so dramatic."

"Dramatic… I come here to offer my condolences, and you insult me. I will not forgive you for this, Jameson. Oh, by the way, don't tell anyone I was here. I don't want my sister to find out. I'd become a laughing stock, and that just wouldn't do. If this were to become public, my father would have to defend my honor."

"Please leave, Belle. I'm tired of this already."

"I'll go, but you'll regret letting me slip through your fingers, Jameson Hartford."

Annabelle stormed out of the house. Jameson turned to look at Delilah and Nanny. He sighed and said, "Well now Beau Lansing has another reason to hate me. I guess we better get going."

Delilah hugged him. Nanny just shook her head in disbelief.

He had lost his appetite and could not finish breakfast, so they decided to leave immediately. Uncky helped Jameson load the wagon with suitcases, guns, ammunition—all they would need for their journey northward.

Nanny packed the leftovers in a basket then couldn't help but speak her mind. "I hope you know what you're doin', Mista Jameson. No one is gonna look kindly on a white man and a black woman travelling together like they're husband and wife. They just ain't gonna accept it."

Jameson told her, "Don't worry. We'll be fine".

"If you say so; everything's worked out so good for you so far, hasn't it?" she answered sarcastically.

He ignored her, shook Uncky's hand, and thanked him for all his help and kindness. They climbed into the wagon and started off.

They stopped at little Eve's grave and placed fresh-cut flowers on it one last time. Unexpectedly, Delilah ran off to the side and appeared to be sick. She threw up a lot of the food she had just eaten.

"Are you all right?" Jameson asked.

"Yes, yes, I feel fine. I just had a little too much to eat. I'm not used to eating so much food, that's all," she assured him.

This had happened to her once before, she recalled to herself, and pretended not to be concerned. Delilah knew what was probably causing her indigestion, and she was worried, but she was afraid to tell Jameson, unsure of his reaction.

They both climbed back into the wagon. She sat proudly right next to Jameson and held her head high. She was so excited to be all dressed up and leaving her prison behind. It was all so new. She couldn't wait to meet up with her friends. The air was fresh and sweet, and the sun was shining bright. The songs of a thousand birds filled the sky as the journey to freedom began. It was all just too beautiful, too perfect. It was like a dream come true.

Chapter 13

HARD ROAD TO FREEDOM

They were making good time, traveling farther than Jameson had thought they would.

"At this rate we should catch up to them this evening," he said eagerly. "We'll reunite and head north."

Delilah began singing a spiritual hymn he had heard many times before. The workers used to sing it in the fields as they toiled. He enjoyed listening to it, as it was a rousing song, instilling strength into him he thought he had lost. He tried to join in, but his voice only ruined the moment and sent Delilah into fits of laughter. She tried to teach it to him, but singing was not one of his strong points.

Evening was near as they came over a hill and saw something in the field ahead. There were clothes and food strewn everywhere.

"I recognize those clothes," Delilah said. "They belong to my people. Somethin' happened here, somethin' bad."

They came around a bend, and Delilah screamed. There hanging from a tree was Eli. He had a sign pinned to his lifeless body. It read, "Beware! This is what happens to runaway slaves with guns."

Jameson stopped the coach, got out, and ran over to Eli and cut him down. His body was not yet cold, indicating that this atrocity must be a relatively recent occurrence. They dug a grave and buried him under that tree with a cross and a marker that read, "Eli, a fee man. Rest in peace."

"What happened?" Delilah asked in a panic-stricken voice.

"They must have run into a band of vigilantes or slave catchers," Jameson said.

"But they had their freedom papers!" Delilah exclaimed. "Why would anybody do this, and where are my friends?"

"I don't know," Jameson said with a sigh. "Let's look around and see if we can find any clues."

They scoured the grounds, picking up the clothes and assorted items. Jameson found a pool of blood. *Someone must have been shot*, he thought. This was not good.

"It's getting dark. Let's make camp here and spend the night. In the morning we can follow the tracks of the horses and the wagon and see if we can find them."

Delilah reluctantly agreed. They started a fire to ward off the night chill and tried to eat some of the food Nanny had packed for them, though neither one was very hungry. Finally they just settled down for the night and wondered what the morning light would reveal. Would they discover the fate of their friends? How could such a promising day turn out to be so hideous? It was a long and restless night as they stared up at the millions of stars and prayed for the safety of the small group of lost souls.

In the morning the wagon tracks were clear. They followed them east, heading straight toward Charleston. Jameson had the horses going as fast as possible. The roads were rough and full of ruts and holes. It wouldn't do them any good to break an axle or a wheel or have one of the horses go lame, as then they would never catch up. They were both very anxious to find their friends and solve the previous night's mystery.

Charleston loomed in the distance, and many other horses and wagons obscured the trail they were following. Their only alternative was to go straight into the city and hope they could spot them. He told Delilah to keep a sharp eye out for her friends. They frantically looked left and right and into other wagons as they neared the city and the train depot that had brought Jameson and his wife here a few short days ago.

"There, there! I see 'em!" Delilah screamed. "Over there in that crowd."

Jameson looked to see what Nicholas Mansfield had described to him a few days earlier as a slave auction. Someone was trying to sell his freed workers.

He jumped out of the wagon, grabbed a rifle, looked at Delilah, and said, "Stay here, Lilah. Do not talk or look directly at these people. They are not your friends. Don't trust anyone. I'll get them back safely. Stay put! I mean it!"

"Okay, James, I'll be waitin' right here for you. Be careful," she pleaded.

As he approached the platform, he could hear them trying to sell Becky and Sara and their children.

"Now what do you bid for these fine, strong women and these two strapping youngsters?" the auctioneer shouted.

"I'll take the women, but I don't want no brats who can't work. They're just extra mouths to feed," a voice from the crowd declared.

"We can separate them. No problem," said the auctioneer.

Jameson ran over to the auction area, pushed his way through the crowd, and jumped on the platform. He fired his rifle into the air, and the crowd instantly became quiet.

"Who brought these people here?" he demanded.

No one said a word.

"I said who brought these people here?"

"What's it to you?" came the reply from a stranger on the sidelines, his face concealed under a large Stetson hat.

"Because, sir, these are my people. They are not for sale."

"Can you prove that?" the voice came back.

"Of course I can. I have the paperwork back at my plantation."

"Then why were they traveling alone in a wagon with clothes, food, and guns? Why did one of them take a shot at my brother? It grazed him right across the cheek. Good thing that slave couldn't handle the gun, or my brother would be dead now."

"Well you took care of him, didn't you, sir? You hung him for no reason."

"No reason! He shot at us. We were defending ourselves from a crazy darkie."

"And why, sir, did you stop them in the first place?"

"A bunch of Negroes all alone in a wagon travelling north, who wouldn't have stopped them?"

"They were travelling north because I gave them their freedom, all of them. They had their papers with them."

"They didn't have no papers with them."

"Well, what did you do with the papers?" Jameson said accusingly.

"Are you calling me a liar?" he responded.

Jameson turned to address the crowd. "I am Jameson Hartford. Let it be known that any man who buys any of these people is wasting his money. I will prove that they are mine and are now legally free. You will have nothing to show for your hard-earned money."

The crowd started to disperse. No one wanted to take a chance that Jameson was lying. It would be better to purchase a sure thing.

The stranger climbed up on the platform. To Jameson's surprise, it was one of the Wrabble brothers. He accused Jameson of first killing his brother and now cheating him out of slave-trading money.

"I invested time in these slaves, and I got one dead brother and another one with a huge gash on his face. You owe me, Hartford."

"I don't owe you a thing except to hang you for killing two innocent men."

"You'll regret this, Jameson Hartford. Me and my brother will get our money one way or another." He scoured at Jameson and jumped off the platform.

While all this was going on, Delilah grew impatient and decided to try to get a closer look in order to hear what all the yelling was about. She crept and snaked her way through the crowd, trying not to draw attention to herself. Her bonnet became snagged on a low hanging branch and was pulled off of her head, revealing that she was a Negro. She gasped and grabbed for the elusive bonnet but it was too late. People were all shocked and pointing at the black girl in the fancy clothes trying to look like a white woman. She panicked, turned and tried to make her way back to the wagon.

"Hey there, sweetie, you trying to look white?" came a voice from behind a large tree.

A white man with a large gash across his cheek came forward. "Come with me, darlin'. I'll make you feel white."

Delilah turned to run. He grabbed her arm, pulled her toward him, and dragged her away toward his horse. She tried to resist, but he was too strong for her. Delilah looked around yelling and pleading for help, but no one seemed concerned. They were either pointing and laughing or totally ignoring the situation. After all, it was only a black woman, nothing for the supposed upstanding white citizens to be worried about.

Jameson gathered up all his former workers and ushered them back to his wagon. Unbeknownst to him, he was being stalked by an angry Dawson Wrabble, who was stirring up the crowd.

"Who is this guy to free slaves? We should stop him before he starts an uprising."

The crowd was beginning to get loud and unruly, listening and believing everything Dawson had to say.

Upon returning to the wagon, Jameson noticed Delilah was missing. He called out to her. He jumped on the wagon and frantically searched the crowd, looking for any sign of her. He memorized the dress she was wearing and thought he might be able to easily spot it. He began to ask the people around the wagon if they had seen her, describing her perfectly to them. One of the older men said he saw a man forcibly taking her away. He thought she was his slave and didn't do anything.

"Who was it?" pleaded Jameson.

"I don't know," he replied, "but I believe he had a huge gash across his cheek. Yes, sir, I'm sure of that." Jameson thought it must be the other Wrabble brother.

"Thank you, thank you very much," said Jameson.

"That must be one special slave," muttered the older man.

"She is a special lady," Jameson said, "a very special lady."

He told the rest of the freed workers to get on the wagon and stay there. He was going to search for Delilah.

"I think I see her over there, Mista Jameson!" Sara yelled.

Jameson looked to see her far off in the distance being forced onto a horse. He instantly recognized the younger Wrabble brother as the kidnapper and began to head in that direction as the angry crowd drew near. The mob of irate men stopped him in his tracks.

"Hey, slave lover!" someone yelled.

"You lousy Yankee, we'll teach you a lesson."

They set upon him, pushing and prodding him, spitting, and cursing him out. There was even talk of a lynching. Luckily the sheriff was close by, and the commotion brought him quickly to the scene. He instantly set about dispersing the mob.

"I'm sorry about that, sir," he said. "Come down to my office, and you can press charges against these folks, and I'll arrest them."

Jameson was thinking only about Delilah. He had to find her. "Forget it," he said.

"Are you sure, sir?"

"Yes, I'm positive. I have to find someone," he stated as he looked in the direction where he had seen her only moments ago. She was not there. The horse and rider were gone.

He looked all around, but there was no trace of the familiar figure. Fear welled up inside him. He had to find her. There was no telling what the two Wrabble brothers would do to her, especially if they figured out Delilah belonged to him.

He asked the freed workers if they knew where their wagons were hitched.

Daniel told him, "They're over there by the big flowering tree with the low hangin' branches."

Jameson hurried them over to the two wagons and split the group into smaller numbers for faster travelling. Then they all started back in the direction of Serenity.

"We're sorry, Mista Jameson, but those two men attacked us for no reason. They wouldn't accept our freedom papers. Eli only used the pistol to try and protect us. We didn't start anythin'," Nate said.

Jameson replied, "Forget it. It wasn't your fault. It was mine. I should have known better than to send you out there alone. I thought they would honor the freedom papers. I had no idea they would try to hurt you."

"Where are we goin' now, sir?" asked Daniel.

"I'm taking you back to Serenity so I can go after Lilah."

The small caravan was travelling as quickly as possible. Anxiety filled Jameson's thoughts. He could not get to the plantation fast enough. The trip had seemed much faster when he and Abigail had followed the same road a few days earlier.

They finally arrived back at Serenity, but it was already sundown. Nanny and Uncky were quite surprised to see them. He quickly related his story as to what had occurred and how he had to find Delilah. Nanny said the Wrabble boys were from the Spanish Moss Plantation, and it was only a short ride west of here, down Blue Jay Way then left to the end of Hollow Road.

"Them's not good, folks," said Uncky. "They is white trash."

"All the more reason I have to leave immediately," Jameson replied.

"I'll saddle you a fresh horse, Mista Jameson, right now," said Uncky.

The horse emerged as Jameson gathered up his rifles, making sure they were loaded. He took his last pistol, tucked it into his belt, and set out.

"God be with you!" yelled Nanny. Then she added to herself, "You're gonna need all the help you can get."

Jameson had the horse at full gallop, dodging low-hanging tree limbs and jumping any obstacles in his path. The moonlight illuminated the road, such as it was, but holes, fallen branches, and nocturnal creatures always posed a constant threat. The thick, humid air caused the sweat of his brow to roll into his eyes, making visibility even worse. Fog was rolling in to easily mask any trail he might be able to locate. Adrenalin was pumping through his veins as he raced onward.

Jameson kept pushing his horse faster and faster when he suddenly realized he was halfway to Willow Hills, and he must have inadvertently missed the turnoff. He had to swing the horse back around and return down the same road he had just travelled to look for the elusive Hollow Road. In his haste he had wasted a lot of precious time. Why was he having such difficulty finding the road? Had he gone the wrong way? There were no road signs, but perhaps he could find freshly made horse tracks. He dismounted and walked with his horse in tow, searching frantically for some hoof prints, a wagon wheel track, anything. He was beginning to panic as fear for Delilah's safety welled up inside of him. Nothing was going to stop him from finding and saving her, nothing.

Suddenly, he found those new tracks disappearing down what appeared to be an old road, but it was obscured by brush, tree limbs, and thorny bushes. Could this be the road he was so fanatically searching for? He had no choice but to follow it. He had to keep his hopes alive.

Chapter 14

SPANISH MOSS

Jameson had finally found Hollow Road and couldn't believe the condition of the plantation. It wasn't really a plantation any longer, just a rundown, seedy house needing a lot of repair. It was now less than an acre of land that hadn't been farmed in quite a while, full of overgrown weeds. Spanish moss hung off all the trees, blocking the road and any path leading up to the house.

The Wrabble brothers inherited the plantation from their father. They were all shiftless and lazy. They were not interested in running a plantation, only in having a good time. They squandered their inheritance then started selling off their slaves. When they were gone, they sold parcels of the land to accommodate their carefree lifestyle and need for alcohol. A once-great plantation was now reduced to a mere shadow of its former self. It was a sad ending. The only humor in the entire situation was their name. It aptly described them. They were indeed rabble.

Jameson tied his horse to a large Sycamore tree and proceeded on foot, taking a rifle with him. He crept through the underbrush, past rubbish and dead tree limbs, snagging his shirt and pants on sharp thorns and finally reaching the house. There was a light on in one of the rooms. He worked his way up to the window and peered inside. The room was sparsely furnished, and what was there was dirty and needed attention. He could clearly see Dawson and Brandon sitting at the table, unshaven in their rumpled clothing and drinking a bottle of whiskey, but he did not see Delilah anywhere. Fear again filled him, and the damp night air forced the perspiration to leach out of his body. Where could she be? Could he have been mistaken as to the identity of the kidnapper?

Then Dawson spoke," Come on, brother. Let's go out to the barn and have a little fun with our new slave."

"Just a couple more swigs, and I'll be right behind you, but I get her first."

"You? Why you?"

"I stole her, that's why."

"I'll arm wrestle you for firsts."

"Okay, okay, let's go."

Jameson saw an opportunity to hurry to the barn and find Delilah. He made his way as quickly and quietly as possible through the brush and twigs. He opened the barn door. It squeaked horribly. He hoped they were too inebriated to hear it. Once inside he scanned the darkness for her. He found her in a corner, bound hand and foot and gagged. Her gown was torn off and tossed to the side, leaving her clothed only in a small cotton undergarment.

He ran up to her and removed the gag.

"Oh, James," she cried. "You found me. You came for me."

"Of course I came for you, Lilah, I told you no one would ever hurt you again, and I meant it. Are you all right?"

She nodded.

"Did they do anything to you?"

"No," she whispered. "Not yet."

He pulled out his knife and sliced through the ropes, cutting her free.

"I'm going to teach those boys a lesson!" he exclaimed.

"No. No. Please take me home, please, James," she begged.

He knew that was the right thing to do. He would get her to safety and come back and make them pay for this. Jameson helped her up, put his jacket on her, took her in his arms, and started to carry her out of the barn.

"I won!" The cry came from the house. "I get her first! Whoopee! I'll see you later, brother."

The door swung open with Dawson Wrabble charging forward from the house. Being drunk, he tripped and stumbled, almost falling to the ground in his haste to satisfy his manly urges. Jameson with Delilah quickly dashed off to the side of the barn into the darkness undetected and out of sight. They made their way down the path, avoiding the low-hanging branches but getting caught again and again on the ever prickly thorns, finally reaching Jameson's waiting horse. He got on and pulled her up behind him, turned the horse, and galloped for home and freedom. She hung on tight to her hero, hoping they would succeed in their escape.

Dawson ran into the barn screaming, "Here I come, darling. Get ready." He stopped abruptly, noticing she was not where he had left her. He looked around, figuring maybe she crawled off somewhere. Trying to entice her, he said, "Come out, come out, wherever you are. I ain't gonna hurt you...much."

Brandon entered the barn and found his brother searching feverishly for Delilah. "What's the matter, brother? She too smart for you?"

"I can't find her, Brandon."

"Hey, look over here, brother." He found the ropes and carefully examined them. "These have been cut. She couldn't have done that. Somebody must have come here and taken her."

"But who would have done that? Who knew we even had her?"

Dawson picked up the dress, shook the dust off of it, and said, "Well, they forgot her clothes."

Something fell out of one of the pockets. Brandon bent down, picked it up, and unfolded it. He read it aloud. "This officially states that this slave known as Delilah has been legally set free by her former owner, Jameson Hartford."

He stopped and looked at his brother. "Jameson Hartford. That's the third time that man cheated us. First he killed our brother. Then he took money out of our pockets by claiming those slaves we picked up were legally his, and now he steals that little black doll from us."

"We were gonna have such a good time playing with her too."

"He's not gonna get away with this. We're gonna get him and take what's rightfully ours."

"You said it, brother. Let's get him good. But we'll need a plan."

"Yeah, let's get back to the house. I need a drink so I can think. Hey, I made a rhyme."

"Shut up and give me the bottle."

The pair of worthless drunks staggered back into their house to formulate a plan. They managed to grab their seats and sit down before they fell. They took large gulps from the bottle, passing it back and forth. They were in no shape to think clearly and summarily fell asleep at the table. Revenge would have to wait until tomorrow, tonight was for sleeping it off.

Chapter 15

GROWING CLOSER

Jameson and Delilah rode up the path to Serenity. Nanny and Uncky were anxiously awaiting their return.

"Thank God. Thank God," said Nanny. "Are you all right, Mista Jameson? Lilah?"

"We're okay, Nanny. I found her before anything happened."

"I'm fine, Nanny, James saved me."

"Come on into the house," said Nanny. "I saved some supper for you, and I'm boiling some nice hot water for you both to take some nice baths." Then she added, "You both need 'em, you know."

"Thank you, Nanny, but I have to take care of those two thieves."

"No, no, James, please stay with me tonight. I need you. I don't wanna be alone," pleaded Delilah.

He smiled and agreed to stay for her sake. They ate the delicious feast set before them, as both of them were famished.

Then Jameson declared, "Let's have those baths, Nanny!"

The hot water was brought in buckets from the stove to the tub. Several buckets were required to fill the beautifully crafted porcelain bathtub.

"You want me to scrub you?" asked Nanny.

Jameson laughed out loud. "No thanks, Nanny. I'm a little too old for that. I think we can manage from here," he said as he ushered Nanny from the room, leaving the two of them alone.

He watched Delilah remove the small cotton undergarment she was wearing and then helped her into the tub first. The water was hot and took a little getting used to as she gradually settled in. He started running his soapy hands first along her arms, then her legs and finally across her body, kissing each spot, in turn, as he cleansed them. She washed her face and hair. Then, laughing, he dunked her under the water. She rose up out of the lather and laughed as he escorted her out of the tub. He placed a towel around her and tenderly dried her off. Now it was his turn.

She helped him remove his clothes, and then he lit a cigar as he climbed into the hot, steamy water.

"I haven't had one of these in a while," he remarked. "I forgot how good they were."

She followed suit and soaped up his body, copying his every move. He took another puff, curled his lips, and blew out three perfect smoke rings.

She was amazed by this bit of talent, and as they wafted away, she asked him, "How did you do that?"

"It's a family secret, but I might be coerced into revealing it to you if you can convince me that you're worthy."

She grabbed the cigar out of his mouth and, laughing, pushed his head under the water. When he came up and cleared his eyes, he saw her puffing on the cigar, inhaling and then blowing a stream of smoke out of her pursed lips. He had never seen a lady smoking. Southern belles did not do that, at least not in front of the men. She took another puff.

"I didn't know you enjoyed cigars."

"Is it bad, James? Do you not want me to do it?"

"No, no," he replied, "go right ahead. Enjoy. Where did you learn to smoke?"

She exhaled a large plume of smoke and said, "After we harvested the tobacco and the leaves were cured, Mista Josiah used to give the slaves the leaves that he could not sell, you know, the bad ones. We would roll 'em up and smoke 'em in the evenin' after supper. I didn't like it at first, but I got used to it, and now I like it a lot." She took another deep puff.

"Aren't you going to share that?"

She slowly blew out a long cloud of smoke as she sauntered over to Jameson. Sitting on the edge of the tub, she took the cigar out of her mouth and placed it in his mouth. He took a puff and then returned it to her lips. As she inhaled a large puff, he pulled her close. She slid halfway back into the tub, sending a small wave of water tumbling to the floor as he gave her a deep, loving kiss. She exhaled and exchanged her breath with his as he sucked the smoke from her lungs deep into his own. As their lips parted, he blew out the remnants of her smoky breath. Their relationship was transcending to another level, drawing them closer and enabling them to become one in spirit and hope.

He arose from the tub, toweled off, donned his robe, and carried Delilah up the stairs and into the bedroom. They fell on the bed into each other's arms, kissing passionately and then becoming one in love. They wanted and needed each other. Nothing else mattered—not color, not public opinion, not a forgotten wife. Bigotry and hatred be damned. They would be together again tonight. Their lust for each other was stronger than anything.

They shared the end of the cigar. Delilah curled up into his arms and fell asleep. Jameson's thoughts turned to the Wrabble brothers and what revenge he should enact upon them. Then he remembered something more unsettling. All the letters of freedom were gone. He would have to go into town to Nicholas Mansfield and request replacements. What type of reaction would he receive from the townsfolk this time? He wasn't looking forward to that. But for tonight he was quite content and slowly fell asleep.

Chapter 16

LOOSE ENDS

Jameson awoke the next morning and reached over for Delilah. She was not there. The bed was empty. He rose quickly, threw on a robe, and called her name.

"Lilah? Delilah, where are you?"

He heard whimpering coming from the bathroom and hurried in the direction of the cries. He entered to find her standing in front of the mirror with strands of her hair lying on the floor all around her. She had taken a pair of scissors and cut her hair very short, all over her head.

She looked at him with tears in her eyes and said, "You told me you wanted me to keep my hair short for you. I just want to make you happy." She sort of smiled and then said, "Do you like it?"

She was a strikingly beautiful woman, and the short hair only defined the gorgeous lines of her face and huge, brown eyes. He walked over to her, ran his hands through the little bits of hair that remained, and told her how beautiful she was. They kissed.

He asked her, "Did you want to cut your hair that short?"

She only stared at him as tears welled up in her eyes and began to roll down her cheeks. He decided to pursue a different line of questioning.

"Why are you crying? Are you all right?"

She spoke in a trembling tone. "I cut it short so no one can ever pull me by my hair again and make me do things I don't want to do." She half laughed and added, "There's not enough hair to grab." Then she rebelliously stated, "Besides, it makes me feel free."

"Delilah, you are free, and nothing like that will ever happen to you ever again; I promise."

"James," she said, "slavery isn't somethin' you can forget that easily. A piece of paper don't erase years of toil and bad treatment. Besides, it don't seem that we can be free. Look at all that's happened—the killings, the fights, the hatred. I'm afraid that all the plantation masters and townsfolk will never let us be free. They would rather kill us than allow us to be free. We will never make it."

"I understand how you feel," he said, "but I vow to you that no one will ever hurt you as long as I'm alive."

"Then I must die first," she said defiantly. "Nobody else cares if I live or die."

"Don't talk like that," Jameson pleaded. "We're going to be all right. We will make it."

He hoped she was not being prophetic. He took her and held her close in his arms, offering her a safe refuge from her fears. He repeatedly kissed her head and the short wisps of hair, telling her how beautiful she was and how much he cared for her. He also kept reassuring her that everything would be okay, though he had serious doubts. She finally calmed down but held on tightly to her knight in shining armor, not wanting to relinquish the safety that his arms provided. The somber mood was broken.

"Breakfast is ready!" Nanny yelled. "C'mon down now. Hurry it up. It ain't gonna keep 'til lunch."

They went down to breakfast. Jameson said he had to go back into town to get new letters of freedom for all the former slaves.

"Do you still have yours, Lilah?" he asked.

"I had it in that dress I wore yesterday."

"You mean the one those two brothers tore off you and we left in the barn?"

She nodded yes. Jameson realized the Wrabble brothers might figure out who Delilah belonged to and that he was the one who came to rescue her. Surely they would retaliate, but where and when? He sadly came to the conclusion that he would never be allowed to prove his hypothesis; the populace of Willow Hills would never allow it. Delilah was right; they would rather kill them all than permit Jameson to succeed. He told Delilah, Nanny, and Uncky that he would have to sell the plantation and escort all the freed men and women personally up North and stay with them to help them acclimate to their new lives.

"Are you sure of that?" asked Nanny.

"Yes, I'm sure of it now. The attitude and atmosphere around here tells me I would never be allowed to hire people to work the fields and abolish slavery. I believe it would take an act of Congress or a war to accomplish that."

He didn't know how right he was.

Jameson asked Uncky to saddle a horse for him and make sure his rifle and pistol were loaded and ready. As he got up to go, Delilah quickly rose and ran off to the bathroom and once again vomited.

"Are you sick, child?" asked Nanny.

"No, no. I'm fine. I just can't get used to this food," she said.

"I'll bring Doc Pritchard back with me," Jameson said.

"No, no. I'm fine, James."

"I won't take no for an answer. He's coming back with me," Jameson said as he mounted his horse and rode off.

He went straight into Willow Hills and wondered what kind of reception he would receive this time. The town was sort of indifferent toward him, tolerating him but wary of him all the same. He tied up in front of Nicholas Mansfield's office and entered the building. Mansfield was surprised to see him.

"I thought you'd be gone by now, Jameson."

"So did I, Mister Mansfield, but I ran into a little trouble. I'll need new letters of freedom for my people, and you can draw up the papers for the sale of Serenity. You once told me you had an interested party. Do you think they might still want it?"

"I'll check, but I'm almost certain they do. What changed your mind, Hartford?"

Jameson said, "Let's just say my eyes were opened."

"Well, you've made a wise choice. I wish you luck, my boy. I'll draw those papers up immediately."

"Who is the buyer, Mister Mansfield?"

"I'm not at liberty to say. Sorry, sir."

Jameson said he would be right back and left for the bank. He could see Shelby Mathison watching him and then running into the lawyer's office. *I guess everyone will know my intentions before the end of the day*, he thought. I'm certainly not a threat to them if I just leave with my freed slaves. He turned into the bank and asked to see Thaddeus Bordeau.

"Good morning! Good morning, Mister Hartford," Thaddeus said. "What can I do for you?"

"First, how is Bethany Sue?" he inquired.

"She is receiving the help she needs and getting better. Thank you."

"That's real good news. Tell her I was asking for her, will you?"

"Yes, I will. She'll be happy to know you are interested in her welfare."

Jameson then told Thaddeus about his plan to sell the plantation. Bordeau was happy, to say the least, maybe a little too happy. He would like the money from the sale wired to his bank in Boston. Jameson was assured that would not be a problem. His next stop was Doc Pritchard's.

On the way he noticed the townspeople looking at him and whispering. *The news is spreading already*, he thought. He turned into Doc's office.

"Well, Jameson, my boy, I heard the news. I for one am sorry to see you go. You're a real gentleman, more so than a lot of these other self-proclaimed gentlemen.

"Thanks, Doc, but I came to see you for a different reason. Lilah is sick. She's vomiting a lot but insists she's all right. I'm worried."

"You know I don't treat darkies, Jameson. If the town found out, I'd be out of a job."

"But Doc, you took an oath to help all human beings. Aren't the so-called darkies humans?"

"Yes, yes, of course they are." He pondered for a moment then said, "Oh, all right. I'll come out to your place this evening and have a look at her."

"Thank you, Doc, I appreciate it. I'll pay you whatever you ask."

"Just have Nanny prepare one of her delicious meals. That's all the thanks I need."

"I'll make sure of that, Doc. Anything in particular you would like her to make for you?"

"It's been a long time since I had some good old-fashioned southern fried chicken, uh with all the trimmings of course."

"You'll have it tonight, Doc, with all the trimmings. Thanks again."

Jameson headed back to Mansfield's office. Upon going in, he was surprised to see Shelby Mathison there.

"I heard the news, Hartford," the sheriff said. "I can't say I'm sorry to see you go."

Jameson replied sarcastically, "I'm sure the town and you are real happy now."

Then he told the sheriff about the Wrabble brothers and what they tried to do. Jameson wanted them arrested.

The sheriff said, "I'll have a talk with them. They're just rambunctious boys, and after all, these are Negroes we're talking about, not whites."

"It's a crime to steal someone else's property, isn't it?" questioned Jameson.

"Yes, but you freed them, so really they didn't belong to you anymore, and well, those things will happen around these parts. Besides, you got everybody back, so it's really not a crime anymore."

"They killed an innocent man, sheriff."

Shelby Mathison shrugged in an attitude of indifference.

Jameson just shook his head. As usual, nothing would be done. He couldn't win.

Mansfield handed over the deed with a surprisingly ample sale price attached to it but no buyer listed. Jameson eagerly agreed to the price, and the paper was signed.

"We'll be gone by the end of the week," he told Mansfield.

"No hurry, my boy," he replied. "It's good doing business with you."

They shook hands. Jameson took his copy of the signed sales record and the new freedom papers and departed.

"I'm glad he's going," said the sheriff.

They all agreed.

As he walked outside, Jameson was surprised by the sudden appearance of Abigail. "Hello, Abby."

"Hello, Jameson."

They stood in silence for a moment, and then Abigail said, "I'm divorcing you. I should have known better. You ruined my life. You embarrassed me and shamed me by taking up with that, that... black hussy. Her anger boiled over, and she slapped him across the face then quickly said, "I'm sorry. I didn't mean to do that."

He did not deny the affair this time; he was guilty as charged. Perhaps he should have felt some remorse for his infidelity, but he didn't. He truly cared for Delilah and was falling in love with her, if he wasn't already.

He did not want to cause Abigail any more pain and sorrowfully said, "I didn't mean for all this to happen either, Abby. I'm sorry for your hurt. I really am."

"My sister told me she went to see you to offer her sympathy, and you tried to seduce her."

"That's a lie, Abby. I would never do that."

"I know. I don't believe her. We both know Annabelle is prone to flights of fantasy and theatrics. She likes to fabricate stories to make herself feel needed and loved. It's sad really."

"Yes, it is."

A long silence ensued. There was nothing more to say, although Abigail probably wished there was.

Jameson finally broke the silence. "I hope you have a good life, Abby. Take care of yourself."

He turned, walked away, mounted his horse, and rode off. She stood there looking at him. Tears welled up in her eyes. She still had feelings for him. She was hoping he would fight for her like a true Southern gentleman. Instead he just walked away, leaving her with a broken heart.

Jameson was contentedly travelling down the road when he spotted another wagon coming toward him. He became leery as this was a lonely road, and he seldom met another traveler during his excursions.

There was something familiar about that particular coach, and as it drew nearer, he recognized the driver in the sailor outfit. It was Petey, which meant Captain Mordechai Le Brute the slave trader was inside the coach. Jameson reproached himself for not remembering the mother and daughter slaves he had agreed to purchase. What with all that had occurred he had completely forgotten about them. He waved to the driver to stop the carriage and called out to the captain.

Mordechai emerged from the coach, demanding to know why Petey had stopped, when he spied Jameson. He did not say anything, merely ran his eyes up and down Jameson's frame.

"Good day, Captain." There was no reply, so he continued. "Why did you not return to my plantation with the two women I agreed to purchase from you?"

Again, no answer, so Jameson continued, "We had a deal, sir. You reneged on your word."

Mordechai finally spoke, "You are right. I did renege on me word."

"Why would you do that, sir?"

Mordechai thought for a moment, and then said, "I sold them."

"You sold them. Sir, we had a verbal gentleman's agreement."

"Look, I'm no gentleman. However, I do keep me word, and if you must know, I was warned by your neighbors not to sell you any slaves because you are against slavery and would only free them. Personally, I don't care what you do with them after I get me money, but it's awfully important to a lot of people around here. They gave me an ultimatum. If I sold them to you, they would not buy any slaves from me ever again. I'm a businessman. I'm only in this for the money, you understand. I need their business more than yours, so I was forced to sell those two to somebody else, and mind you they paid me far less than you were going to pay me, but for future business I was forced to accept their less than generous offer. You understand, don't you?"

Jameson replied, "Sadly, I understand your reasoning, but I don't agree with your principles. Can you at least tell me who purchased them?"

Mordechai said, "I can't. It was part of the agreement."

"Well, thank you for nothing then," Jameson said as he readied his horse to leave.

Mordechai thought for a moment and then said, as he was getting back into the coach, "You must be really hated for your views. None of these people like you very much. It must be hard to have no friends."

"I have friends," Jameson said, "just not the color you and your like would approve of, and believe me when I tell you; they are better people than any of your friends."

The only consolation Jameson received was from Petey, who said, "I wish you luck, sir. I wish I had your courage and could do more, but, well—"

"Let's go, Petey," the captain yelled from within the coach.

Petey slapped the reins, and the coach started to roll away as Jameson did the same with his horse. The two people of opposing views galloped off in opposite directions. Jameson wondered which one of his so-called neighbors had purchased the two women and why it was such a secret. He probably knew the answer to that question. He hoped they were at least being treated fairly. He turned to the problem at hand—getting his people out of Willow Hills safely.

Chapter 17

FEELINGS

On the road back to Serenity, Jameson wrestled with his conscience over the last few days. He had won the battle, but lost the war. He had freed his people but had not convinced anyone else that they did not need slavery to run a successful plantation. It became clear to him that they did not want to abolish slavery, and nothing he said or did would convince them otherwise. The freed workers had no skills other than what they were trained to do. They could not read or write and would be unable to survive on their own. Perhaps Nicholas Mansfield was right when he told Jameson that he was not in the South long enough and did not understand the situation or complications of what he wanted to do. Jameson was saddened by the whole situation. Maybe he should have just left everything as he found it, but no, that was not an option to him. He could not save everyone, but at least he could still save his workers.

Since it was on his way home, Jameson decided to stop at the Spanish Moss Plantation and teach those murderous thieves a lesson. He tied his horse at the same tree as the night before, took his rifle, and crept up to the house. It was even more rundown and weed-ridden in the daylight than last night. He looked in the window. The house was empty; no one was at home. He made his way to the barn. The door was ajar. He slipped inside. Again no one was around. He saw Delilah's dress on the ground. He picked it up and searched through the pockets for the letter of freedom. It was not there. Panic filled his body. Had they gone to Serenity to seek revenge? He ran back to his horse and galloped home.

As he approached his plantation, all seemed normal. He thought he would pass slave row and ask them if everything was all right and tell them he had secured new letters of freedom for all of them. When he arrived, the place was empty. No one was around. He wondered if perhaps they were at the main house. He had wanted them to stay in the now largely vacant house, but Nanny would not hear of it. If Abigail or Bethany Sue returned, they would be upset with her if slaves were living in the same house as they were. He acquiesced to her wishes but thought maybe she had a change of heart. He rode up to the mansion.

Uncky greeted him. "Is everything all right here, Uncky?"

"Yes, sir, everything is fine. Why do you ask?"

He did not respond but ran up the stairs into the house. Delilah was waiting for him.

She ran to him, threw her arms around him, and said, "I missed you, James."

He was afraid for the missing workers and asked her, "Are your people here in the house?"

"No. Aren't they down at slave row?"

"I just passed there, and they're nowhere to be found. I'm concerned. Nanny, have you seen the workers?"

"No, sir, Mista Jameson, I ain't seen them since they all came back with you last night."

Jameson added, "I passed them this morning when I rode out. What could have happened?"

He grabbed his rifle and ran down to slave row, Delilah following closely behind.

They arrived to find empty shacks, not a soul.

"Maybe they're in the fields," Delilah said.

They hurried down to see the cotton and tobacco plants unattended.

"Where could they be?" asked Delilah.

"I have a strange feeling this has something to do with those Wrabble brothers," muttered Jameson.

They started back toward the house. Along the way they were met by Doc Pritchard's coach. He was coming to examine Delilah as he had promised.

"Can I offer you two a ride?" Doc said.

"Thank you, don't mind if we do."

Jameson told Delilah he had asked the doctor to come by and check her over. She panicked at the thought of a physical examination and insisted she was all right.

Doc said, "I'll be the judge of that, girl. We'll find out if you're ill or not."

Back at the plantation house, Doc took Delilah into the study and asked Jameson to wait in the hall. Delilah had never had a doctor look at her before, and she was visibly nervous.

"Calm down, child. I'm not going to hurt you. I just want to listen to your heart, look in your throat, things like that. You just relax. Now tell me, how long have you been vomiting?"

"It's nothin'," she insisted. "I just get ill sometimes."

She jumped every time the doctor went to touch her. He could see how scared she was, so he took extra time and explained each item to her before he used it. He let her listen to her own heart and showed her each tool and its purpose. He was very kind and understanding, putting her fears to rest. She was very interested in all the doctor's tools of the trade and paid strict attention to how each one was used, marveling at the wonders of medicine.

Meanwhile, Jameson was pacing back and forth, wondering what was taking so long.

"You're gonna wear out that floor," said Nanny. "Come on. I have a nice meal prepared for you and the doctor."

"I can't eat just now. I have too much on my mind. Nanny, I want you to know I sold the plantation today. I will be leaving Serenity forever. I'm heading back to Boston with Delilah and the rest of the freed workers, that is, if I can find them again."

Nanny curiously asked, "What about Miss Abigail?"

"She does not want to be with me any longer. She's going to stay with her parents at Tall Oaks."

Nanny rolled her eyes and sighed. "It's none of my business, Mista Jameson, but she is your wife."

"That she is, Nanny, but she and I have drifted apart. We don't agree on many things any longer. She is content with the status quo, and I can't accept it. She doesn't understand that these poor people need me to get them to freedom. I can't just let them fend for themselves. Look what happened the first time I left them. I have to provide them support, protection, guidance, and hope. It's something I have to do. Even if I fail I have to try to make a difference. Maybe it's my destiny. I don't know, but I intend to see it to the end." He paused and then added, "You know I would like you and Uncky to come with us."

"I believe we'll stay, Mista Jameson. Uncky and I are too old to set out on an adventure with you young folks. As long as we stay here, we'll be okay."

Jameson added, "I'll make sure the new owner will let you stay here, and I will ask that they treat you kindly." He gently kissed her on the cheek.

Back in the study, Doc Pritchard told Delilah his diagnosis. She already surmised the results but asked him anyway.

"Are you sure?"

"To the best of my abilities and without further tests, I'm pretty positive. You get dressed. I'll tell Jameson."

"No! Please doctor, don't."

"He has to be told," said Doc. "This is important. It can change all his plans."

"I know. Please let me tell him," pleaded Delilah.

"You promise you'll tell him?"

"Yes, I promise."

"How can I be sure?"

"Because I wouldn't hurt him, I love him."

"Love," Doc said in a huff. "Love comes and goes. He still has a wife, you know?"

"I know," said Delilah sheepishly, putting her head down.

Doc shook his head and left the room.

Jameson was waiting anxiously. "What is it Doc? Is she okay?"

"I promised I would let her tell you."

"Come over here. Sit down and have some delicious fried chicken, doctor," Nanny said.

"I can't wait. You are one great cook, Nanny, simply the best." Doc settled into his chair and proceeded to enjoy the feast prepared especially for him.

Delilah came out of the room, looking frightened. "What is it, Lilah? Please tell me."

"James…" She hesitated. "The doctor thinks—" She stopped again and drew a heavy breath.

"What, Lilah? What is it? You can tell me anything."

"James, I'm afraid that the doctor says that he thinks I'm—"

Abigail burst in through the front door, interrupting the confession.

She said, "I'm sorry to disturb you, Jameson, but I just found out you sold the plantation and are preparing to leave for Boston. Is that correct?"

"That's right, Abby," he said.

"Jameson, I just wanted to tell you that I'm sorry for what happened this morning in town. I didn't mean it. I still love you, Jameson. I never stopped loving you. I'm hoping we can work it out."

Abigail's eyes caught Delilah's, who was standing in the shadows in back of Jameson. They stared at each other. Abigail's eyes filled with jealousy and contempt, Delilah's with fear and worry. Then Delilah bowed her head and walked back into the study. She stopped just out of sight but within earshot. Jameson walked toward Abigail, temporarily forgetting the scared and frightened Delilah.

"I can't let you go, Jameson," she continued. "If you're going to leave, please take me with you. I don't want to lose you. I don't care about what you did with that girl. I only care about us. We can start over. Take me back. Let it be like it used to be. I need you, Jameson. I love you."

She hugged him and kissed him. He did not fight her. He gave in and returned the kiss. Delilah, watching from the study, started to cry.

Chapter 18

CONFRONTATION

Jameson was confused. He thought his life with Abigail was over, yet there he stood, holding her in his arms. Then he remembered Delilah. He looked around, but she was not there.

"I have to go find Lilah for a minute. I'll be right back," he said softly to Abigail.

"No, Jameson, please forget her. Take me back to Boston with you," she pleaded, placing her arms tightly around him so he could not leave her.

Just then, as if on cue, a shout came from out in the front yard. "Hey, Hartford! Jameson Hartford, you in there? Come out and face us."

It was the Wrabble brothers. Jameson looked for his rifle then realized he had left it in Doc's coach. All he had was the pistol he had hidden in his jacket.

"Come out, Jameson Hartford, or should we burn you out?"

"Don't go out there," said Abigail. "They're crazy."

"I have to," said Jameson. He nudged her aside, opened the door, and walked onto the porch.

"What do you two boys want now?" he said.

"Don't you want to know what happened to your slaves?" queried Dawson.

"What did you do with them? Where are they?" demanded Jameson. "You better not have hurt them or you'll pay."

"They're all right, Jameson Hartford. They just aren't yours anymore. That's all."

The brothers were drunk as usual, babbling, and not making much sense.

"What do you mean? What have you done?" yelled Jameson.

"We took 'em and sold 'em."

"You had no right. They weren't yours."

"They weren't yours either, Jameson Hartford. You freed them. You gave up any legal claim you had to them. They were free, and we helped ourselves to the free goods." Brandon Wrabble laughed.

"That's a good one, brother," Dawson said.

"I want them back," demanded Jameson.

"We got rid of them. You'll never find them. They're gone for good this time. You killed my brother and cheated us before, when we were trying to sell them. I told you we'd get even, and now we almost have. Just one little thing more, Jameson Hartford: we want that little girl you stole from us. Bring her out, and we'll go in peace."

"That's never going to happen," said Jameson.

Abigail came out of the house.

"Don't come out here, Abby. Go back in."

"Now listen here, you two," Abigail began. "You both know my father Beau Lansing. He and the rest of Willow Hills are not going to look kindly on what you've done. Just leave and we'll forget everything."

"We want that little slave girl, and then maybe we'll tell you what we did with the other slaves!" yelled Brandon.

Abigail turned toward Jameson and whispered, "Give her to them, Jameson. She's only one, and you'll get the other five, six, eight, however many there were back again. You can save more of them if you just sacrifice that one. That's what you want, isn't it, to free a lot of slaves?"

He looked at her in disbelief and said, "You don't even know how many people we have, do you? How many men and women toiled these many years so you could have an easy life? Yet you're willing to send an innocent person into hell with the likes of them."

Abigail should have looked ashamed, but she wasn't. She didn't understand him at all.

He turned to the brothers and yelled, "No, you can't have her. You'll have to kill me first."

"That can be arranged," Dawson said as he raised his rifle.

Jameson reached for his pistol. Dawson aimed.

Abigail screamed, "Watch out Jameson!" as she lunged forward and tried to push him out of the line of fire.

The rifle exploded. Abigail fell. She had saved Jameson, but the bullet had found a new victim.

"You shot her!" Jameson screamed. "You shot her!"

The two Wrabble brothers knew they would be severely punished for shooting Beau Lansing's daughter, accident or not. They turned and fled.

Jameson took Abigail in his arms and held her close. "Doc, Doc Pritchard," he called frantically. "Help! Abigail's been shot."

He held her close and said softly, "Why did you do such a foolish thing?"

"I love you, Jameson. I always have and always will."

Blood was seeping from the wound. Abigail saw Delilah watching from a distance and decided to take advantage of the situation. She was never one to let a good crisis go to waste.

She moaned in pain and grabbed at Jameson's arm, begging, "Do you love me, Jameson?"

"Yes, Abby, I love you."

"Kiss me," she whispered.

He bent down to allow their lips to meet. Delilah, witnessing the kiss, turned and ran out the back door into the fields, weeping uncontrollably.

Doc emerged from the house, took one look, and told Jameson to take her inside quickly.

"Get my bag. I'll need boiling water and clean towels. Take her into the study and place her on the couch."

Jameson dutifully obeyed, all the time asking himself *why*. Once Abigail was safe, the anger welled up inside of him. He was determined to settle the score with the Wrabble boys once and for all. He ran to grab his rifle from Doc's coach and went out in pursuit of retribution.

Chapter 19

REVENGE

The Wrabble brothers were running tripping and stumbling to their horses when they spied Delilah scurrying across the field.

"Isn't that our little girlfriend?" said Brandon.

"Let's go get her and get out of here!" yelled Dawson.

They mounted their horses and rode after her, yelling and screaming. Brandon pulled out his rope and twirled the loop in the air, charging at her.

She saw them coming and screamed, "Help! Help me!"

Jameson heard the cries and ran as fast as he could in the direction of the screams. In the clearing he could see them trying to lasso her like a wild animal. Delilah was weaving and ducking, trying desperately to avoid the rope. After a few unsuccessful attempts, Brandon managed to get the noose over her head and around her body. He yanked her to the ground and dragged her several feet before stopping the horse. They both dismounted and went after their prey.

Jameson was still many yards away and realized he could not reach her in time. He stopped, cocked his rifle, aimed, and fired, hitting Brandon squarely in the chest. He fell to the ground. Dawson, seeing what had occurred, grabbed Delilah and held her up in front of him as a shield.

"Brandon, are you okay? Speak to me, brother. Say something, anything."

Brandon just lay there motionless, staring up into the sky with lifeless eyes. Dawson was forced to turn his attention to Jameson.

Crying, he shouted, "You killed my brother. You killed both my brothers. I'm all alone now. I have no one. I hate you, Hartford. I hate you."

Jameson started running toward the captor and his prey.

Dawson screamed, "You stop where you are." He pulled a large knife out of its sheath and put it up to Delilah's throat. "Stop or I'll cut her throat. I swear I'll do it."

Jameson froze in his tracks. He tried to speak gently to avoid any rash reactions from the distraught brother. "Don't do anything you'll regret, Dawson."

"I'm leaving, and I'm taking this here girl with me as insurance. Don't follow me or she dies. Do you hear me, Hartford?"

Jameson knew Dawson was unstable and tried to reason with him, using a soothing voice to calm him down. "I hear you, but I have a better deal. You let her go, and I let you go. You have my word on it. I promise I won't come after you. What do you say?"

Dawson was visibly perplexed, should he trust Jameson or not? Jameson took the opportunity to inch forward, a few steps at a time, being careful not to be noticed.

"I don't trust you, Hartford!" screamed Dawson. "She goes with me, or she dies right here."

Jameson countered, "Dawson, listen to me. Your brother shot Abigail. You didn't. Right now all you're guilty of is stealing my workers and selling them. You tell me where they are, and I forget everything. I won't press charges. You'll be free." He kept inching closer and closer, trying not to be detected. "If you kill her," he continued, "that's murder. You'll hang."

"It's not murder to kill a slave," Dawson said.

"She's not a slave. She's a free person. You said it yourself. That makes it murder."

Dawson looked confused and was panicking. Delilah was crying, shaking, and scared beyond belief. The standoff felt like it was going on for hours, but in reality it was only a few tense minutes.

All of a sudden, Dawson realized Jameson was edging forward. "You're trying to sneak up on me. You're trying to trick me!" he screamed. "I'm gonna have to kill her."

Delilah, determined not to die like this, threw her foot up from behind and connected with Dawson right between his legs. He screamed in agony and loosened his grip. She pulled away. He grabbed her arm and wielded the knife ready to silence her forever. Jameson reached into his jacket, pulled out the pistol, cocked it, and fired, hitting Dawson just as the knife came toward Delilah. He fell to the ground, unable to complete his final act. Jameson ran to get Delilah. She was moaning on the ground. Blood was oozing out from between her legs. Jameson lifted her into his arms and ran back to the house, reassuring her everything would be okay.

He ran through the front door of the mansion, yelling, "Doc, Doc, I need you. Lilah's been hurt."

Doc had just finished stitching Abigail's wound. "Bring her in here, Jameson."

She was placed on the other sofa opposite Abigail. Doc began to exam her.

"What happened?" he said.

Jameson explained and told him he had shot both brothers. They were lying in the field. Again, Jameson was instructed to wait in the hall while Doc tended to Delilah.

After what seemed like an eternity, Doc emerged.

"She's all right, Jameson, but whatever occurred out there caused a miscarriage. She lost the baby. I'm sorry."

"She was pregnant?" Jameson was stunned. "I didn't know. I had no idea."

"She didn't tell you?" Doc said.

"I think she was trying to tell me when Abigail came and then the Wrabble Brothers showed up. I never let her finish. I stopped her from telling me. No wonder she was so upset and crying." Jameson stared off into space.

"Don't you want to know about your wife?" Doc said.

Jameson snapped back to reality and answered, "Of course I want to know. Is she all right?"

"She's going to be fine. The bullet passed through her. It narrowly missed some vital organs, but she will have a full recovery."

"That's great, Doc. Thank you."

Nanny came out of the study. "They're both asking for you, Mista Jameson. You better go in."

"Don't upset them, Jameson," Doc said. "They need their rest. I gave them something to help them sleep. Keep it brief."

Jameson entered the study. He looked at both of the women, stopped for a moment, wondering which person he should speak to first, then proceeded to go over to Delilah. "You're going to be all right," he said as he knelt down next to her and took her hand while gently stroking her head.

"James," she started, "I wanted to tell you something."

"I know," he said. "Doc already told me."

"My baby's dead, James. The baby's gone. Why do I keep losing my babies? Why do they keep dying?"

"I'm sorry, Lilah, I really am, but you can get pregnant again."

"I would have made a good mother, James. I would have brought that child up right. I would have taught them not to judge people by the color of their skin, not to hate, not to give up.

"I know. I know," said Jameson. "And you'll still get that chance. You'll be a great mother."

"Do you really believe that, James?" She looked at him, pleading for a yes.

"Yes, yes I do, now don't upset yourself," he said. "You need to rest and get your strength back."

He bent over her and kissed her head. She closed her eyes, but tears were rolling down her cheeks.

He got up and walked over to Abigail. He knelt down beside her, not sure if she was asleep, but Abigail opened her eyes.

Jameson whispered, "Why did you do that? Why did you move in front of me and get shot like that?"

"I'd do anything for you, Jameson, even take a bullet for you. I love you," Abigail said in a weak voice.

"Doc says you're going to be fine. He expects a full recovery. Don't disappoint him, just get better," Jameson said.

"Tell me you love me, Jameson."

"Okay, okay, now get some sleep."

He bent over and kissed her forehead then quietly slipped out of the room.

Unbeknownst to Jameson, Delilah was watching and listening to every word, pondering her own destiny, she wondered if her hopes and dreams had exceeded real life; would she live happily ever after with her knight in shining armor, or would she remain forever a slave, having only briefly tasted sweet freedom? The drug finally did its job and she drifted off into a deep sleep never finding an answer to her question.

Chapter 20

CHOICES

Jameson emerged from the study with a fresh bottle of whiskey, looking quite forlorn. He gently closed the door, gazed at the inquisitive stares, and said, "How about a taste, Doc?"

"No, none for me," Doc said as he finished his dinner. "That was delicious, Nanny, as usual. How are my patients, Jameson?"

"They're both sleeping, Doc."

"Well, that's fine. That's what they both need. I have to go now, but I'll come around tomorrow to check on them."

"Thank you, Doc. Thank you very much," Jameson said, shaking his hand.

The doctor left, and Jameson walked over to the table. He sat down and poured himself a large drink.

"You want something to eat with that drink, Mista Jameson?" Nanny said.

"No, thanks, Nanny, I have some serious thinking to do."

"That bottle gonna help you think?" asked Nanny. "If you ask me, it's gonna cloud your mind and cause you to make mistakes."

"Oh, and I suppose you know what I should do?" Jameson retorted.

"Yes, I do, Mista Jameson. You should stay with your wife and go back to Boston with her where you belong. You can't marry Delilah. A Negro woman and a white man, that just ain't acceptable. Nobody ever heard of such a thing. People will hate you and her and make your life hard, real hard."

"I can't just reject Lilah. I care very deeply for her. She and I have something special. It's hard to explain," claimed Jameson.

"It's called sex, Mista Jameson. Don't confuse it with love."

Jameson was stunned by Nanny's candid remark but replied, "You're wrong, Nanny. It's more than that. I think about her all the time."

"When you're miles away from here and back in Boston with your wife, you'll forget her, and she'll be better off with her own kind. In time, she'll forget you too."

Jameson added, "Maybe I don't want that to happen."

"Well you should. Take my word for it."

"Thank you, Nanny. I'll take that all into consideration. Now please, I want to be alone."

"Good night, Mista Jameson."

"Good night, Nanny."

Nanny retired to her bed. Jameson sat at the long, lonely table, drank, and thought and drank some more. What should he do? Who should he take with him, and who should he reject? He believed he loved them both but for different reasons. Exhaustion finally took its toll as his head grew too heavy to support. He reluctantly gave in to gravity, placed his head on the table, and fell asleep.

He awoke the following morning still at the table. Nanny offered him some hot black coffee. It was just what he needed.

"I better check on our two ladies," he said.

"I been checkin' on them a couple of times during the night. I guess you were too…uh, tired to hear me, besides, I was just in there," said Nanny. "They're both awake and feelin' better. I'm gonna make them some toast and juice. You better stay here, Mista Jameson. You don't wanna be starting anything."

Jameson mumbled, "You're right as usual."

In the study both women were lying opposite each other on facing couches. They were eyeing each other up and down.

Abigail started, "I don't know what Jameson sees in you. You're not refined. You're short hair makes you look like a man. You're hands are all calloused, and you're, well, you're a Negro. I just don't see it. Besides, now that I'm back, I'm sure he will cast you aside."

Delilah was visibly hurt but countered back, "No he won't, James promised me he is takin' me back up north with him and I believe him."

"James. Don't you even know his given name is Jameson, not James?"

"He likes me to call him James. He told me so."

"Men will say anything to get a girl in bed, even a black one," taunted Abigail. "Believe me, you're out. I'm back in."

Delilah lifted herself off the sofa, wincing in pain.

"Where do you think you're going?" Abigail said sarcastically.

"I'm leavin'. I'm not stayin' here with you," retorted Delilah.

"Well, bring me some coffee and toast, and hurry it up," snapped Abigail.

"I'm not a slave anymore," claimed Delilah. "James gave me my freedom."

"Well, after he and I leave, the new owner will surely make you a slave again, so learn your place now," chided Abigail.

Delilah left the room and slammed the door.

The noise roused Jameson. He turned to see Delilah shuffling out of the study. He rose and went to help her, taking hold of her and leading her into the kitchen.

"You shouldn't be up and around yet, Lilah."

"I couldn't stay in that room with her. She kept sayin' you were goin' to take her with you and leave me here to be a slave again. That's not true, is it James?"

"I wouldn't let that happen to you, Lilah, never."

He held her close and kept stroking her hair, trying to allay her fears. As she calmed down, he gained enough courage to pose a very pertinent question.

"Delilah, please forgive me, but I have to know. We were only intimate three times in the last few days. You could not be with child and have had a miscarriage. It is too early, medically impossible…unless…the child was not mine." He gave her a quizzical stare.

Delilah looked scared, and tears welled up in her eyes. Her voice quivered as she spoke, "Oh, James, I wanted to tell you so many times, but I was so afraid that you would hate me, but the baby… it wasn't yours… it was Mista Josiah's baby. He came for me again, maybe a week before he died. I'm so sorry. Please don't hate me, please."

She began to cry again as Jameson tried to comfort her, and Nanny whispered, "Tsk. tsk, tsk, poor child, poor, poor child."

Jameson said, "That's not your fault. There's nothing you could have done about it. How could you possibly think I would blame you and hold it against you? My poor little Lilah, you've gone through so much, and all I can do is offer you yet another apology for the horrible actions of my brother. What has he done to you? Even after he's dead his evil stench lingers on, still hurting somebody as wonderful as you. I'm so sorry, Lilah. Please try to forget the past and live for the future…and me."

They looked deep into each other's eyes, and just as their lips met, as if on cue, the study door suddenly opened, and Abigail stood there propping herself up against the wall. Jameson had to run over to her and escort her to the table.

"You shouldn't be up and around either, Abby. The doctor said for you to stay in bed."

"Did you expect me to stay in there while this little whore tries to seduce you again?"

"Don't call her that, Abby. She's not like that."

Abigail was determined to finish the confrontation, once and for all. "Jameson, tell her you and I are husband and wife and belong together. There is no room for her."

"Abby, try to understand, I came here to free these poor people and run the plantation with hired help. I failed. I not only caused two of them to be murdered, but I lost the rest of the people. They were stolen and probably sold into slavery again. I can't even find them. The only two people who knew where they were, the Wrabble brothers, I had to shoot dead."

Abigail interrupted, "You had to shoot them because of her." She pointed at Delilah. "You should have traded her for the rest of the slaves. Then you would have at least freed a few people instead of just this one," Abigail said derisively. "What can she possibly give you that I can't?" Abigail hesitated for a moment then realized what she had just said. "Is it true she was pregnant with your child?"

Jameson looked stunned.

"Yes, I heard you last night. You made her pregnant, didn't you?" Abigail was starting to raise her voice. "Just because we were having a hard time conceiving, you decided to have a baby with a slave?"

"It wasn't like that," said Jameson reluctantly.

Abigail screamed, slapped Jameson across the face, called him a cad, and then collapsed on the floor. Jameson picked her up and carried her back to the sofa in the study. Nanny got the smelling salts and revived her. She lay there, crying hysterically. He told her he was sorry. Nanny told him he should leave her alone for a while and not upset her any further.

When Jameson returned to the kitchen, Delilah looked at him with sadness in her eyes and said, "I understand if you want her instead of me, but know this, James, you didn't fail. You tried to do more for us than anybody else ever had. It didn't all work out the way you wanted, but you gave us all hope. You have to understand that we didn't know there were men like you alive who hated slavery and would fight for us. You gave us the faith to believe that one day we would all be free. And all those people you freed, they were proud to be free, even if it was just for a little while. You're not a failure. You're a great man, James. I guess you should go back to Miss Abigail. She needs someone to look after her. I'll manage somehow."

Jameson smiled at her and said, "I told you this once before, that you were a very wise woman, and I meant it. Abigail does indeed need someone. I'm just not necessarily sure it's me. You're so sweet and kind. You're caring and giving. You're everything she's not. You worry about me and everyone else, even those that would hurt you. Maybe I'm just a dreamer, but I don't care what the other people say. I don't care what the rest of the world thinks. I do love you, Delilah."

He hugged her as tears of joy ran down her cheeks.

Then he hesitated and added, "But Abigail is still my wife, and I love her. She and I have to talk about our respective futures. It's the proper thing to do."

"I understand," said Delilah. "I'll be here waitin' for you and your answer."

As he walked away, she thought, *Please come back for me, James. I love you.*

Jameson went into the study, sent Nanny out, and closed the door. Delilah and Nanny stared together at the sealed entry, waiting for the storm.

Jameson boldly faced the hysterical Abigail and stated, "Abby, I made up my mind. I will be taking Delilah back to Boston with us."

"How could you do this to me?" she screamed. "You chose a Negro over me? Why it's an insult and humiliating. What will all the neighbors, for that matter, the whole town say about me?"

"I can't leave Lilah. If I did she would wind up being a slave again. No one would care if she was free or not. All they see is she's black. She's a slave. Lilah is too smart and kind to end up like that. I won't let it happen."

Abigail added, "What about me, your wife? We're still married. You're breaking your wedding vows to be with a Negro. People will think something is wrong with you and me."

"We can all travel back together."

"I won't share a house with that whore. It would be worse in Boston than here. All my committees—the mayor, the church council—I simply couldn't bear it."

"Then you're saying you'd rather stay here," declared Jameson.

"No. I demand you get rid of that—"

"Don't call her a whore again, Abby. I won't stand for it. You know what your problem is? You look at her, and all you see is a woman with darker skin than yours, and you instantly dislike her for that reason and no other. I don't see color when I look at her or any of the others. I only see people like you and me who need help and a chance to be free and just...live their lives."

Abigail made no reply, perhaps because she knew Jameson was right and she could not rationalize her hate and bias.

Jameson then calmly stated, "Why don't you think of helping Delilah instead of condemning her?" He paused for a brief moment then added, "I've made my decision, and I'm bringing her back with me to Boston. If you don't want to come along, that will be your choice."

The rage once again filled the face of the uncharacteristically sedate Abigail, and she screamed, "You're a horrible man, Jameson! I don't know what I ever saw in you. My father and the others should have hung you out on that road. Then I would be the poor grieving widow instead of the shamed wife. It's a scandal. I'll never be able to show my face in public again."

Jameson retorted, "It's always about you. It's always been about you. You never cared about anyone, just your status in life and how important you are. You always managed to believe the worst about me, even when all I was trying to do was right a terrible wrong. Lilah actually cares about me, my feelings, my needs. I won't cast her aside, and I don't care what you want."

Abigail screamed, "Oh no! Go. Get out of here! You'll regret it. I'll get even with you. I hate you." She fell back on the couch in tears.

Out in the kitchen, Delilah and Nanny could hear yelling, crying, and more yelling. Then Jameson emerged, sad and confused. He walked over to the table and sat down for another large drink and to plan his next move.

He gazed at Delilah and softly said to her, "I'm taking you to Boston with or without Abigail. Judging from the conversation I just had with my wife, I suspect it will be just the two of us. You're very important to me. I need you, Lilah."

She replied, "You'll always have me, James, as long as you want me."

They embraced, each wishing the moment could last forever, but reality always had a way of intruding upon them, for tomorrow never knows.

Chapter 21

LOOPHOLES

Jameson had Uncky hitch the horses up to the buckboard, and he drove out into the fields to check on the bodies of the two Wrabble brothers. His plan was to bring the brothers' bodies into Willow Hills and report to the sheriff what had happened. Perhaps he could convince someone, anyone, to help him look for his missing workers, but he doubted it. After he delivered the brothers to the undertaker, he would ride into Charleston and try to locate his freed workers; maybe they tried to sell them at auction again.

He checked the two dead bodies, hoping they would have some sort of bill of sale on them for his missing people. The brothers had a sum of money in their pockets, probably from the sale, but no paperwork whatsoever. Jameson shuddered with disgust as he realized he needed proofs of ownership and bills of sale for livestock and land sales, but the poor blacks were strictly a cash business where they vanished into obscurity. There was no way to track them now. He loaded the two bodies into the wagon and proceeded into Willow Hills.

He arrived to a lukewarm reception, mostly curious onlookers who wondered what was covered up in the wagon. He stopped at Sheriff Shelby Mathison's office and told him what had transpired. The sheriff did not completely believe the story but could not press charges against Jameson, even if he wanted to. After all, he was married to Abigail, and her father was too well respected to drag his daughter through a trial.

The sheriff would offer no help toward recovering the missing workers. He told Jameson to be happy they were gone and his problem was over, and now he could just leave. Jameson shook his head and left for the bank. He needed to insure that his funds from the sale of Serenity would be forwarded to his bank in Boston. He also wanted an addendum added to the contract providing Nanny and Uncky would be able to remain at the plantation and would be treated fairly. He was assured that would not be a problem. They were both well liked and highly thought of, as slaves, that is.

Lastly, he stopped in the dress shop and bought Delilah a new wardrobe consisting of dresses, shoes, a new bonnet, everything a Southern belle needed for her first train trip. He guessed at the sizes but relied on the clerk to advise him as to the latest fashions and colors. He knew very little in such matters. When he was completely satisfied, he left the store and bid a final farewell to Willow Hills.

On the way back to Serenity, Jameson decided to stop at Tall Oaks and inform Beau Lansing, his father-in-law, of Abigail's gunshot wound. As he passed the fields, he thought he glimpsed a few of his freed workers laboring under the hot sun. He rode toward them, and there, to his amazement, were Zeke, Daniel, Nate, Becky, Sarah, and all the rest. He yelled out and queried them as to why they were there. Daniel told him that they were all gathered up under threat of death by the Wrabble brothers, brought here, and ordered to go to work.

Sara added, "They wanted to know where you had Lilah. We were threatened unless we told them that she was up at the mansion with you. We didn't cause you any trouble, did we, Mista Jameson?"

"Don't you worry. The Wrabble brothers won't be bothering you or anyone else ever again. I've permanently removed both of them."

The anger welled up inside of him as he tried to figure out why his freed workers were once again slaves working on his father-in-law's plantation. The workers were also confused and full of questions. He told them he would try to uncover the answers.

The outraged Jameson rode up to the mansion to find out exactly what caused this anomaly. He met Beau Lansing outside in front of his house.

"Why are my freed people working for you?" he demanded.

"Calm down, son," said Beau. "I had the Wrabble boys round them up for me. They were freed by you, captured by them, and delivered to me. It's all legal, unless you want to start more trouble."

"They're free, or at least should be, and belong at Serenity," Jameson claimed.

"They will be back at Serenity, my boy, since I purchased the plantation from you. I'll need them to work the fields."

"You purchased it, but why?"

"I'm expanding. I only had cotton fields. Now I have additional cotton and also tobacco crops. Besides, what do you care? You're leaving."

"I want my workers set free. I have papers."

"They're not yours anymore. They're mine. Those papers are useless. I purchased the plantation before you gave them the papers. Therefore, they were part of the property, and I legally own them. Trust me, son. I'm doing you a favor. I'm saving your life. You just don't understand it all yet. We did it for you and Abigail. I don't want my daughter to be a widow. Now why don't you just go and leave well enough alone before you create more trouble. You know you can't win."

Jameson knew he was beaten. The law would not help him. What was he to do in a place surrounded by unfriendly, unsympathetic faces? Abruptly his thoughts turned to Delilah.

He had to get her out of Lansing's reach before Beau remembered her and demanded she be returned to him as a slave also. He turned his horse, kicked some gravel up in Beau's direction and quickly rode off in anger, sadness, and dismay. He was so ashamed he could not even face his former workers. What would he tell them—that they were slaves again? He could not bring himself to tell them he failed. He did not even care to tell Beau about his daughter and her gunshot wound. All that mattered now was Delilah.

Upon returning to Serenity, he was relieved to see Delilah coming out of the house. He jumped off the wagon and held her tight, prompting a curious inquiry from Delilah.

"Is everything okay, James?"

"Yes, I'm just so glad to see you, that's all. Here, I have something for you."

He delighted in showing her all the items he had purchased for her. He watched as her face lit up like a child on Christmas morning. No one had ever given her a gift, let alone so many presents. She had never owned new store-bought clothes.

"Are they really all for me?" she asked in disbelief.

He nodded a yes. She thanked him over and over again, grabbed the packages, and ran upstairs. She couldn't wait to try them on and model them in front of the full-length mirror in the bedroom.

Jameson went into the study to see Abigail and tell her his freed workers were now captives at her father's plantation.

Surprisingly, she laughed and said, "So what. The Wrabble brothers and my father did you a big favor."

He stopped her. "How did you know the Wrabble brothers delivered them to your father? I didn't tell you that. You knew all about this. You were in on the plan all along, weren't you? You didn't want those people set free, so you schemed to keep them here."

"Don't be so dramatic, Jameson. You ruined the first attempt by rescuing them in Charleston. We had to get them away from you to save their lives and yours. They would never have made it to freedom. Trust me. It's better this way for all concerned."

"Not all, Abby, not those poor workers, and not you! I'm leaving you, Abby. I'm going back to Boston with Delilah... alone."

"You're a horrible person. I should have married your brother when he made advances toward me."

Jameson was taken aback. He had heard the rumors about Josiah and Abigail but refused to believe them.

"That's right, Jameson, your brother wanted me also. I guess I should have chosen the real Southern gentleman."

"Don't delude yourself, Abby. Just for your information, and to preserve my own honor, the baby Delilah was carrying was not mine. It was my brother's. Yes, your so-called good Southern gentleman was the father, not me! Good-bye. Give my regards to your conniving father."

Abigail was startled by this revelation, and as Jameson turned to leave, she cried, "No, wait, Jameson! I'm sorry. I forgive you. Everything I did, I did for you...for us. Jameson, come back! Please, please! Don't leave me."

He slammed the door to the study and went upstairs to see Delilah. Nanny could hear the muffled cries of despair and sadness coming from behind the closed door. She wanted to know what had transpired but felt it was better to bide her time.

Meanwhile, Jameson told Delilah all that had taken place. How they had fooled him into accidently selling his workers along with the plantation using a legal loophole and how he could not stay to help them because he feared for her safety. He related his most recent encounter with Abigail and the result of that conversation.

"Abby made my decision easy. You and I are going to Boston, alone."

Delilah should have been happy, but her thoughts were for the welfare of her friends. "Was there no way to save them?" she inquired.

"Not without a lengthy legal battle, I'm afraid, and one I couldn't possibly win here in Willow Hills. Maybe I can try to do something from Boston. Then there's the question of you. If he tried to take you, I don't know what I would have done. I love you, Delilah."

"I love you too, James."

He took her in his arms, held her close, and kissed her passionately. They held on to each other, never wanting the dream to end. After a few minutes they separated and gazed deeply into the other's soul. They knew it was a love that was meant to be.

"I wish this moment could last forever," she whispered in his ear.

"It will my love, it will. I promise you," he assured her.

The day's festive mood was only spoiled by the fact that the former workers would not be able to join them. Jameson felt somehow responsible and he needed reinforcement for his failure.

"Delilah, do you think there was anything I should have done so that I could have saved everyone? Maybe I could have done something more."

Delilah told him, "There was nothing more you could have done." But with her next breath, she begged him, "But please try to save my friends once we get to Boston."

He reassured her, "I will, I promise you. I'll do everything in my power, but for now we just have to concentrate on you and me, getting out of here while we're still alive. Okay?"

She understood but was not happy about the predicament. Trying to cheer her up, he asked, "How do you like your new clothes? Does everything fit properly? I had to guess at the sizes. I'm not too good at picking out women's clothes."

She beamed a broad smile and said, "Wait here and let me show you."

The first item she chose was a light-blue silk dress with lace around the neck and a ribbon tied around the waist.

"Do I look pretty?" she asked him coyly.

"You look ravishing."

"Is that good, James?"

"It means you look beautiful."

And she did. The fashion show continued with outfit after outfit being paraded in front of the sole judge for his approval. He loved every outfit, or maybe he was just in love with the model.

The rest of the day was spent packing their bags, as they were leaving early the next morning to catch the train for Boston.

Chapter 22

MAKING TRACKS

The last night at Serenity was spent in anxiety for Jameson, hoping to escape with Delilah before anyone could stop them. Delilah, on the other hand, was so excited she could not sleep, so they rose early. It was her first train ride, and she was going to a strange city where she did not know what to expect. They got dressed and went down to breakfast.

"My, my, Delilah, you sure look pretty!" exclaimed Nanny.

"Thank you, Nanny. I feel pretty too!"

"How is Abigail this morning?" Jameson queried.

"She's better. She's asking if you're still here. I told her you were. She wants to see you."

Jameson sighed. "It's better if I don't go in there. It would only mean trouble." He paused then added, "Don't tell her we've gone until you absolutely have to. I need to be sure we get on the train without further incident."

"Whatever you say, Mista Jameson, I'll try to help you all I can. You can always rely on me."

"I know, Nanny. I know."

As they were preparing to leave, Jameson added long arm-length gloves to Delilah's outfit and told her to keep her bonnet on and try not to be noticed.

"Are you ashamed of me?" she asked.

"No, not at all," he retorted. "I just don't want the conductor to try to force you into the slave car at the rear of the train, that's all. I want to avoid any more trouble."

"I hope you won't always try to hide me," she said.

He stared at her for a second then removed the gloves and the bonnet and said, "I'm proud to be with you Delilah. I'll never be ashamed of you… or us."

She smiled.

Then he added, "You better keep the bonnet on. All Southern women wear bonnets when they are outside, exposure to the sun or some such nonsense."

Uncky helped Jameson load the carriage. They both kissed Nanny good-bye.

"I'll miss you very much," Jameson said. "Here is my address in Boston. If you ever need me for any reason, get a letter or telegram to me immediately, okay?"

Nanny hugged him. He reached into his pocket and gave her the cash he had taken from the Wrabble brothers. At first she refused it, but upon Jameson's insistence to use it for emergencies and treat herself to some luxuries too, she finally accepted. Jameson and Delilah climbed into the coach, and Uncky drove them away.

"Nanny, Nanny!"

Screams were emanating from behind the den doors. Abigail had heard all the commotion and the horses galloping off. Nanny rolled her eyes and reluctantly entered the room.

"Has Jameson left for Boston? Did he take that…whore with him? Did he really leave me behind? Tell me, Nanny. I have to know."

Nanny sadly shook her head yes to all three questions. Abigail began to cry. Nanny tried to comfort her.

"There, there, child, you still have your family."

"Did you tell him I wanted to speak with him before he left?"

"Yes, Miss Abigail, I did."

"He didn't even care to say good-bye to me?"

"I think he didn't want to upset you anymore," Nanny said, trying to cover for Jameson.

"Upset me? Didn't he think I would be upset when I found out? Oh, Nanny, what have I done? I've lost him, haven't I?"

Nanny just stood there, not knowing what to say as Abigail began to cry again. Nanny slowly and silently backed up until she reached the edge of the room. Then she slipped out and closed the door behind her, leaving Abigail to wallow in her own self-pity and tears.

A short time later, Beau Lansing came riding up to Serenity to find out when Abigail and Jameson were leaving for Boston. He did not know Abigail had been shot or that Jameson had left her behind and was heading to Boston with Delilah. Nanny was surprised to see him but had to tell him that his daughter was in the study.

"Where is Jameson?" he asked.

"You oughta ask Miss Abigail, Mista Lansing. She knows more about it than I do," answered Nanny.

He entered the study. "What happened, girl?" he said as he closed the door behind him.

Nanny could only hear, "You were shot! He did what? He left you for a slave! That one! She belongs to me too! He stole her! I'll kill him! I'll kill them both!"

The door swung open, and Beau shouted at Nanny, "Did he leave yet? Tell me now!"

Nanny had no choice but to confess all she knew. "He left a while ago. I don't think you can catch him, Mista Lansing, sir."

Beau turned to Abigail and said, "I'll be back in a little while, darlin'. I'll kill that two timin' cheater and that little whore… she'll come back with me, dead or alive, her choice." He stomped out of the house, mounted his horse, and rode for the train station. He had death in his eyes.

The station was unusually crowded with boisterous people as Jameson and Delilah climbed out of the coach.

"What's going on?" Jameson inquired of one of the passing men.

"What? Didn't you hear? We fired on some of them damn Yankees today at Fort Sumter, right here in South Carolina. There's going to be a war, a real revolution. We're all enlisting. We're gonna whip those Northerners. Yee Hah!"

Jameson became concerned. He knew what war meant. The world would never be the same. He and Uncky carried the luggage to the conductor, who had it delivered to their private car. He shook Uncky's hand and told him to be careful.

"What does a war mean, Mista Jameson?" Uncky asked.

"It means you all might be free someday, anyway. In the meantime, just take care of yourself and Nanny."

"I will. Don't you worry yourself about that."

Delilah hugged him good-bye, and they turned to fend their way through the crowd. The people were all in a frenzy, chomping at the bit to go to war and defeat the evil North.

"What does all this mean, James?" Delilah asked.

"It means a lot of people will die, each believing their cause is the right one, unnecessary deaths. If only I could have gotten the chance to prove my theory, maybe all this wouldn't have been necessary."

"You did all you could, James. Nobody ever did more," Delilah said, trying to calm him down.

She could see he was very upset watching all the men, old and young, trying to enlist, rushing off to certain death.

Beau Lansing had his horse at a full gallop. Hate filled his face, and death was in his eyes. He wanted Jameson to pay for disgracing his daughter and making him look foolish in front of the whole town. He would not let Jameson escape, even if he had to chase the train on horseback. Delilah would be the spoils of his war, just another trophy for his amusement. He kept whipping his horse, demanding the steed to go faster, faster. He would not accept defeat.

At the station Jameson grabbed Delilah's hand and said, "We better get aboard before this gets unruly."

Jameson and Delilah proceeded, arm and arm, onto the train amid looks and whispers.

"This is why we have to fight those Yankees."

"It's a disgrace."

"It's horrible is what it is."

These were just a few of the comments they heard as they walked proudly down the aisle and into their appointed car. They had effectively passed their first hurdle. There would be many more to come.

Beau Lansing had arrived at the train station. Amazed at the huge throng, he decided to remain on his horse and force his way through the crowds. He kept screaming, "Look out!" and "Get out of my way!"

The unruly mob kept pushing and shoving, screaming and jeering. It was all at a fever pitch now, making it extremely difficult for him to get by. He continually pushed his horse forward, not caring if he trampled anyone—young, old, male, female, black, or white. It did not matter as long as he reached his destination. Extreme hatred made him persevere, and he pressed onward.

Jameson and Delilah sat down in their compartment and held each other tightly as the conductor yelled, "All aboard!"

The train began to chug slowly out of the station. Jameson pulled a cigar out of his pocket and lit it in a symbol of triumph. He blew out the smoke in a sigh of relief.

Delilah looked adoringly at him and said, "You gonna share that or what?"

He laughed and handed the cigar to her. She took a deep puff, inhaled it, and blew out a large billow of smoke in a sigh of relief, just as he had done. They laughed like little children who had just succeeded in making all the adults look foolish. Neither one saw the figure of an angry Beau Lansing sitting atop his horse on the platform, waving his fist at the departing train.

Beau's lust for revenge would not let him admit his loss. He forced his horse to jump onto the tracks and began to chase the departing train. Racing along the narrow strip of earth between the tracks and the dense overgrowth to the side, he seemed to be gaining on the locomotive. He managed to pull within inches of the elusive caboose. Beau extended his arm and tried to grab the stairway railing on the last car, determined to get aboard the train and enact his retribution. He almost succeeded as his fingers touched the rail. Then, in a burst of power, the iron horse gained momentum and pulled away, proving it was faster than its real-life namesake. Beau swore up and down as he and his horse were left in the dust. He finally admitted defeat and returned to the overcrowded train station.

Chapter 23

WILMINGTON

Beau Lansing would not be thwarted. He dismounted and pushed his way back through the crowd, running straight to the telegraph office. A wire was dispatched to the sheriff in Wilmington, North Carolina, claiming Jameson Hartford had stolen a female slave from Mister Lansing and was fleeing to Boston on the train. Jameson was to be arrested and returned, along with the girl, to Willow Hills where he would stand trial. The reply from the sheriff was in the affirmative. The law would board the train when it stopped and apprehend the robber and his illegal property.

The sheriff and his deputies were at the station as the train pulled into Wilmington, North Carolina. They informed the conductor of their intentions to search every compartment in every car. The conversation was overheard by a Negro baggage handler, who had helped Jameson and Delilah with their luggage. He immediately knew they were in danger and calmly but hastily made his way to their private car.

Jameson and Delilah were still reveling in their triumph when the knock interrupted their celebration.

Jameson warily approached the door and asked, "Who is it?"

The voice from the other side whispered, "Mister Jameson Hartford, sir, please open the door. It's an emergency, sir. I must warn you."

Jameson was leery, but he unlatched the lock and opened the door. He could see the panic on the poor man's face.

"Mister Hartford, there's lawmen on board the train looking for you and the lady. I heard them telling the conductor they're going to arrest you for stealing the girl. You got to hide, quickly. They'll be here real soon."

Jameson thought for a second, looked at Delilah then the baggage handler, and said to him, "I need your help. I didn't steal her. She was one of my workers. I freed her and fled because the people there didn't want any slaves to be free."

Delilah spoke up, "That's right! He's telling you the truth. I was his slave, but he freed me."

"What do you want me to do?" the baggage handler replied.

"I need you to change clothes with her so they'll think she is the baggage handler. Here, you can wear one of my suits," Jameson said as he opened his suitcase and produced a handsome jacket, matching pants, and white shirt and tie.

The man agreed. The transformation began, and when the exchange was over, no one was sure the charade would be successful. Jameson and the baggage handler were close in size and stature, but Delilah's outfit was a bit large, to say the least. The baggage handler produced pins and thread from the pocket of his jacket and proceeded to try and fit the costume to the model. When he was done, all agreed it just might work; it had to.

"What is your name, sir?" Jameson queried.

"I'm Kirby, sir," he replied.

"Thank you, Kirby. We are forever indebted to you."

"It's my pleasure, sir. I'm already a free man, and I am happy to help someone else become free."

"How come you have pins and thread?" Delilah queried.

"I have to be ready for any emergency our passengers might have," Kirby stated.

"Whatever the reason, I'm just glad you're here," Jameson assured him.

They shook hands. Then Kirby took Delilah and left the cabin to try and blend in with the other passengers. Jameson awaited the patrol.

Within minutes the knock came on the door.

"Who is it?" Jameson said.

"It's the Wilmington sheriff. Open up, sir."

Jameson answered, "The door is unlocked. Please come in."

They entered and looked around.

"What can I do for you gentlemen? I'm always happy to assist the law in any way I can."

"Are you Jameson Hartford?"

"I am, sir."

"Are you travelling with a Negro woman slave?"

"No, sir, I am not."

"You were seen boarding this train with a woman."

"I'm travelling with my wife."

"Where is she, sir?"

"She went to the dining car. She was hungry."

"I have a report that you stole a female slave from a Mister Beau Lansing in South Carolina and you were taking her to Boston."

"That's a false accusation, Sheriff. We found a female stowing away in the back of our coach on the way to the train. We turned her over to the authorities in Charleston. She managed to escape from the sheriff amid all the crowds and chaos at the station, but that's hardly my fault, is it?"

"No, sir, it isn't."

Jameson felt he had pulled the wool over their eyes when the sheriff added, "Would you mind accompanying us to find your wife so she can corroborate your story?"

Jameson hesitated then said, "It's not a story. It's the truth, and I do not like being called a liar, sir. You are insulting me."

"I'm sorry, sir, but I need someone to verify what you've told us, or I'll have to ask you to leave the train and come to the police station with us until I can contact the sheriff in Charleston to attest to your recollection of the incident."

His bluff having been called, Jameson had no alternative but to comply with the sheriff's wishes.

"Okay, Sheriff, let's go and try to find my wife."

They left the cabin and proceeded down the walkways to the dining car, passing from one car to the next amid nameless faces and quizzical stares. Suddenly, there before them lay the disguised Delilah and Kirby.

Jameson spoke, "Baggage man, please be sure I locked my cabin in car three. I am going to find my wife in the dining car and may not return for a while."

"Yes, sir," Delilah replied in her best gravely man's voice.

Jameson was trying to alert Delilah, should he get caught. The dining car was dead ahead and was very crowded.

Jameson turned to the sheriff and said, "Would you mind if I went in alone and brought my wife out here to talk with you? I don't want to upset her."

"That would be fine, sir, but we will be watching and waiting. You have two minutes before we come in."

"Thank you for the vote of trust, Sheriff," Jameson said sarcastically as he entered the car.

Jameson scanned the crowd, looking for a way out of the predicament he found himself in. He spotted a young lady who was smiling and flirting with him. She was quite attractive and well dressed with just a hint of mischief in her eyes. It made her seem like the right person to help him pull off this charade.

He approached her and said, "Excuse me, miss, I don't mean to be so forward, but I was hoping you could help me out of a jam?"

"What did you have in mind, sir?"

"My name is Jameson Hartford, and I need you to tell a little white lie to the sheriff who's waiting in the next car for me and just pretend to be my wife."

"My, my, whatever did you do, Mister Hartford? You didn't kill anyone, did you?"

"No, no, I assure you it's nothing that bad. I stole a female worker from my father's plantation because he left the entire place to my brother in his will. I felt I was cheated, so I took one of his workers to compensate for my loss. My brother wired the sheriff, and now they're questioning me and could possibly arrest me. I told the sheriff I turned her over to the authorities in Charleston before I got on the train. I just need you to verify my story, that's all."

"Where is your wife, Mister Hartford?"

"I'm not married, Miss, uh, Miss—"

"Prudence. My name is Prudence."

"So, Miss Prudence, will you help me?"

"If you're not married, won't they get suspicious if I pretend to be your wife?

"The conductor saw me get on the train with a woman. I had her disguised in a dress, long gloves, and a bonnet."

"Where is she now?"

"In the slave car, of course...oh no, here they come. Please help me, dear Prudence."

The sheriff approached Jameson and said, "Well, is this your wife?"

Jameson swallowed hard and looked helplessly at Prudence. She stood there for a moment, weighing her options.

The sheriff spoke, "Madam, is this your husband?"

Prudence looked at the sheriff then at a panicked Jameson and spoke right up. "Sheriff, how can you doubt my husband? Jameson is a very honest man. Of course we didn't take any slaves. That's just a downright lie perpetrated by my husband's conniving brother. And, if you remove my husband and me from this train, I shall call my daddy, who's a renowned lawyer, and sue you for everything you have. You won't be sheriff for much longer, I can assure you of that."

"Sorry, ma'am, sorry sir, I hope you understand we have to check out all complaints and all stories. Sorry to trouble you. Let's go, boys. We've held this train up long enough."

The sheriff and deputies departed.

Jameson smiled and thanked Prudence. "You saved my life. How can I ever repay you?"

She replied rather seductively, "I'll think of something, Jameson, my darling husband."

He purchased a whiskey and downed it rather quickly. The train began to move. He thanked her again and excused himself, saying, "I'll see you later, perhaps tomorrow."

"What's the hurry, handsome?"

"I left my compartment unlocked. You know you can't trust anyone these days."

"I'll come with you."

"No, no you better not, just in case the authorities are waiting for me. We don't want to push our luck. It would be safer if you remained here, but thank you again."

Prudence grabbed Jameson's hand and seductively added, "I'm in compartment C3. Don't be a stranger."

Jameson had solved one problem but seemed to have acquired another. He tried to be polite, lest Prudence have a change of heart and confess her sin of lying to the conductor.

"I really need to go check on my belongings and be sure she, uh, they are still in my compartment, but I'll be sure and remember your room number. Thank you again. Good-bye, Prudence."

He slid his arm free and quickly made his way out of the dining car and back to his own compartment, counting himself lucky to be rid of the sheriff, Lansing, and a rather bold Prudence.

She kept watching him with a doubtful gaze, wondering what the real story was and if she had been the one who was inadvertently duped.

Jameson jockeyed his way through the various train cars and crowds of nameless riders, finally reaching his private compartment. He knocked on the door, saying, "It's me, Lilah. Everything is okay. Open up."

Delilah unlocked the door. They embraced and kissed.

"I fooled them," he said as Kirby looked on, suspiciously wondering what was really happening.

"I was so scared," Delilah said.

"It's over now. We're moving. Soon we'll be in the North, and they won't be able to touch us."

Jameson knew that by the time the sheriff was able to verify or disprove his story, the train would be long gone, hopefully out of Beau Lansing's reach.

"Lilah, you better give Kirby his uniform back."

Jameson told Kirby to keep the suit of clothes. He also gave him some money and his business card. They both thanked him immensely, and Jameson told him to contact him if he ever needed anything.

Kirby said, "I'm glad to be of service, sir, but with all due respect, you two need to be real careful. The world is a cruel place to things they don't understand or accept." He smiled as he left the compartment and said, "Lock the door behind me, sir. There's no sense inviting any more trouble. Good luck, sir, ma'am."

They both settled down in each other's arms and felt at peace. The next test of acceptance would be Boston, and it was still a long train ride away.

Delilah gazed out the window, watching the landscapes roll by. The train proceeded over trestles, through large towns, and along the shore of a vast ocean. She had no idea the world was so large or so diverse. She had never left the confines of her plantation prison and just assumed the rest of the world existed as she did. She grew nervous and afraid that she had made the wrong decision to leave the place she knew for the great unknown.

Jameson was exhausted and sleeping soundly next to her on the seat. Not wishing to disturb him, she eased herself closer to him, and he instinctively placed his arm around her. She felt safe and content for the moment, and she too fell asleep. Boston and her new home were still hours away.

Chapter 24

BOSTON

The journey was finally nearing an end as the train pulled into the Boston station. Jameson gathered their belongings and he and Delilah made their way to the street. Jameson heralded a hansom cab, and the two of them prepared for the short ride to their new home.

Also disembarking from the train, Prudence caught a glimpse of her one-time husband, Jameson. She decided to surprise him when she noticed his female accomplice all dressed up, looking totally unlike a black servant woman. She watched as Jameson held her hand and helped her into the coach. Clearly this was not a slave-master relationship. She continued to view the scene suspiciously, deciding Jameson had lied to her and did, in fact, steal this woman from a plantation. She vowed to uncover the mystery, but she would bide her time, as she did not want to create a spectacle on the street. She would definitely check on this Jameson Hartford and confront him at a future date and time.

Delilah had never seen such a large city before. The streets were all paved with cobblestones, the buildings large and lifeless. All the people rushed, helter-skelter, along the walkways. Small plots of grass and trees were scattered sparingly. Where were the farms and plantations? The cab driver was a Negro, like her, but the majority of the people she could see were light skinned. She became worried and frightened. *I won't be accepted*, she thought and grabbed Jameson's hand unconsciously.

He held her hand in return and seemed to know what she was feeling. "It will be okay. Don't worry. I'll take care of you," he said.

She smiled nervously.

The ride was short, but each stride of the horse made Delilah realize how large and foreboding this city could be. The cab pulled up in front of a large two-story colonial house with a well-manicured, green lawn, large trees, and flowering shrubs. The home was smaller than the plantation but large nonetheless. It was a welcoming sight for Jameson, another frightening unknown for Delilah.

A short path led up to the front door. Jameson helped Delilah out of the cab, paid the coachman, and carried their bags up to the front door. The door swung open, and they were greeted by Millie the maid and Belle the cook, the two members of the house staff. They enthusiastically welcomed Jameson then eyed Delilah suspiciously.

"This is Delilah, ladies. She will be staying with me. She's my lady friend."

The eyes of the two employees grew wider, but they welcomed her nonetheless.

Belle asked, "Where is Miss Abigail?"

"She decided to stay in South Carolina with her family. Belle, could you please fix us something to eat? We're famished."

"Certainly, Mister Jameson," Belle replied.

"Thank you. Come on, Lilah. Let's unpack upstairs." He led her by the hand through the hall and up the staircase to one of the three bedrooms.

They were closely followed by prying eyes and curious looks.

"James?"

"Yes, Lilah."

"Are these people your slaves?"

"Heavens, no! They work for me here during the day. I pay them a weekly wage, and at night they return to their homes and families."

Delilah thought for a moment and then asked, "Why couldn't they do that on the plantation?"

"That is the question I asked so many times. I don't know the answer. I wish I did."

"James?" she said again.

"Yes, Lilah?"

"What am I to you?"

"What do you mean?"

"Well, I'm not your slave. I'm not your wife. So, what am I?"

"You're my...lady friend. I'm still married to Abigail, so we can't be married or even engaged until I can secure a divorce from Abby. Until then, you have to be content with lady friend. And to avoid a scandal, you better stay in a separate room."

Delilah looked hurt and confused.

Jameson continued, "I don't want rumors running rampant throughout Boston until I am officially a single man again. I'll start the proceedings when I get back to work on Monday. This room is right next to mine. You'll be comfortable in here. Start unpacking and change into something nice for dinner. I'll be just next door. I'll come get you, and we'll go down to dinner together."

As he walked away, she found herself all alone in completely new surroundings. She looked around the huge room, tried out the soft mattress on the bed, opened the drawers in the armoire, and looked at herself in the large full-length mirror. She couldn't quite figure out who she was or what to make of her new life. She was anxious to come to Boston, but now that she was here, she was unsure of her decision. She had not thought everything through in her desire to be free and to be with Jameson. Did she make a mistake? Should she have stayed with her own kind? She was jolted back to reality when Jameson knocked on the door. As he entered, she just stood there staring at him.

"Are you okay?"

She nodded an unsure yes.

"You're not ready. You haven't unpacked or changed. What's troubling you, darling?"

"Oh, James, I don't fit in here. I'm not like these people. I'm below them. They're better than me."

"No, they're not. You are just as good, no, you're better than anyone. That's why I love you."

"But they act and talk so different, so perfect. I don't fit in."

"That's not the Lilah I knew in South Carolina. She was determined, sure of herself, and knew what she wanted."

"James, I don't speak right or act right. I'm nothin' but a common worker who belongs back on the plantation."

"No, you're not. You're a special woman, my special woman, and I won't have you saying those things about yourself. If it would make you feel better, I can send you to a kind of charm school, a place people go to learn proper etiquette, manners. Do you think that will help you have confidence?"

"Maybe. I'd like to try it."

"Okay, I'll enroll you in Mrs. Barrington's school. She's a neighbor and lives right next door. I can introduce you tomorrow, okay?"

"Thanks, James."

He kissed her on the head and proceeded to unpack her valise. He helped her place her clothes in the drawers and hang her dresses in the closet. She picked out a nice outfit and changed. Then they both went down to dinner.

The prying eyes of Millie and Belle were disturbing the delicious food.

Jameson finally spoke up, "You might as well know. Abigail and I are getting a divorce. We don't agree any longer on what's important in life. You both know how I abhor slavery and wanted to free the workers on my plantation. Well, Abigail and her father thwarted my every effort, and eventually her father secretly purchased the plantation, took ownership, and annulled my attempts to free my workers.

"Delilah was the only person I was able to free, and she was responsible for saving my life down there. I fell in love with her and intend to marry her when my divorce is final. Please welcome her and be kind to her. She's been through a lot and could use some friends."

The two staffers looked at each other, rolled their eyes, sort of shrugged, and then Belle walked up to Delilah followed by Millie.

"Welcome, Miss Delilah. I hope you'll be happy here," they both said in unison.

Delilah rose from the table and hugged them both. Jameson smiled.

When dinner was over, Delilah walked around the house, looking in all the rooms and noticing all the fine furniture—rich, luxurious rugs and draperies, lamps and knickknacks. Her thoughts turned to the friends she had to leave behind at Serenity. They would have been thrilled to live in such a fine house and would have been satisfied with just a fraction of all the items she surveyed. She went from room to room, touching and selecting certain items, picking some of them up, and examining them in closer detail.

There were paintings on all the walls of places she didn't know existed and would love to have visited. Abigail's portraits were hung prominently in several locations, but she only found one of Jameson. Peculiar, she thought. He looked so serious and scary in the picture. The gold emblem on the bottom was etched with his full name: Jameson Lee Hartford. She wondered if she had another name. Sadly, only her mother knew, and Delilah did not know where her mother might be.

Then her eyes were drawn to a large framed oil painting of people she did not recognize with bold wording emblazoned across it in a language she could not pronounce. She inquired of Jameson as to who they were and what the wording meant. He told her it was a picture of the founding fathers of the United States, and the quote was a Latin proverb. Latin was a language of the Romans, an ancient civilization that no longer existed. Latin was a dead language that no one spoke any longer, but well educated people still used it to impress other people.

The proverb read, "Verba movent. Exempla trahunt," which meant, "Words move people. Examples lead them."

She thought the saying was quite impressive and vowed to remember it.

When her curiosity was satisfied, she and Jameson climbed the staircase and retired to their separate bedrooms. He bid her a goodnight and kissed her on the cheek. He closed the door and told her he would see her in the morning. She stood alone in the large room with only a flickering candle for company. Slowly she disrobed and climbed into the companionless bed.

After a few minutes, Jameson returned and burst into Delilah's room. He entered, swept her up in his arms, and carried her into his room.

She shrieked, "But, James, what about people talkin' and the scandal?"

"To hell with them all, I love you, and I don't care who knows it. The world be damned!"

Alone together in Jameson's bed, they undressed one another and kissed passionately. They could not contain the love they felt for each other. In eager anticipation, their lips exchanged the delicious, exotic tastes of one another. Excitement was at its height, and they bathed in each other's heated breaths. In an imperfect world, they seemed to fit perfectly together. They danced wildly in rhythmic passion to the music of love. When it was over, they fell asleep in each other's tender embrace. Love shows no bias or prejudice; all seemed right.

The next morning after breakfast, Jameson took Delilah next door to introduce her to Mrs. Barrington and enroll her in the School of Charm and Grace for Young Ladies. Her large, white house was perfectly manicured and situated on the picturesque St. Charles River.

Due to her anxiety, Delilah hadn't even noticed the scenic beauty of the surroundings until today. The fear quickly returned as she approached the foreboding manor. Jameson knocked on the front door, and a rather graceful, dark-skinned woman answered.

"Good morning, Anna. May we see Mrs. Barrington?"

"Why hello, Mister Hartford, please come in. It's nice to have you back. When did you return?"

"We just arrived yesterday. Oh, this is Delilah."

"Hello, Anna," Delilah said politely.

Anna did not acknowledge her but simply said, "Please be seated. I'll get Mrs. Barrington for you."

The room was so feminine with fresh flowers in small, dainty vases, pink walls, lace curtains, and frilly rugs covering the floors. Everything was so prim and proper, as if it was a model home and no one actually lived there.

"I'm scared, James. I'm not like these people." Delilah sighed.

"You're right! You're better than they are… Just don't let them know it," Jameson whispered and winked at her.

Mrs. Barrington entered the room and seemed to command instant respect. She was an imposing figure, impeccably dressed with perfectly coiffed grey hair and her nose slightly in the air. Jameson rose, took her hand, and kissed it.

"Good morning, Mrs. Barrington."

"Good morning, Mister Hartford. I'm so glad you and Abigail have returned." She spoke perfect English, pronouncing every syllable carefully. She paused and looked around, right through Delilah as if she wasn't there, and asked, "Where is Mrs. Hartford?"

Jameson explained Abigail's absence and introduced Delilah. He said she would like to attend Mrs. Barrington's school to learn the fine art of becoming a lady.

Mrs. Barrington laughed. "Mister Hartford. She's a Negro."

Jameson cut her laughter short by stating, "You don't instruct Negroes? I didn't know you were unable to teach them."

Mrs. Barrington shot back, "I can teach anyone, but why does she want to become a lady?"

"She wants to learn so she can be accepted. Me, I like her fine just the way she is, refreshingly honest. Will you take her in as a student? I would appreciate it very much if you could help her."

Mrs. Barrington let out a sigh and reluctantly stated, "I'll do it for you, Mister Hartford, as a special favor."

"Thank you very much, Mrs. Barrington."

She looked at the frightened Delilah and said, "Come along, child. The other students will be arriving shortly."

Jameson turned to Delilah and said, "I'm off to work. I'll see you tonight."

He tenderly touched her face and added, "Don't change too much."

She smiled nervously. As she followed Mrs. Barrington into the study, Jameson departed.

The other students arrived in due time. They were Elizabeth, Josephine, Catherine, and Penelope. They were all from wealthy aristocratic families and immediately took Delilah to be beneath their status. Daughters of doctors, lawyers, politicians, and bankers, they imagined themselves of greater importance than they actually were. They never missed an opportunity to laugh at her or insult her. From day one they started the relentless teasing and mocking. They made fun of the way she spoke, how she looked, and how she should be respectful and learn her place.

"She speaks like an alley cat. She can't pronounce anything correctly, slurring all her words."

"What do you expect? You know where she was raised, don't you?"

"Why is a black person trying to be like a white person?"

"Why is your hair so short? You look like a man."

"She can't help it. That black hair is impossible to style."

"Her hands are all calloused, not smooth like a real lady."

Whenever she would try to fight back, they told her, "Be careful or we'll have our fathers ship you back to that plantation to be a slave again where you belong."

Mrs. Barrington tried to contain the ridicule, but as soon as she left the room, the spiteful, bullying remarks started again.

While practicing the proper techniques for serving a perfect tea party, it was Delilah's turn to walk balancing a book on her head with a tea cup and a plate of cakes in one hand while greeting guests and ushering them to their assigned positions. As she walked past the girls seated on the settee, one of them extended her leg and purposely tripped Delilah, sending the book, tea, cakes, and china, flying to the hardwood floor.

"Oops, I'm so sorry," Elizabeth said sarcastically as the other girls giggled uncontrollably.

Delilah was not physically harmed, but sometimes mental cruelty can be far worse. Through it all, Delilah held her head high and tried to learn proper etiquette and speech. At night, she would return to Jameson in tears, but come the next morning, off to school she would go.

Jameson was her rock, always consoling her and telling her how great she was. Every day he would notice subtle changes in her speech and demeanor. She was growing and learning, becoming a lady of stature. He was so proud of her and never missed an opportunity to praise her and give her ego a needed boost. He couldn't help beaming every time he saw her. The strength she received from Jameson helped her to face the next day with an unquenchable fire. Mrs. Barrington also admired her perseverance and tenacity in the face of all that ridicule and bullying. Delilah was emerging from the cocoon of bondage, transforming herself into a beautiful butterfly right in front of their eyes.

One evening at dinner, Jameson was telling Delilah that his lawyer was having a difficult time getting answers from Thaddeus Bordeau and Nicholas Mansfield back at Willow Hills. They were not responding regarding negotiating the freedom of her former friends and the whereabouts of the funds from the sale of Serenity. In fact, he could not even get in touch with Abigail to sign divorce papers. He assumed the shadow of Beau Lansing was hovering over everything and extending all the way up North, even into Boston. The discussion was interrupted by a knock on the front door.

Millie opened the door to find an attractive, unknown woman standing before her. She looked mysterious bathed in the yellow lamplight from the street.

"Is this the home of Mister Jameson Hartford?" she asked.

"It is," answered Millie.

"I would like to see him, please."

"Whom shall I say is calling?"

"Tell him it's his wife, Prudence."

Millie looked startled and confused.

Prudence clarified, "It's a private joke. He'll know who it is. Just tell him."

Millie invited the stranger into the foyer and asked her to wait while she announced the visitor to Jameson. Millie departed the room. Prudence looked around, admiring the residence and all the expensive accoutrements. She thought to herself, *I certainly picked the right man to help on that train. This could be a very lucrative arrangement.*

Jameson emerged from the kitchen, surprised to find Prudence in his home.

"Prudence, I'm shocked. How did you find me?"

"Is that any way to greet your wife?" She laughed.

Delilah walked into the foyer and said, "James, aren't you going to introduce me to your friend?"

Jameson answered, "Of course, Delilah. This is Prudence, the woman who helped me on the train. Remember, I told you about her."

"Oh, yes, Prudence. Thank you for all your help," Delilah said as she extended her hand in friendship.

"So it's true. You have taken up with…her. You told me she was your slave."

"I did," Jameson said. "And she was, but I set her free, and now she's my lady friend."

Prudence was visibly shocked but calmly uttered, "Oh, so you used me. No one uses me, no one." Prudence thought for an additional second then added, "You know this arrangement won't be viewed positively by your employer. In fact, it is a detriment to your job, your career, and your life."

"My life and career are none of your business."

"Oh, but it is, my dear husband. You made me lie for you, remember? On the train to the police, and I intend to get even for that outrage."

"I'm sorry I lied to you, but I had to. Try to understand, Prudence."

"What I understand, Jameson Hartford, is that I can make your life a living hell unless you decide to ease my conscience."

"What do you want, Prudence?"

"I want money. You have it, and I want it."

"Are you talking about extortion?"

"That's such an ugly word, darling. Let's just call it hush money. You pay me, or I tell my influential father, who is a big depositor in your bank. He withdraws his money, and his friends follow suit, and voila, you no longer have a job."

"You can't mean that, Prudence. I told you on the train I needed you to lie for me, and you agreed to do it."

"Did I? I don't recall. All I know is you start paying me, oh, let's say fifty dollars every month, or I start talking."

Delilah could no longer hold her tongue and spoke out, "Why would you do that? Why do you want to hurt him?"

Prudence defiantly replied, "Shut up. I'm not talking to you."

Jameson jumped to Delilah's defense. "Don't talk to her like that."

Prudence retorted, "Don't tell me what I can and can't do. I have influence and a great deal of sway in this city."

"Get out, Prudence. I won't succumb to your delusions, and I won't pay you a cent. No one here in Boston cares whether Delilah is black or white. There's equality up here in the North."

"Oh, but you are so wrong, dear Jameson, so wrong. Think long and hard before you dismiss me, for once the wheels start turning, even I won't be able to stop them."

"Get out now!"

"All right, hubby, but you'll be sorry. I'll come to see you when you are in the poor house. Ta-Ta."

Prudence turned and strutted out of the house and down the path to her waiting coach.

"I'm afraid I made another enemy. For a man who wants peace, I seem to start a lot of wars," Jameson declared.

Delilah tried to calm him down as Millie watched from the sidelines. Leading him back into the kitchen, she poured him a rather large glass of wine, hoping it would dull the senses and help him forget the last five minutes. The next day, however, would not prove to be much of an improvement.

The Bostonian people were beginning to notice that Jameson was living with Delilah, and Abigail was nowhere to be found. The girls at Mrs. Barrington's school did not stop with tormenting only Delilah. Their resentment also targeted Jameson as well. Spoiled rich girls bring home gossip to rich fathers who threaten big bankers where they keep their fortunes. A scorned woman with connections can also wreak havoc in a man's life, and

Prudence was stirring the pot and igniting a controversy through her father's many influential contacts.

Jameson was called into the bank president's office and questioned about his living situation. He explained, though he felt it was none of their business. He was told to evict Delilah or face the consequences. Jameson defiantly refused. He was told his fellow bankers were not bigots, but too many depositors threatened to close their accounts if he were kept on, so he was unceremoniously fired. Jameson left the bank in disgrace.

That evening he related the incident to Delilah. It was her turn to console him. He told her how the rich girls spread the rumors and caused him to be removed from his job.

Delilah said, "Perhaps you would be better off if I left."

"Don't talk like that, Lilah. I never want you to go."

"What will we do for money, James?"

"The cash from the sale of Serenity should be deposited shortly. We can live quite nicely on that for a good period of time. We'll be okay as long as we're together."

They kissed, and somehow everything felt better.

The following morning, Delilah was angry. She had every notion of quitting the school, but first she was going to tell off those rich brats. When they had all arrived, Delilah began yelling at them for what they had done to Jameson. They laughed and said he deserved it for being with a Negro. Delilah lost control and grabbed one girl by her hair and threw her to the ground. Another was slapped across the face. A third was thrown into the wall. The last one ran out of the room screaming for help, at which time Mrs. Barrington entered.

They all accused Delilah of attacking and abusing them. Of course, they claimed they did nothing to provoke such behavior. It was four against one, and Delilah was sent outside to the back patio to await her punishment. She did not argue. She simply turned her back on all of them and calmly strutted out the door. Once outside, she paced back and forth for a while then reached into her purse and fumbled around until she found a cigar. With trembling hand, she finally managed to light it. She took a large puff, inhaled it, and expelled the smoke out through her nose, not fully exhaling it, before deeply inhaling another puff. She sat on a bench and patiently waited for her judgment.

Minutes later, Mrs. Barrington emerged, but surprisingly she was not angry at all. "That was most unladylike behavior, my dear."

Delilah said, "They're not ladies, at least not the kind of lady I want to be."

Mrs. Barrington looked kindly at Delilah and said, "My dear, I heard what happened to Mister Hartford. I'm sorry. Excuse me, but the cigar—"

Delilah thought she would be reprimanded for smoking.

"Do you have another one of those?"

Delilah looked confused but reached into her purse and produced another cigar, which she handed over to Mrs. Barrington along with a match.

Mrs. Barrington ignited the cigar and said, "Don't look so surprised, my dear. I also enjoy an occasional cigar. After all, if a man can smoke, why can't a woman?"

Delilah smiled.

Mrs. Barrington continued, "I admire you for defending your man. I'm beginning to think you and I are a lot alike. You see, my husband, God rest his soul, was rich. I, on the other hand, was poor. His family threatened to disown him if he married me. He did anyway, because he loved me, and I him. They ridiculed me every time we were together. Finally, one day I had enough, and I too fought back, although I did it verbally, not physically.

"I would have enjoyed hitting them, but I was not as strong as you, my dear. After that they didn't dare provoke me again. When they passed, my husband inherited all their wealth, and when he died, he left it all to me. I am now one of the wealthiest women in Boston. I might be able to help get Mister Hartford's job back for him or at the very least secure him another position."

Delilah perked up. "Oh, can you do that, Mrs. Barrington? That would be wonderful. Thank you so much." Delilah hugged her.

She, in turn, hugged Delilah. "I misjudged you, my dear. You are quite a woman. Mister Hartford is very lucky to have you."

Delilah smiled. "He's lucky to have you for a friend also, Mrs. Barrington."

"Call me Martha, Delilah. After all, we are friends. You know I never cared for that Abigail. She was so stuffy and false, always kept everyone at arm's length. You, my dear, are the real thing."

Delilah said, "I'm sorry for the fight and any broken furniture. I'll pay you for it."

"Nonsense, my dear, they had it coming. I sent all those girls home for the day. I'm sure they'll try to make another scandal out of it, but they'll be afraid to taunt you anymore."

They both laughed.

"And those old items, I didn't care for them anyway; time to go shopping for something new. Any excuse to go shopping, right, Delilah? Maybe you would like to go shopping with me. I'd love the company."

"Oh, yes, I would love to go shopping." Delilah beamed.

"Fine, we'll set it up. Now how about a nice cup of tea, my dear? You can show me how much you've learned concerning serving a proper tea."

They drank, talked, and smoked, becoming close friends. Then Delilah ran home to tell Jameson the good news.

As she came through the front door, she saw Jameson sitting in the shadows, on the parlor chair holding a piece of paper. His lit cigar, glowing in the dark, provided the only light.

Instinctively, she knew something was wrong and rushed over to him.

"James, what's the matter?"

He looked up and said, "I received a telegram today from South Carolina. It seems there will be no transfer of funds. Beau Lansing has reneged on his decision to purchase Serenity. He does not want it any longer, so the title and the entire plantation, along with all my freed workers, your friends, now reverts back to me. I have to go back to Serenity, Lilah."

"James, no, it's a trap. Beau Lansing wants you in jail. Maybe he wants you dead."

"You're probably right, but at least he can't say I stole you if he didn't buy the plantation. I still have the freedom papers, and I hope I can still free the rest of my workers. I have to go, but you should remain here where it's safe."

"Oh, no, I'll not stay here and worry everyday whether you're safe or not. If you go, I go too. That's final!"

He looked at her and smiled. "What did they teach you over there?"

They both smiled. There was no time to spare. They had to pack and leave as soon as possible. Nanny, Uncky, and the others needed them. Their safety was in jeopardy.

The rest of the day was set aside for planning and preparing to travel once again to South Carolina and Serenity. He already knew what kind of reception awaited him and was afraid for Delilah. Beau Lansing would stop at nothing to destroy Jameson and place Delilah back in bondage, but he had to go, as fate, once again, was giving him a chance to vindicate himself and give the gift of freedom to his deserving workers. They had no idea what was really waiting for them. All they knew was that it was not going to be pleasant. It would, in fact, be far worse than they could ever imagine.

Chapter 25

RETURN TO SERENITY

The coach was waiting at the curb as Jameson and Delilah hurriedly attended to last-minute details before leaving. They bid good-bye to Belle and Millie and assured them they would return; at least they prayed they would. Delilah told Jameson that they had to tell Martha Barrington what had happened as she had wanted to help him secure employment again. They turned the luggage over to the coachman and walked over to their neighbor's home. Delilah related the particulars of what had occurred to Mrs. Barrington and thanked her for all her help and support.

Jameson also thanked her and then remarked, "You know that I lived here all these years, and I never knew your first name was Martha."

She replied, "That is because your wife, Abigail, only wanted to be distant acquaintances. Delilah and I are close friends. Take good care of her, Jameson, and if you need me, I will help you in any way I can."

He thanked her again, and Delilah hugged her. The journey back to Serenity was about to commence.

Mrs. Barrington beckoned Delilah to remain behind for a second and secretly asked, "Are you all right, my dear? I believe I see a certain glow in you. Are you with child, Delilah, darling?"

Delilah looked surprised but answered straightforwardly, "I think I am, but please don't tell Jameson, or he won't let me go with him."

"Please be careful, Delilah, and come home safely."

"I will, Martha. I will."

They hugged again, and then Delilah ran to join Jameson waiting by the coach. They embarked and were whisked away to the depot.

The train station was not as crowded as normal. No doubt, the escalating war made people uneasy about travelling, especially South. They arrived just in time to board and find suitable accommodations in a private car. They settled in for the long trip.

Last time, Jameson recalled, there was excitement and anticipation. This time there was fear and dread. His plan was to get the workers to freedom as quickly as possible and then resolve the land problems, but even the best laid plans go astray.

Delilah looked beautiful in her pink dress. Her whole demeanor had changed. She now acted like a lady of means. She held her head up proudly, as she should, and possessed a lot more confidence. There was something else, however, but Jameson couldn't quite put his finger on it. He remembered his other business—to get Abigail to agree to a divorce. This was not going to be an easy trip. The plantation would be overgrown and neglected—or worse, ravaged by looters. He tried to put the thoughts out of his head and settle in for the long ride. Delilah cuddled in close, and that seemed to make all the difference.

As the train crossed into Virginia, it came to an unexpected halt. Confederate soldiers entered and searched the train, seemingly for spies or perhaps eligible draftees. They eyed Jameson and Delilah and questioned them at length.

"What is the purpose of your trip?"

"I don't see what business that is of yours, soldier."

"Just answer the question unless you want to be detained and maybe arrested," the soldier shot back.

"I'm returning to my plantation in South Carolina," Jameson acquiesced.

"Why is a colored girl all dressed up like that and in this cabin with you instead of in the slave car where she belongs?"

Jameson had to think fast and replied, "She's mine, and I want to keep her close by. Do I have to tell you why?

The soldiers smirked as an evil look enveloped across his face.

Jameson grew apprehensive, ready to defend Delilah if necessary, when he received a reprieve. Shouts, screams, and then gunfire coming from another car drew the soldiers' attention away from them. Then an order to come immediately forced them to leave. There was more gunfire then silence, and finally the train began to move again. They witnessed a body being removed, clothed in a blue uniform. Apparently, they found whoever they were looking for, the poor soul. It was just another nameless casualty in another hideous war. The excursion proceeded without further incident, and finally the train pulled into Charleston, South Carolina.

The city was different than either one had remembered. The anxiety of impending war was everywhere, and the lack of able-bodied men was blatantly apparent. No one paid them much attention, but they felt the fear and hurried to get out of the troubled city. They were forced to purchase a horse and wagon for their trip to Serenity.

The weather was exceptionally hot, and everything was dry. There was a drought. The little ponds and swamps were reduced to puddles or just cracked earth. The only positive note was a blessed lack of gnats and mosquitoes. They pushed the horse to make time, fearing for their safety.

As they approached Serenity, Jameson was surprised to see it was in good condition. The workers were not at their homes, and they both wondered where they might be. The horse followed the path up to the plantation house, and again all seemed to be in good condition. They disembarked from the wagon and went up the stairs to the front door. Nanny threw open the door and greeted them enthusiastically. Uncky came scurrying from the barn. They were overjoyed to see each other again. Nanny and Uncky knew what had occurred with regards to the sale and the reason for it.

"You better be careful, Mista Jameson. That Mista Lansing, he hates you for leavin' his Abigail, especially because you left her for Miss Delilah here. And don't you look pretty, like a regular Southern belle, you are. But Mista Jameson, you got another problem. Mista Jebediah is back with his new wife, Miss Madeline, and he wants to take over this here plantation."

The door opened wider, and Jebediah, Josiah's son and Jameson's nephew, appeared. He was still the same self-centered, loud-mouthed boy they remembered, just older, but alas, not wiser. He stood there defiantly in a partly unbuttoned shirt and an unknotted tie draped loosely around his neck.

"Well, welcome back to my home, Uncle Jameson," Jeb said. "Oh, and is this the little slave girl that replaced Aunt Abigail. I heard a lot about this one. Good in bed, is she? I'll have to give her a whirl."

Delilah slapped Jeb across the face and sternly said, "Don't you ever address me in that manner again. I'm a free Northern woman, and I will not be maligned by the likes of you."

Jeb was startled for a moment then said, "I will not be hit by a Negro in my own house."

Jameson stepped in, "First of all, if you ever talk like that again about Delilah, I'll hit you myself and a lot harder than she did. Second, this is my house and my plantation. She is welcome in it, and if you want to be, you will mind your manners."

Jeb confronted Jameson. "This was my father's plantation, and so it should have been willed to me when he died, not you."

"Well, it wasn't. You were nowhere to be found, so it is legally mine, and you would be wise to remember that."

"We'll see about that," said Jeb. "I'll go into town tomorrow, get a lawyer, and fight you on this. Oh, and I'll be sure to tell Beau Lansing you're back. He will be very interested." He walked defiantly off to the barn.

"I've got trouble already." Jameson moaned. He turned to Delilah and said, "That was something the way you slapped Jeb. I'm very impressed. I liked it."

She smiled. "I'm not that scared slave girl any longer, and I won't be treated like one either."

Nanny and Uncky stood there in amazement.

Uncky helped them transport their luggage and travelling items upstairs. They changed, freshened up, and went back downstairs.

Nanny fixed them dinner, and as they were eating, Madeline entered. She was young and sweet, spoke softly, and had a kind face and gentle smile that seemed so sincere—the exact opposite of Jeb. He intimidated her constantly, and she just agreed to whatever he wanted to avoid any trouble. Her dress was simple yet elegant, unlike the ornate gowns all the other Southern ladies wore.

"Good evening, I don't believe we've been formally introduced. I'm Madeline." She was the quintessential Southern belle.

"Hello, Madeline. I'm Jameson, Jeb's uncle, and this is my lady friend, Delilah."

"How do you do, Miss Delilah, I'm pleased to make your acquaintance."

Madeline was different. She did not care that Delilah was a darker color. It did not matter to her. She was polite and courteous to everyone.

"Hello, Madeline. I'm happy to meet you," Delilah said. "Come sit with us and have some dinner."

"No, thank you. I have to wait for Jebediah, or he'll be angry."

Jameson inquired, "How is your mother-in-law, Bethany Sue?"

Madeline hesitated then spoke, "I believe she has passed."

Jameson, surprised, looked at Nanny, who shook her head "no."

Jameson said, "Madeline, your mother-in-law was sick under a doctor's care. She hasn't died. You mean Jeb hasn't even gone to see his own mother since he's been back?"

Madeline, visibly shaken, simply said, "We'll speak about this again later."

She excused herself and slipped away into the den to ponder this new fact and await Jebediah.

Jameson asked Nanny how Abigail was doing.

"She's fine, like nothing happened. In fact, she's been seeing Ned Barrows, the town mayor."

"That's not surprising, but good for her. I'm glad to hear it, because I want her to give me a divorce."

"I think she'll say yes to that, Mista Jameson. She wanted to contact you in Boston to talk about it."

"Funny, I had my lawyer in Boston send papers down here for her to sign, and I never heard a thing back from her."

"I'll bet that's Mista Lansing's doings. You watch out for him, you hear?"

"Nanny, where are my freed workers?"

"Oh, Mista Jeb got them in the fields working. He hired a nasty overseer who works them like dogs."

"Well, we'll have to put an end to that immediately."

Jameson and Delilah rose from the table and headed out to the fields. Jeb watched them as they passed by, then quickly snuck back into the house.

Madeline was waiting as he entered and began questioning him on his mother.

Jeb replied, "That uncle of mine is a liar."

Madeline pursued the questioning but was quickly put in her place by Jeb.

"Are you calling me a liar? Do you believe your husband or a complete stranger? Now let me hear no more of this kind of talk."

Madeline was confused but frightened, so she acquiesced to her husband's wishes.

Meanwhile, Jameson and Delilah had reached the fields and encountered the new overseer, Reuben Rutledge, who was berating Jonas for not working fast enough. He was pushing him, slapping him, and threatening him with the lash.

Reuben was of average height, muscular, and smartly dressed for a man of this occupation. His hair was long and unkempt, and he had a large scar running down the length of his right cheek.

Jameson spoke up. "What are you doing there, sir? Leave that man alone."

The workers were shocked to see him and Delilah back at the plantation.

"Who are you?" Reuben demanded. "Mind your own business."

"I am Jameson Hartford, the owner of this plantation, and you will not treat these people in that manner."

"Oh, yeah, well, I'm Reuben Rutledge, the overseer, and Mister Jebediah Hartford, the owner, hired me to get these slaves to work."

"Jebediah does not own this plantation, I do, and you'll do as I say."

"I'll be glad to listen to whomever is in charge, sir, but you have to let me do my job."

"Not if that includes hurting these people. I won't stand for it."

Ruben continued to boast. "I wasn't going to hurt him much. You see I am quite skilled with this whip. I could knock a fly off of someone's face with a single flick without so much as a scratch to the face, or I could place a nice gash right on the lobe of your ear with equal precision."

Jameson shrugged and said, "I am unimpressed with your skill, just leave my people alone. Do you understand?"

"Maybe you would like to see a demonstration, perhaps with one of the slaves, uh, what did you say your name was again, sir?"

"I don't want you to ever use that whip on these people ever again, and the name is Jameson Hartford. You would do well to remember it."

"Jameson Hartford, where do I know that name from? Oh, yeah, I heard about you. You're the one who took up with a slave. Is that the little whore all dressed up?"

Jameson grabbed Ruben, throttled him, and shoved him to the ground. "You're fired! Get out now!"

"You'll be sorry for that, Hartford. I'm going to speak to Mister Jebediah about this."

"Go ahead. He has no say in the matter."

Ruben sneered at Jameson and bragged, "You see this here scar on my face? I got this from a slave who thought he could beat me. He couldn't, and that was the last time any man or slave ever laid a hand on me. Oh, and by the way, I'm also the only one left alive from that fight to tell the story, if you know what I mean."

He laughed as if that was something to be proud of as he left for the main house.

Delilah and Jameson proceeded to greet the rest of their friends. They were met with coldness and indifference, upset that they were promised freedom and left behind. They accused Delilah of becoming a white woman and forgetting her roots.

Jameson explained how he was tricked by Beau Lansing and had to get Delilah far away for her safety. Now that the plantation was his again, he came back to set them free. He still had the freedom papers all legally signed in his suitcase. They were skeptical and untrusting of both of them. They had left them once, why should they believe him now? Delilah begged them to understand, saying Jameson's hands were tied.

Delilah noticed Lizzie was not there and inquired as to her whereabouts. Becky told her Lizzie was ill, but the overseer made her work anyway. The poor child had to go out in the fields, and one day she just couldn't take anymore, and she fell over...dead.

Delilah and Jameson were appalled, and they both expressed their deepest sympathy over her grief and vowed she would not have died in vain. They would all be freed. Jameson said he had better get back up to the house to be sure Ruben would go, but Delilah stayed behind to talk to her old friends and try to make them understand.

At the house, Jebediah acknowledged Jameson's ownership, but he assured Ruben the plantation would soon be his.

"You tell Beau Lansing that Jameson Hartford is back at Serenity and to gather some of the men together and come get him tomorrow morning around ten o'clock. I want to be sure I'm not here. I'll take my wife into town so I can establish an alibi, and no one can blame me for his death or deny me my inheritance. Once the plantation is mine, you, my friend, can have your job back. You can even have that little black whore who thinks she's white. You can make her an obedient slave again."

"Yeah, I'd like that." He sneered. "Okay, I'm off."

Ruben Rutledge was leaving as Jameson came into view. Ruben tipped his hat and laughed as he rode away. Jameson looked toward the house and saw Jeb at the window. He quickly closed the curtain, hiding his face.

A guilty gesture if ever there was one, Jameson thought.

Jeb turned around to find Madeline standing there. "How long have you been there?"

"Long enough, Jeb, you can't want your uncle murdered."

"He stole this plantation from me. Why should I care about him?"

"You can't do this. I won't let you."

"You'll do as you're told if you know what's good for you. Don't make me hurt you, Madeline. You keep your mouth shut, or so help me, I'll… Well, you don't want to know what I'll do to you."

Madeline, crying, ran up the stairs to her bedroom. Jeb, smirking, couldn't wait for tomorrow. Jameson was left wondering what his nephew was planning.

Jeb kept close to Madeline for the rest of the day, lest she have an opportunity to divulge his plans to an eager ear. He felt certain the plantation and all its belongings would soon be his. The wheels were turning. Beau Lansing hated Jameson enough to murder him, and no one in the entire town of Willow Hills would condemn him. They all wanted Jameson Hartford to disappear and would jump at the chance to get rid of him once and for all. It was a perfect plan, or so Jebediah thought. He could hardly wait for tomorrow to perpetrate his crime.

Reuben Rutledge rode onto the Tall Oaks plantation and straight up to the main house. He dismounted and proceeded to the front door. Using the fancy bronze door knocker, he banged the plunger over and over.

Margie the house servant opened the door. "Can I help you, sir?"

"I want to see your master, Beau Lansing. Go get him," Reuben ordered.

"Please, sir, may I say who is calling?" Margie politely inquired.

"Tell him it's Reuben Rutledge from the Serenity Plantation."

"I'll tell him, sir," Margie answered and carefully closed the door.

A few minutes passed, and Margie reopened the door. "Mista Rutledge, Mista Lansing doesn't wish to speak with you. Good day."

Margie tried to close the door as Reuben put his foot on the threshold, preventing her from completing her task.

"Wait?" Reuben said. "You tell him Jebediah Hartford sent me. I got information he wants to know. Tell him, you hear me?"

Margie replied, "All right, sir. I'll be right back." She again closed the door.

Another few minutes passed as Reuben grew ever more impatient. Finally the door opened, and Beau appeared.

"You have some kind of information for me, Rutledge?" he said matter of factly.

"Yes, sir, Mister Jebediah Hartford told me to come here and let you know that Jameson Hartford has returned to Serenity.

Beau's eyes glared, and his demeanor changed as he became something evil. He demanded to know all the particulars. "When did he come back? Is he at Serenity now? Is he still with that slave girl?"

Reuben tried to calm him down and related Jebediah's plan in all its horrific details.

Beau beamed a sly smile. "That will be just enough time for me to get some men together and finish him off once and for all."

"Count me in, sir. I want to be there for the kill."

"Good, Rutledge, good, be here tomorrow morning at nine. We'll all meet here and ride out together. I can't wait. It's been a long time, and now it's finally the end of Jameson Hartford." Beau laughed an evil, diabolical laugh that scared even Reuben as he rode off.

There in the window stood the silhouette of the only person in Willow Hills who still cared about Jameson Hartford... Abigail. She wondered what all the excitement was about and why her father was speaking with the overseer from Serenity. She questioned him upon his re-entry, but he would not divulge a single word.

He was abnormally happy, which made Abigail suspicious. She vowed to herself, *I will find out.*

Chapter 26

UNEXPECTED CONSEQUENCES

The following morning at breakfast, Jameson spoke of his plans to Delilah and Nanny. He felt that since it was late summer and the drought was killing the crops, they should bring in the harvest, sell it all in Charleston at the market, and raise enough money to transport everyone North on the train. He asked Delilah if she thought the workers would be willing to labor in the fields one last time.

She felt she had regained their trust, and they would be willing to help.

Jameson remarked, "You must really love Nanny's cooking, you're eating enough for two people and gaining a little weight."

Delilah, looking stunned, stared at Jameson as if he had just uncovered a deep secret.

Realizing he was in trouble, he added, "You look good darling. You were too thin before. You needed to gain a few pounds."

This time he was given glaring looks from both Delilah and Nanny.

Recognizing that he was not helping himself, he jumped up from the table and left, mumbling something about a lot of work that needed to be done. Once Jameson was out of the room, Delilah glanced up at Nanny, who was not one to mince words.

"You're having a baby aren't you child?"

Delilah hesitated, then said, "Yes Nanny, but I don't want James to know yet. He will be too protective of me and won't let me help him. Please keep it a secret for a while."

"I think he ought to know."

"Please, Nanny, for me?"

Nanny nodded in the affirmative though Delilah could tell she did not like keeping a secret from Jameson.

Madeline appeared seemingly out of nowhere and grabbed Jameson in the hall. Speaking in an urgent tone, she said, "Uncle Jameson, I have to tell you something important. Please come with me for a moment."

Jameson arose and started to accompany her as she spoke.

"My husband, he'll punish me if catches me talking to you."

"What is it, Madeline? What's the trouble? You can tell me. I'll protect you."

"Oh, Uncle Jameson, he's decided to—"

"There you are, Madeline. I've been looking for you."

Jeb had found her.

"You're not bothering my uncle with your stories, are you? Come along. Let's eat. Then we'll be going into town."

"No, no, I don't want to go," pleaded Madeline.

"Of course you do," Jeb insisted.

"Let her talk, Jeb," Jameson said.

"She doesn't have anything to say to you. Do you, Madeline?"

Madeline sheepishly shook her head "no" as Jeb grabbed her arm tightly and led her away.

She glanced back at Jameson, who wondered what his nephew was planning. The sooner they could get the crops harvested and sold, the sooner they could all leave.

He told Delilah, "I'm going into the fields to help."

She replied, "I'll come too, James, the more pickers, the faster the harvest."

He couldn't argue with her logic and she wouldn't have listened anyway.

It was hot and dry in the fields. The drought was continuing. All the more reason to get whatever cotton and tobacco they could into the barn before it all dried up. The work was hard. They spent their days bent over picking cotton bowls or breaking tobacco leaves from their stalks.

The carriage with Jeb and Madeline passed by as Jeb yelled out, "You belong out there, Uncle! I think you found your true talent. Maybe you should consider joining them permanently. Good-bye."

He sped off laughing. Jameson, Delilah, and the other workers continued to toil away under the blazing sun with only water in earthen jars to quench their thirst and cool them down.

It seemed like hours had passed when the sound of horses could be heard approaching the plantation. Jameson, Delilah, and the others looked up to see hooded riders, six strong, kicking up a trail of dust as they trod the hot, dry roadbed. Jameson knew who they were and what they wanted. They wore the same disguises as the riders who had threatened to hang him that fateful day in April as he was returning from Willow Hills a mere six-and-a-half months earlier.

He told Delilah, "They're here to kill me, and I don't have any means of defense way out here. I can't run back to the house. The best thing to do is remain here and try to blend in. Perhaps they won't bother the workers."

The riders rode straight up to the house, dismounted, and split up. Two men went into the barn. The rest went up to the house. They forced their way in, pushing Nanny aside.

"Where is he?" they demanded.

"Who are you looking for? Get out of here. You don't belong here," Nanny said defiantly.

They ignored her and spread out, searching all the rooms, upstairs and down. Then they went out to the yard, where they met up with the other two men coming out of the barn.

"He's not here. He must have gone somewhere. Get the housekeeper to tell us," the lead rider ordered.

They dragged Nanny out of the house and questioned her. She would not tell them anything. They grabbed her, shook her violently, slapped her and finally tossed her to the ground.

"Don't make us hurt you. Just tell us where Hartford is."

"I ain't got nothin' to say to you," Nanny belligerently answered.

"Okay old woman, let's see how much pain you can endure before you break."

"I don't want to hurt Nanny," one of the riders said.

"Shut up you fool," the lead rider demanded, "Get the rope and tie her to that tree, now!"

The other riders obeyed and took hold of the helpless woman.

Uncky came running from the barn, screaming, "Let her go! Get out of here!"

One of the riders threw a rope around Uncky and began to ride away, dragging him behind his horse for several yards.

Nanny cried out in horror. "Stop, please stop! Mista Jameson went to Charleston on business. He's not here."

The rope was dropped as the riders turned to Nanny and said, "There that wasn't so hard was it? Oh and you better not be lying to us."

"I'm not lyin'. I swear, sir."

"And don't say anything about this to Hartford, or we will return and kill you both. Do you understand? Well, do you?"

"Yes, sir, I understand," cried Nanny as she ran over to Uncky, whose lifeless body was just lying there.

In the fields they could hear the screams coming from the house. Jameson wanted to run to Nanny's defense but was dissuaded by Delilah.

She tried to reason with him. "You're the one they're after. If you go up there, they will kill you and then kill Nanny for hiding you."

They did not have to argue long, as they could hear the riders returning. This time they were coming to check the fields.

Jameson wanted to run for cover, but there was no place to hide. Delilah had a better idea. Using water from the earthen jar, she mixed it with the rich brown soil and made a paste. She lathered it onto Jameson's face, neck, arms, and hands, making him appear to be as dark as the other workers. She told Nate to put his old jacket and hat on Jameson as the riders approached.

"James, don't look directly at them, and try to speak to them as a common worker would speak, not as the owner."

They rode right through the fields, trampling crops, looking at all the workers and asking them Jameson's whereabouts. Jameson noticed that his sweat was causing the mud to liquefy and to run off, revealing his light skin. His nervousness made him sweat all the more. He hoped the disguise would last long enough and was good enough to fool these vigilantes.

One by one they asked the workers, who in turn shook their heads and said politely, "I dunno, sir."

As they came by Delilah and Jameson, they posed the same question. Jameson positioned himself with the sun at his back so when he lifted his head, the glare would blind his inquisitors' eyes.

He looked up ever so briefly and uttered in his best Southern drawl, "I dunno, sir." Then he put his head down and went back to picking.

One of the riders looked at Delilah and said, "Aren't you the slave Hartford took up with?"

Delilah spoke confidently but obediently, "Not me, sir. I'm just a picker."

She knew the white men never looked closely enough at any of the Negroes to be able to accurately identify them.

He eyed her for a moment, then said, "Yeah I guess you wouldn't be picking cotton if you were Hartford's darkie."

Then another rider addressed the captive crowd. "We will be coming back, and if you want to live, you will say nothing of today's visit. You understand? Don't tell Hartford we were here."

One of them fired a shot from his rifle into the air, scaring all the field workers.

Nanny heard the shot as she attended to Uncky and said a quick prayer for Jameson.

The hooded men turned and rode off, causing another dust storm in their wake. A sigh of relief went out across the fields.

Nate said, "Mister Jameson, I guess you really did have to leave us before. These men really want to kill you. I'm sorry we doubted you."

All the workers agreed and apologized, each in their turn.

"Don't worry about it. We'll all get out of here together this time." Jameson tried to reassure them.

The questions of doubt and distrust were laid to rest. Everyone was frightened, but slowly, one by one, they all went back to the job at hand—harvesting the crops.

On the road to Willow Hills, Jeb's wagon was casually rolling along when he also heard approaching horses. Turning around, he saw a company of Confederate soldiers who stopped his wagon.

"Why are you out of uniform, soldier?" the lieutenant queried.

"I'm not a soldier," Jeb replied.

"Why is a young, able-bodied man like you not in the service defending our beloved Confederacy from those filthy Yankees?"

"I have a plantation to run."

"We all did, son. We all left something behind for the greater good. Consider yourself drafted. Take this man, Sergeant. We'll process him at camp."

"No, no! You can't do this!" Jeb protested.

"It is an honor to serve the Southern cause, son. It's bad enough you're a draft dodger. Don't be a coward as well."

"I'm not a coward. I have some business I must complete."

"You can complete it after the war. Say good-bye to your wife. Take him, Sergeant."

"Wait, let me finish what I have to do, and I'll enlist. I promise," Jeb pleaded.

"I've heard that too many times, and not one of them has ever enlisted yet. You're coming with us right now."

They pulled Jeb off the wagon as he begged and complained.

The lieutenant turned and addressed Madeline. "You better turn this wagon around and go straight home, miss. There are Yankees all about. Sorry for the inconvenience, but we need every available man for the Confederacy. Good day to you."

They turned and rode away. Madeline, with a sly smirk, did just as the lieutenant had suggested and headed back to Serenity. She was hoping she would be in time to alert Jameson.

Delilah and Jameson ran up to the house to find Nanny crouching over Uncky. He was badly bruised, but nothing appeared to be broken. Jameson carried him into the house and placed him on the couch. Uncky said he was all right and just needed to rest. Jameson wanted to pursue the riders but was again discouraged by Delilah and his lack of firepower.

Nanny insisted they leave her to attend to the ruthlessly battered Uncky and head back out to the fields. It was now more imperative than ever to finish the harvest so they could all leave at once. Jameson grabbed a towel and wiped the sweat and remaining soot from his face, and then he and Delilah walked back out into the blazing, sun-drenched fields. Delilah felt some unfamiliar twinges and then doubled over with pain. She tried to muffle a scream and then grabbed her abdomen.

Jameson was concerned. He took her in his arms and asked her, "Are you all right? What's the matter?"

She replied, "It's nothing. Too much excitement, too much sun, I don't know, I'll be alright, you worry too much about me."

"Of course I worry about you, I love you."

"I love you too, James, but I want to help."

He insisted, "I think you should go back to the house and rest. I can finish the harvest with the others. I'm worried about you."

"James, I want to help. The more people there are in the fields, the quicker we can finish the harvest and leave here."

"No, I won't hear of it. You go back to the house now, or I'll carry you back there myself."

Reluctantly, she turned and walked back to the house, hoping her little secret would be safe, wondering what Jameson would say if he only knew. She entered the house and walked slowly up the stairs to her bedroom. She rested for the remainder of the day, feeling guilty for lying down while everybody else was working.

Madeline was driving the carriage back to Serenity as a group of three Yankee soldiers, separated from their unit, spied her.

One soldier stated, "Let's go get her. Maybe we can have us a little fun with that sweet little southern gal."

The others all nodded in agreement and began the pursuit. They were stopped by the sound of horses coming in their direction. The hooded riders came rushing past Madeline and disappeared into the woods. She panicked and hurried the horses as best she could, hoping Jameson was still alive. The Yankees decided to follow at a safe distance.

The carriage came into view of the plantation, moving rapidly alongside the fields. Jameson's and Madeline's eyes met. She let out a sigh of relief as she stopped the carriage, disembarked, ran, and hugged Jameson.

"I'm so glad you're all right. They didn't get you, thank God. Jeb wants you dead so he can inherit the plantation. I wanted to tell you, but I was so afraid of him. You don't know what he is capable of. I'm so sorry, Uncle."

Jameson held her and said it was okay. He told her what happened and that he did not hold anything against her.

"By the way, where is dear Jeb?"

"We were stopped on our way to town by Confederate soldiers. They forced him to join the army."

"They took him. Well, well, I'd like to say I'm sorry, but I'm not. Why don't you go up to the house and help Nanny with Uncky."

"Thank you, Uncle. I'm sorry I didn't stand up to him. You know I'm sort of relieved that my husband is gone. That's horrible of me, isn't it?"

"Not at all, maybe he'll learn something from the whole experience."

They both smiled. Jameson went back to the fields and Madeline up to the house. He hoped Jeb's absence would buy them some time from the vindictive Beau Lansing.

The Yankee scavengers watched from a safe distance, surprised to see a white man on the grounds. Most men had joined the army, and only children, old men, slaves, and women were left to run the plantations. They were hungry and exhausted and decided to bide their time and see what developed. Maybe an opportunity would show itself.

Uncky was resting comfortably on the couch being waited on by an ever-caring Nanny. Madeline entered and rushed over to them to offer her help and condolences. She explained her story and the abduction of Jeb by the Rebel forces. Neither Nanny nor Uncky could feel remorse for the loss of Jeb, but both felt sorry for Madeline. They fussed over Uncky for the rest of the afternoon, wiping his brow, fluffing his pillow, serving him tea and cookies, although he would have preferred whiskey. Nanny secretly poured a shot into his tea, even though no one would have cared anyway. They doted on him hand and foot until the hungry workers came in from the fields. Although he was in a lot of pain, Uncky kind of enjoyed all the attention.

"Don't you be a fussin' all over me now, I'm no baby," he said.

Nanny made dinner for the weary workers, and for the first time they all sat together, black and white, at one table, enjoying the fine food and each other's company. With all the dissenters missing, for one reason or another, there was no reason they could not share God's bounty. They laughed and ate every crumb in sight, wondering why this simple act had not occurred before while hoping it would always be so from now on.

The former indentured servants would now live in the great house for as long as needed until they could all leave for freedom in the North.

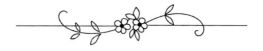

Chapter 27

Surprises

In the following days, the harvest was completed. It was not large due to the drought, but it would still command a good price on the market. It was all neatly bundled into sacks and loaded to capacity onto two wagons for delivery to Charleston. Jameson planned on going with Nate and Zeke right after breakfast.

Uncky was improving although still in a lot of pain. Jameson asked Madeline if she knew where the guns were kept. Nanny interrupted and told Jameson they were hidden in the barn under the bed where Uncky used to rest. She had stashed them there after Jameson left, waiting for him to return home while keeping them away from the hands of the wicked Jebediah.

He went and retrieved three rifles and two pistols along with ammunition. They appeared to be in good condition. He tested each one to be sure. They all fired successfully. He kept a pistol in his coat and a rifle on each wagon. The others he brought into the house and told the ladies to hide them in the kitchen cupboard for protection. The harvest-laden wagons pulled out, bound for Charleston. Daniel, Jonas, and Ozzie went out into the fields to glean them and gather all their tools into the barn. There was nothing left for the ladies to do but bide their time until the men returned. Nanny made lemonade, and they all relaxed and talked of better days to come. Madeline then retired upstairs to rest in her bedroom.

A short time later, the front door was thrown open, and three rag-tag Yankee soldiers barged in.

Dirty uniforms, unshaven faces, with guns drawn, they burst into the hall yelling, "Everybody stay where you are. Don't do anything foolish. We don't want no trouble, just do as we say. Everyone into the kitchen, let's go! Move it!"

Clearly they were deserters, dangerous and capable of almost anything.

Nanny aggressively ordered them, "You get out of here now. You hear me?"

"Shut up woman," they yelled as they pushed her into the kitchen along with everyone else.

They demanded, "Get us some food, old lady. You got any guns? How about gold or silver? Any cash lying around? We don't want any of that confederate cash, you hear."

They rummaged through the rooms, breaking vases and lamps, overturning tables and chairs, throwing dishes and cups on the floor, all the time threatening the defenseless hostages.

They eyed up Delilah and asked her, "Where's the pretty white girl?"

She told them, "There's nobody here but us."

Uncky limped in and asked, "What's going on here?"

They knocked him to the floor and repeated the question, this time pulling out a knife and threatening Delilah.

"I already told you. We're all alone," she said as Madeline came out from her room to find out what all the clamor was about.

The leader of the small band told the other two to keep an eye on the women and ran upstairs.

He grabbed Madeline, shoved her back into her bedroom, and told her, "I ain't had me a pretty little thing like you in a long time. I'm gonna enjoy this. If you don't fight me, maybe you'll enjoy it too."

Downstairs in the kitchen, Nanny, Delilah, and the others heard Madeline scream and cry out.

"Don't! Please leave me alone. Don't hurt me. Please, no, no."

"Shut up, or I'll shut you up."

They heard slaps, and then the screams turned to whimpers as the other two got antsy for their turns.

"I wish he'd hurry up. I can't wait forever," one of them stated.

"You can always have one of the slave girls if you're in that much of a hurry."

They laughed, but then he took a long, hard look and replied, pointing at Delilah, "She ain't half bad for a slave girl."

He started toward Delilah, leering and giggling, when the other one interrupted, "Hey, take a look at these silver candlesticks. Come on. Help me pack this stuff up."

His attention was diverted for the moment. He was obviously more interested in money than sex. Delilah knew this was her one chance to help Madeline. Although visibly scared and nervous, she worked her way, unnoticed, closer and closer to the cupboard. Then waiting until the soldiers were fully engrossed in their search for riches, she undid the latch on the door and carefully opened it. She slid her arm into the opening and felt around for the rifle, inadvertently knocking a mop handle to the ground. The sound brought the soldiers eyes directly to hers. She was shaking as she knew her plot was uncovered.

"What are you doin' there?" the soldier yelled as he started toward her.

Delilah threw the door open, grabbed the rifle, cocked it, as Jameson had shown her, quickly aimed and fired. The loud bang and recoil sent Delilah back against the wall as the bullet hit the onrushing enemy, sending him to the ground.

The other soldier dropped his booty and rushed at Delilah. She quickly turned and fumbled around in the closet finding the last pistol. She grabbed it and turned to fire as the soldier rushed upon her. They collided and wrestled for possession of the weapon. The encounter lasted only a short time when the pistol went off and for a brief moment they both stared at each other; then the second soldier fell dead on the floor. Delilah was relieved but knew the threat was not yet over.

The shots brought the upstairs soldier out of the bedroom with his pants still around his ankles, waving his pistol.

He waddled to the top of the stairway, screaming. "What's going on down there?"

The two guns were empty. Delilah was feverishly trying to reload the pistol, but in her haste was spilling gunpowder all over the floor. Nanny rushed over to help her.

The solitary soldier grabbed for his pants and yelled, "I'm coming down there, and God help you if you hurt my friends."

A frightened figure silently darted out of the bedroom and pushed the soldier forward. He tumbled down the stairs head first, turning over and over. Each thump was clearly audible as his body hit one step after the other. When he finally came to rest at the bottom, his neck had been broken; he was dead. The remaining soldier, only wounded from the rifle shot, ran out the door leaving a trail of blood behind him. He managed to get on his horse and ride away.

"Should we go after him?" Delilah asked.

"He won't get far," said Nanny. "He's hurt bad. Look at all that blood."

They rushed up to Madeline, who collapsed at the top of the stairs. They helped her back to her bed. She was sobbing uncontrollably. Nanny got hot water, soap, and towels to wash the filth off of her. She could easily remove the dirt, but she couldn't erase the memory.

Delilah sympathized with her. "I'm so sorry for you, Madeline. I know how it feels to be raped. I went through it, and I lived. We're here with you to take care of you and give you support. Try to get some rest."

But there was little consolation to be had. Madeline was physically and mentally bruised and battered. The tears kept flowing despite the best efforts of Delilah, Nanny, and the rest of them to calm her down.

The men hurried back in from the fields, but it was too late to offer any assistance. They said they spied a soldier trying to ride away, but he fell off his horse, and upon closer investigation, they discovered he was dead. Everyone helped to clean up the broken glass and blood stains. The dead were brought out to the barn to await Jameson's judgment.

It seemed like an eternity until the wagons carrying Jameson, Zeke, and Nate returned. Delilah ran out to meet them, telling Jameson of the horrible events that had occurred. Jameson ran upstairs to check on Madeline. She was as well as one could expect. Jameson said they had better bury the three soldiers before their regiment came looking for them and blamed the ladies for the soldiers' demise. They were then buried in unmarked graves in an obscure section of the plantation that would not be easily detected.

At dinner, Jameson revealed that they had sold the harvest and he had the money; however, the train was no longer taking passengers North because of the war. They would have to travel by horse and carriage. They would take whatever they could fit and head out in two days. Tomorrow they would pack up the wagons and leave early the following morning. Jameson told Nanny and Uncky it was not safe to remain behind. Everyone, including Madeline, had to go. No exceptions.

A knock on the door brought a temporary halt to the conversation. It was Abigail.

"Hello, Jameson, how are you?"

"I'm fine. It's good to see you, Abby. How are you?"

"I found these on my father's desk after I heard him tell my mother he had gotten them in the mail over a month ago." Abby produced the divorce papers Jameson had sent her from Boston.

"I signed them. They're official. Once you file them, you'll be a free man, so you can marry"—she looked into the kitchen and saw Delilah—"her, if you still want a black girl for a wife. Honestly, I don't understand you at all."

"I don't know what to say, Abby."

"Don't say anything, Jameson. I've found a new man. You may have heard. Ned Barrows, he's a fine Southern gentleman who appreciates me for myself."

"I'm not at all surprised, but I am happy for you, Abby. Thank you for bringing the papers to me."

Abigail started to leave, stopped, turned around, and added, "My father would kill me if he knew I brought those papers to you. He wants to see you dead, as would many others around here."

"Does that include Ned Barrows?"

"He's not on your side, if that's what you mean, but he's not a murderer either. Be careful, Jameson. I saw your overseer talking with my father the other day. I think they're planning to hurt you…maybe even kill you. Watch out for yourself."

"I will. Thank you, Abby."

"Good-bye, Jameson."

Delilah appeared by the door next to Jameson as they watched the coach depart. Abigail turned around to look back one last time at the man she once had and the woman who now held his heart.

"Do you still love her?" Delilah asked awkwardly.

"No, I don't love her, but I still care about her. She was a part of my life for many years. Most of those years were good. It seems the disagreements escalated when we came here and I wanted to free all of you. She just couldn't, or maybe didn't want to understand."

He paused for a moment then added, "Ah, but if I hadn't returned, I wouldn't have met you." He smiled at Delilah and added, "Do you know what this means?" He held up the divorce papers. "It means as soon as these are filed at the courthouse in Boston, I'm no longer married to Abigail."

He took Delilah by the hand and out onto the porch. The sun had painted the evening sky with splashes of brilliant reds and oranges.

He said, "I was hoping this would have been more romantic but—" He knelt down on one knee, looked her tenderly in the eyes, and said, "Miss Delilah, would you do me the honor of becoming my wife?"

She squealed with delight and fell forward to hug him, inadvertently knocking him down.

As she lay on top of him, kissing him, Jameson asked, "Am I to take this as a yes?"

"Yes, yes, I love you so much!"

"We'll officially get married when we get back to Boston, okay?"

"Yes, yes. So Mrs. Barrington, I mean Martha, can be there."

"I love you, Delilah."

"I love you too, James."

Time seemed to stand still for a moment.

Then Delilah, beaming, said, "I've been looking for the right time to tell you something, and I think this is it." She paused for only a second and then cheerfully blurted out, "James, I'm going to have a baby. You're going to be a father!"

"What? When? How long have you known about this?"

"I knew in Boston, but I didn't want to tell you, because you wouldn't have taken me with you."

"You're right. I wouldn't have. You're quite a woman, Delilah, quite a woman. I can't believe it. I'm going to be a father, finally!"

They kissed and kissed, not wanting the moment to end.

Nanny, Uncky, and the rest of their little family heard all the noise and came out on the porch to find out what happened. When they heard the news, there were mixed reactions. Nanny smiled but remained silent. Uncky was just happy for them. The newly freed workers were skeptical, as one would expect them to be. But they all congratulated Jameson and Delilah and wished them the best. Big days lay ahead for all of them, but one hurdle was directly in front of them with the name of Beau Lansing.

Chapter 28

Night Visitors

Night had fallen on Serenity, and all concerned were resting comfortably. The sound of breaking glass was barely noticed. A dark figure had forced his way into the house and was creeping across the room toward the stairway. He slowly ascended the stairs and found his way to Madeline's room. He cautiously opened the door, approached the bed, and carefully put his hand over her mouth. She awoke with a start and tried to scream, but his hand muffled the sound.

The figure spoke in a whisper. "Don't yell, Madeline. It's me, Jebediah, your husband. I've come home to you."

Madeline, realizing it was Jeb, grabbed him and pulled him close. "Oh, Jeb, thank heavens you're back. How did you get out of the army? I missed you so much, and I have so much to tell you. Yankees were here. One of them attacked me. I pushed him down the stairs and killed him."

"Wait a minute," Jeb stopped her. "What did you say? What exactly happened?"

She repeated, "A Yankee attacked me."

Jeb stopped her. "Yankees were in my house. What were Yankees doing in my house?"

The noise woke Jameson and Delilah in the next room. Jameson grabbed his pistol and went into the hallway. The voices were coming from Madeline's room. He threw open the door and was shocked to see Jebediah.

"What are you doing here?"

"I left the army to come back and claim my inheritance," Jeb answered defiantly.

"You mean you deserted?" Jameson countered.

In an attempt to change the topic, Jeb said, "My wife was attacked by Yankees, and you didn't defend her?"

"I wasn't here when it happened. I was in Charleston," Jameson said, defending himself.

"You should have been here to protect the women. I wouldn't have left them alone."

"The women did just fine by themselves. They eliminated all three Yankees."

"But my wife was attacked. What did they do to her? I demand to know. Tell me, Uncle. I have a right to know."

"She's fine, Jeb. They didn't permanently hurt her. Let's leave it at that."

Madeline softly spoke up. "A Yankee raped me, Jebediah, but thanks to Delilah, he was distracted before he could finish."

"What! You were raped! By a Yankee! This is all your fault, Uncle. I suppose they didn't try to rape that black slave of yours, just a pure white woman, huh?"

Jameson warned him, "Hold your tongue, Jeb, before I—"

"Before you what? I hold you responsible for this, and you'll pay!" Jeb screamed as he began to leave.

Madeline cried, "Where are you going? Don't leave me. I need you, Jebediah."

Jeb scornfully replied, "You're tainted with Yankee scum. I can't be near you anymore. I'm leaving!"

Jameson spoke, "Jeb, she's been through a lot. She needs you. Get back here, you coward."

Jeb stormed out as Madeline broke into tears. Delilah again tried to comfort her. Jameson knew Jeb was going to get Beau and the rest of the vigilantes. Now they had to prepare for the worst.

He turned toward Madeline and apologized, saying, "I'm sorry, Madeline, but he didn't care enough to even go see his own mother. He showed you his true self. I know it hurts, but it's best he's gone."

There would be no more rest that night, just a grave concern for the coming storm.

It was very early in the morning as they packed their bags and took them out to the barn, loading them onto the wagons. Vegetables, potatoes, and the like from the garden were picked and preserved for the trip. Chickens were rounded up, caged, and loaded onto the wagons. Extra ammunition was also added to the other supplies.

Jameson called everyone together and set out his plan for defending themselves from the coming confrontation. He made sure all his firearms were loaded. Uncky would be upstairs at one of the bedroom windows with Nanny to reload as he fired each gun. He would be downstairs with Delilah reloading. Madeline would remain in her room for her safety. The workers would remain at their lodging, also safely out of harm's way. They wanted to remain and help, but Jameson insisted that if something happened to him, they could still attain freedom. They had their signed papers and should try once again to head North. They begrudgingly agreed and left for the safety of their dwelling.

After they had departed, Jameson said he forgot to give them a pistol and some ammunition for their protection. Uncky agreed to take the gun down to slave row.

Jameson yelled, "Tell them to be ready to leave as soon as the conflict is over, regardless of the outcome!"

The ground was dry and cracking from lack of rain, and the wind was picking up, blowing from the west. Every indication was that a storm was approaching—in more ways than one.

It was a mere hour until daylight, as the sound of horse hooves broke the silence of the night. Flickering lights could be seen in the distance. They were carrying torches. As they approached, there were no white sheets or hoods disguising them. They were emboldened with revenge and did not concern themselves with recognition. They were determined that no one of importance would be left behind who could identify them.

Jameson could barely make them out in the dim light. Were there eight, perhaps ten riders? He could not be sure. All he knew was that he was outnumbered and could not win this time.

The riders pulled up close to the house.

Beau Lansing shouted out, "Jameson Hartford, come out here and face your fate! You cheating, conniving, no good, Yankee scum. You've disgraced my little girl, not to mention this whole community with your selfish actions. We only want you. We'll leave everyone and everything as it is if you come out and give yourself up. I'll even leave that little whore alive if you come out peacefully."

Jameson responded, "I haven't committed any crime, and why should I trust you?"

"Would your father-in-law lie to you?"

"You're not my father-in-law any longer. Abigail found the divorce papers you were hiding. She signed them and gave them to me."

Beau replied angrily, "She did what? I'll deal with her later, but you, you won't get the chance to file those papers, my boy."

Jameson added, "Oh, but I will, and then I won't be related to you any longer."

Beau replied, laughing, "Jameson, you are so naive, or perhaps just ignorant. Are you still going to marry that little slave girl of yours?"

"That's none of your business."

"Ah, but it is, Jameson, because if you marry her, I'll still be your father-in-law. I'm her father too!"

Jameson and Delilah looked at each other, stunned by this new revelation.

Beau continued, "That's right. I had many enjoyable evenings with her mother, although I don't think she enjoyed them as much as I did. Then when she got pregnant, I sold her so my wife wouldn't find out."

Jameson yelled, "I don't believe you. Prove it!"

Beau replied, "All right, her mother's name was Leah, and I sold her to Charles Higgins at the Moors Plantation. I'd like to tell you to go ask her, but...she's dead."

Charles Higgins chimed in, "That's right. She wasn't a very good worker but really good in the hay."

The two men broke out into unrestrained laughter.

Jameson looked at Delilah, who had tears in her eyes.

She sobbed. "I remember my mother saying my father was not Mister Higgins, but she wouldn't tell me who my real father was. She said it would be better if I didn't know. Now I understand what she meant."

Jameson tenderly wiped the tears from her face and wanted to comfort her, but he had to deal with the problem at hand first. He angrily turned toward the unwelcome intruders and responded to the charges.

"Who are you to judge me? You cheated on your wife, didn't you?"

Beau laughingly asserted, "I didn't fall in love with the girl and leave my wife. I was just enjoying a little midnight lovin' and that's all."

Jameson shot back, "You are far worse than anything you claim I am."

Beau yelled back, "Enough talk! Well, Hartford, are you coming out, or are we coming in to get you?"

Jameson had to try to save the innocent souls with him, so he started for the door but was stopped by Delilah.

"I don't want to lose you, James. I won't let you go."

"Don't go out there, Mista Jameson. I don't trust him. We'll take our chances and fight if we have to," Nanny added.

Jameson smiled at them, thought for a moment, and then responded to the intruders. "Get off my property. I'll kill the first person who comes any closer."

Another rider pulled up with something or someone in tow. "Well, look what we have here! Isn't this your house servant?"

It was Uncky. They most certainly had captured him on his way back from slave row.

"We'll kill him if you don't come out here now, Hartford. You won't escape again, not a second time."

Jameson looked at Delilah and Nanny. He said, "I have to go. I can't let them murder Uncky."

"No, James, they'll kill you."

"Here, Lilah, take the rifle. After they let Uncky go, try to shoot Beau Lansing. He seems to be the leader. If you kill him, maybe the others will just leave."

He kissed her and opened the door. Uncky, aware of what was happening, broke free from his captors and ran for the house.

"Don't come out here, Mista Jameson. They'll kill you!" Uncky shouted. He did not want Jameson to perish because of him.

A rider raised his gun and fired as Uncky fell to the ground. Nanny screamed as Jameson grabbed the rifle from Delilah and fired, bringing down the shooter.

Someone yelled, "Let's get him," and the riders charged forward, forcing Jameson to retreat back into the house.

They all rode in unison, guns blazing. Jameson, Delilah, and Nanny hid behind the door as bullets riddled the dry wood. The intruders stopped at the far end of the property, reloaded, then charged again. Bullets forced their way through the weakened wood and shattered many of the plantation's windows. Jameson pushed the ladies to the floor and fell on top of them in an attempt to afford them as much protection as was humanly possible.

When the riders had passed for the second time, Jameson threw open the door and tried to retaliate with a single rifle shot before disappearing back inside as the third assault began. Again, the hail of bullets flew through the wood and windows as Jameson, Delilah, and Nanny lay helpless on the floor, showered by pieces of broken glass.

When the attack subsided, Jameson opened the door and attempted another retaliatory shot before the next onslaught. Rueben Rutledge, who had remained behind, was waiting for Jameson to appear. He immediately galloped past and cracked his whip, striking Jameson hard on the back, knocking him down. Delilah grabbed him and pulled him safely back inside, slamming the door.

They could hear Reuben laughing and celebrating his successful assault, telling the others, "I taught him a lesson. Now he knows what the lash feels like. He's just like one of his precious slaves."

Blood was oozing from the laceration as Jameson regained his composure. The trio looked at each other, and their faces told the whole story. They were desperately outnumbered and did not stand a chance. They would go down fighting if they must. Jameson grabbed another rifle, determined to avenge this sneak attack. He opened the door and fired. The pellet found its mark as someone fell from their saddled perch. He could not identify the victim, but it was one less person they had to battle.

Watching from behind the barn, the freed workers witnessed Uncky's shooting and Jameson's whipping. They could no longer just stand idly by and let fear prevent them from standing up for their rights. Grabbing axes, pitchforks, shovels, and sickles from the barn; they timed their attack and charged the surprised riders from behind.

Jameson grabbed another gun and fired. This time he could clearly see that the unlucky party was the overseer Ruben

Rutledge. He went down crying like the coward that he was. Payback was almost complete.

Delilah and Nanny were frantically working to reload the guns as Jameson noticed the freed workers attacking the unsuspecting riders. For the first time since this ordeal began, he felt a glimmer of hope. In his delight, however, he let his guard down and failed to notice Beau Lansing galloping ever closer. Beau fired his pistol, and Jameson felt the bullet pierce his flesh. He fell to the ground and dropped his gun.

Delilah raced to Jameson's side, grabbed the rifle, aimed, and fired. The bullet grazed Beau and forced him to drop the reins. The bright blast frightened his horse, causing the animal to rear up, knocking Beau from his saddle. As Lansing hit the ground, he let go of his torch. It rolled and ignited the dry brush around the house. Fueled by the high winds, the house immediately caught fire and it spread quickly through the dry kindling. Beau Lansing stood up and charged into the house before another loaded gun could be fired. He grabbed Delilah and threw her back into the house with such force that she hit the wall and collapsed onto the floor.

"I'll deal with you later," he yelled and turned his full attention to the injured Jameson.

Intent on revenge, he lifted Jameson and pushed his knee firmly into the wound on Jameson's side. Jameson winced in pain. Beau's fist then hit him squarely in the jaw. Jameson tried to defend himself but he was too weak and Beau was too strong.

"What's the matter, Hartford, can't fight your own battle without a woman to help you?"

"Beau, I didn't mean to hurt you or Abigail, I only wanted to free my workers. Was that so bad?"

Delilah arose and ran at Beau. He hit her hard, sending her backwards against the cabinets. Again, she collapsed on the floor.

"Don't worry, daddy will have plenty of time for you later sweetie. Right now, I got to kill me a cheating son-in-law."

"Beau, please leave her alone. She had nothing to do with any of this."

"Don't you worry son, I have big plans for my little girl."

Beau lifted Jameson, pinned him against the wall, and continually hit him; all the while laughing and taunting him. Jameson could no longer stand of his own accord and fell to the floor.

"I'm getting tired of this Hartford. It's time for you to die," Beau said as he reached for a pistol lying on the floor.

It looked like the fight was all over and evil had won when a loud bang was heard. Beau unexpectedly clenched at the sudden pain in his stomach and saw blood oozing out, turning his shirt a bright red. He was stunned and looked into the kitchen. There he saw Nanny holding a smoking pistol.

She said, "Get outta this house Mista Lansing. You ain't welcome here anymore."

Beau, dazed and confused, stumbled back outside about 100 feet and collapsed in the yard.

Delilah and Nanny ran over to Jameson and helped him up. He was beaten but far from defeated. Nanny gave him some whiskey. They bandaged his wounds and he began to regain some strength.

"Thank you Nanny. You saved us."

"I don't know what came over me, Mista Jameson. Lord forgive me, I just had to do something."

They hugged and shared a brief moment of peace and happiness amid the mini war being waged all around them.

The freed workers were able to bring down a few unsuspecting riders before they were even noticed, but once their presence became known, they also suffered losses. Guns were fired, and axes were swung; it was a melee of blood and bodies, each fighting for their survival, their cause, and their way of life. The one-time slaves were no longer afraid and fought with a fury that they had bottled up inside themselves for far too many years. They all had their reasons. Becky wanted revenge for Lizzie's death and others for the unfair treatment they had received, but the best reason of all was for freedom. They would fight to the death for sweet freedom.

The house was filling with smoke. Jameson told Delilah and Nanny they had to get out. He took the loaded guns and told them to run for the barn, and he would give them cover. Once they were safe inside the structure, he would follow. They protested that he was not strong enough to make the escape on his own. He insisted he was quite capable, and they reluctantly gave in. Hand in hand, they left the house, running for the safety of the barn. A rider saw them and tried to head them off, but Jameson was faster and took him down. They finally arrived at the barn, and Delilah frantically looked around to signal Jameson.

The smoke was much thicker now, and Jameson was coughing, trying to breathe as the blood from his wound began to flow again. He left the house and limped and wheezed as he tried to reach the safety of the barn. Jameson was suddenly stopped in his tracks by a blow to his back causing the weakened body to collapse on the ground.

He quickly rolled over and through the sweat in his eyes and the smoke from the fire he could just about make out the figure of a man holding a pistol pointed directly at his head. He could not make out the face until he heard the unmistakable chilling voice.

"You'll not escape this time, Uncle, I'll make sure of that," Jeb boasted as he cocked the pistol.

His hair tousled and his breath reeking of spirits, he was out of his mind with jealousy and hatred.

Delilah, witnessing the event, could not be contained. She left Nanny and the safety of the barn and ran to her man's defense.

Jameson yelled, "No, Delilah stay back, don't come here." He then looked squarely at his assassin and tried to reason with his deranged nephew, "Jeb, listen to me, this is no time for revenge."

Jeb shouted, "Shut up uncle, I don't want to hear anything you have to say. Everything was fine until you showed up. I'm going to kill you first, then her," he added, pointing at Delilah.

Jameson pleaded, "Leave Delilah out of this, it's between you and me."

Jeb's face instantly reminded Jameson of someone he'd almost forgotten, "Jeb, Madeline is still in the house."

"What, what did you say?"

"She'll burn to death if you don't get her out."

"Madeline is in there?"

"Let me help you. There's no time to lose. Help me up and we can both try to save her. Let's go now!"

Jeb hesitated, looked at the house, looked at Jameson, looked toward Delilah, and then with the butt of the gun, hit Jameson in the head, knocking him slightly unconscious.

"I don't need your help to save my wife," he said as he ran off into the inferno, screaming, "Stay right there, I'm coming back for you, Uncle."

Jeb managed to find a point of entry into the blazing mansion and disappeared into the flames and smoke.

Delilah reached the dazed Jameson and tried to revive him.

The mini war had reached a climax as one lonely rider fled, and the few remaining workers felt the thrill of success for the first time in their lives. David had beat Goliath, and the one-time slaves felt like human beings for the first time in their lives. Nanny ran over to Uncky, who was motionless, lying on the ground in a pool of blood. Jameson was finally coming around as Delilah was trying to pull him to safety.

"James, we have to get away from the house. There's gunpowder in there. Come on before it explodes."

She lifted him and managed to get him a safe distance away. As they watched the raging fire, the gunpowder ignited with a deafening blast, sending a ball of smoke and flames high into the sky. The fire now engulfed the whole house, and the explosion had weakened the support beams. They stood helplessly by and watched the once proud mansion be devoured in flames and ultimately collapse unto itself. They looked at each other in horror as the realization of what had happened shuddered in their consciousness. Jeb and Madeline were certainly gone.

Jameson mused, "Poor Madeline, perhaps there was a shred of decency to be found in Jeb after all."

As if in divine judgment, the skies opened up, and a torrential rain poured down, quenching the flames. Crashing, deafening thunder was coupled with howling winds as jagged flashes of lightening pierced the ground. It was an unrelenting assault on the unprotected earth, ensuring an end to the battle and a cleansing of the blood and foul air.

They picked themselves up and walked over to Nanny. She was bent over Uncky and crying, for this was the man she cared for and secretly loved. Nanny knelt down by the fatally injured Uncky and tenderly held his head in her hands.

With his dying breath, he said, "I love you, woman. Don't you cry now. Just go and be free." He exhaled, and his body went limp. He had held on to precious life just long enough to say good-bye to his woman.

Nanny was crying uncontrollably. "Don't leave me. Please, don't leave me. I need you." She kept kissing him, hoping she might somehow revive his lifeless body, but he would only taste freedom in the great equalizer, that is death.

Delilah and Jameson tried to console her, but she had to let her grief come out, knowing she would never see this wonderful man again. He gave up his life so that Jameson, Nanny, and the others could live. They wept right along with her for the kind gentleman who everybody loved.

Jonas, Nate, and Becky also did not survive. They had all fought valiantly for freedom, but only Daniel, Zeke, Sara, and young Ozzie would live to experience it. They wept and mourned, assuring themselves that these brave fighters knew they had died for a worthy cause. Standing in the downpour, the heavenly rain and their tears combined and flowed over their loved ones then softly vanished into the parched earth.

As the precipitation subsided, they all knew they had to hurry and move on, as the smoke and explosion were sure to bring inquisitive neighbors. The first order of business was to properly grieve and bury the dead in the graveyard, right next to where little Eve was buried. Each spot was marked with a cross and a headstone inscribed with each hero's name. The dead riders were left in the field where they fell. No one wanted to expend energy to honor those murders as they viewed the death and destruction that was all so unnecessary.

Jameson took a last walk around to check for any signs of life. Among the dead, Jameson recognized Shelby Mathison, Charles Higgins, and Ruben Rutledge, but wait, could that be Ned Barrows? Jameson didn't realize he was so hated and by people he considered to be his friends and family. He surveyed the disaster and total destruction of his boyhood home. It had finally come to this.

Delilah, who was following close behind him, spat on the body of Charles Higgins as she passed him, saying, "I hate you for what you did to my mother. I'm glad you're dead. "

Jameson tried to console her. "You have every right to hate him. I hate them all for what they did to you and your mother, but now you and I can do something that would have made your mother both happy and proud. We can help these people to freedom."

She agreed but added, "I still hate them."

They started to walk away when Delilah became startled and with a panicked look in her eyes stuttered, "J-J-James, where is Beau Lansing's body?"

The question stopped Jameson dead in his tracks. He hobbled over to where Lansing had fallen earlier, finding only traces of blood, no body.

"Nanny shot him so I'm sure he couldn't have gotten far."

He checked again, asking all the workers to help and try to find the missing corpse. Everyone searched but to no avail, Beau Lansing did not appear to be among the dead, which only meant one of two things; either he managed to crawl off somewhere and die or he was still out there someplace waiting to extract his revenge upon Jameson and Delilah.

They could not worry about that now as they had to beat a hasty retreat and help the survivors attain their freedom once and for all.

Jameson's wounds were cleaned and bandaged by Delilah and Nanny. He hoisted himself upon his horse, wincing in pain, hoping he would not start bleeding again. The survivors gathered together their belongings and loaded them onto the two wagons. They harnessed the horses as each found a comfortable spot and prepared for the long ride North.

The clouds parted, and the sun rose in the eastern sky, beckoning them onward. A last look around at what was the only home some of them ever knew was further saddened by the loss of their friends and families. A new world awaited, and anticipation was high. They snapped the reins, and the horses started to travel.

When the sun had fully risen, a coach containing Abigail rode onto the plantation. She couldn't believe the carnage. Searching among the bodies she came across her fiancé, Ned Barrows. She was heartbroken, but a tiny bit of her was somewhat happy to not find Jameson's body among the dead. She realized he must have escaped and also wondered what had happened to her father; he was nowhere to be found either. Perhaps he had escaped and was back at their plantation, she would alert everyone to be on watch for him. Other folks from the surrounding area were beginning to arrive, brought by the explosion, sounds of gunfire and the light and smell from the once blazing fire.

Around the back, two figures were found lying in the dirt—Jeb and Madeline. They were barely alive, and Abigail ordered them taken directly to the doctor in town. The rest of the neighbors assisted in claiming the dead and removing them back to their homes for proper burials. A lot of questions were beginning to be asked as to what had happened and who was responsible.

Abigail knew the answers but remained silent. Her thoughts turned to Jameson. She wanted to go after him but wondered what she would do when she found him. She did not pursue him, just let him go, hoping their paths would cross again one day. She climbed back into her coach and headed home, tears streaming down her face.

Chapter 29

NORTHWARD

The travel North was difficult at best. They would try to stay off the main roads to avoid running into either blues or grays or just roving troublemakers. Jameson rode ahead on a third horse to try and scout the area and avoid confrontations. If a patrol was spotted, Jameson would ride back to the wagons and stop them, asking everyone to remain quiet until the trouble passed.

After a hard day in the saddle, Jameson's shirt was covered in blood from the wounds he had suffered at the hands of Abner Slycott and Beau Lansing. He would dismount the horse, grimacing in pain, allowing Nanny and Delilah to clean and re-bandage him. Nanny was afraid she would have to use a needle and thread to close the wounds if he continued to bleed. He would not survive the trip if he kept losing blood at this rate.

He steadfastly refused the stitching, acting more like a child than he wanted to admit. She wound the bandages extra tight, hoping that and a good night's rest would control the flow. In the morning the bleeding seemed to have subsided, and Jameson climbed back into the saddle, praying for yet another miracle. He tried to ride a little slower and a lot more carefully to prevent the wounds from re-opening. It seemed to be working as the little band of freedom seekers moved slowly north.

Luckily he had saved a rifle, a pistol, and some ammunition in the barn, so they would be able to hunt for food. There was plenty of fresh water and fish in the streams, and he had money if they needed to purchase anything. The horses were tended to by young Ozzie, who had a real affinity for the animals.

Nanny continued to prove herself invaluable with her skills and knowledge. She could make any kind of meat into a delicacy. She could mend clothes and repair almost anything. She and Delilah tried to teach the travelers how to read and write in preparation for their newfound freedom. They devoured the knowledge eagerly.

They had to get to Boston before the winter set in, or they would not make it. Jameson's main concern was Delilah, who was definitely showing her pregnancy. He would've liked the baby to be born safely in Boston.

Guns flaring and distant cannon fire could be heard in the quiet of the night as they tried to get needed sleep. What would happen to them if they were caught in the middle of a battle between blues and grays? How would they survive? Jameson could not worry about all this right now. He had to get his needed rest; too many people were depending on him.

The next morning, with the wounds healing nicely and the bleeding having stopped, Jameson decided to ride out early to establish a clear route. He returned with good news; the route was clear, so they ventured out onto the main thoroughfare. The horses were able to pick up their gait, and they gained a lot of ground.

The wagons were surprised by a company of Confederate soldiers, who questioned them long and hard. They were looking for spies and deserters. Names were mentioned; Jebediah's came up. Jameson cleverly lied in his best Southern drawl to gain their freedom by telling the captain that Yankees had burned his home and killed everyone except for the people he saw on the wagon. He was trying to take them to his remaining family members in Virginia. The captain asked him the family name. He thought quickly and made one up...Chesterton. The captain shook his head as if he'd heard of it and let them pass.

When he ran into a Yankee patrol, he claimed he was fleeing the Rebels who wanted him dead for trying to free his slaves. This time he spoke in his acquired New England dialect. The captain wasn't sure about them, but the raggedy band of stragglers on the two wagons did not look like any kind of threat to anyone, so they were also permitted to pass.

On the eighth night into their trek as everyone was settled down and sleeping, they heard a rustling in the reeds. Jameson instinctively grabbed for his rifle as the shadowy figure crept into their camp and headed straight for the campfire and kettle of leftover food.

Jameson yelled, "Stop where you are, or I'll shoot!"

The figure replied, "Please don't shoot. I ain't armed. I got no gun."

"Who are you? What do you want?"

"My name is Lewis, and I'm just cold and hungry, that's all. I don't mean no harm to nobody, honest. Please don't shoot." He begged.

In the light of the fire the awakened band of brothers could see a scared, shaking, undernourished black man. Nanny quickly rose and took him by the arm. He meekly followed her lead.

She said, "This man is in need of a good meal. I'm gonna heat something up for him."

Jameson kept his gun cocked and pointed, requesting additional information from the malnourished stranger.

"Where did you come from?"

"Please, sir, I got separated from my master and can't find my way back."

"I don't believe that. You're a runaway, aren't you?"

Lewis looked down and sadly admitted, "Yes, sir. Yes, I am. Please don't send me back there, please. I can't take it anymore. I'd rather be dead."

Delilah spoke up, "Don't be afraid. We won't send you back. We're all heading North to freedom. James, is there any reason he can't join us?"

Jameson said, "It's all right with me, but you all should be aware that harboring a runaway is a crime. It's stealing and abetting, and if we are discovered, we could all be arrested or even worse, we could be hung on the spot. This affects us all, and we should decide this democratically. Let everyone vote on it. All those in favor of taking Lewis along with us, raise your hand."

The one-time servants had never been asked their opinion before. They were always told what to do. This new process of voting was something completely new to them, and they eagerly embraced it. One by one the hands went up; it was unanimous. They all agreed that the stranger should join them on their quest for freedom.

Lewis was ecstatic. He ate, drank, and thanked everyone over and over again, praising God for allowing him to find salvation. Jameson reminded him that he was not yet free, and they had a long, hard journey ahead of them. Perhaps the war would keep the slave catchers at bay, as most of them probably enlisted "for the cause." After this they would take turns standing guard every night, relieving each other every few hours.

Jameson was trying to keep track of the days by notching a piece of wood as the sun set each day. He needed to know how long they were on the road so he could tell what month they were in and how long before winter would be upon them. The days were already growing shorter, and the nights were cooler. They had to keep moving at all costs. He was worried for Delilah; this bumpy wagon trip was not good for her. Moving north every day the long trip was both monotonous and taxing.

Late in the evening of the fifteenth day while all were sound asleep, gunshots and screams could be heard nearby. The sounds could not be more than a half mile to the north. Jameson arose and told everyone to remain calm and stay in camp; he needed to see what was happening.

He crept through the underbrush and weeds, careful to be as silent as he possibly could. From behind a thicket of bushes, he could see into the clearing ahead—men dressed in blue and grey engaged in combat. The war was gaining momentum. A man in grey was shot, and then a man in blue was thrust through with a bayonet. The momentum shifted back and forth as he watched in horror at the waste of humanity. A noise from behind sent shivers down his spine as he sprung up to defend himself. It was only Delilah, worried and concerned for his welfare. He grabbed her and pulled her down to safely conceal her behind the leafy shelter.

"I told you to stay in camp. It's not safe out here," he whispered.

"I couldn't wait. I had to be sure you were all right," she said apologetically.

"Lilah, you're with child. You have to take care of yourself and the baby," he said as he held her tight in his arms. "I don't want to lose you or our baby."

"I'm sorry," she spoke softly, "but I don't want to lose you either."

He kissed her gently as the fighting seemed to subside. There was no way to tell who won or who lost. Most of the soldiers lie dead on the ground. The few remaining survivors rushed back to their units for help and supplies. The two observers remained unnoticed.

Jameson and Delilah were worried for themselves, their friends, their baby, and most of all, for their country. Could it survive such a terrible war? They started back to camp for needed rest. They would have to be on the alert for small skirmishes such as these in the future.

As they returned to their wagons a familiar but eerie voice called out to them.

"Just stop right where you are, Hartford."

They were surprised to see Beau Lansing standing there with a rifle pointed at them. His shirt was still bloodstained from where Nanny had shot him, and he had that crazed look in his eyes. All the workers and Nanny were neatly lined up against the wagons and all of Jameson's firearms were in Beau's possession.

"I been tracking you for some time now Hartford, you keep veering on and off the main roads, going deep into the forest and then emerging on a different path. But it seems my patience has paid off, because I not only get you, I get all my slaves and… my daughter as well. And look, she is pregnant, no doubt with your child, huh Hartford? So, I'm going to be a grandfather after all, that is rich," Beau said laughing a hideous laugh.

"Why are you here and still carrying a grudge? The feud is over, we all lost comrades and loved ones. Let it go already," Jameson declared.

"I won't be satisfied until you are dead and that little whore is back on my plantation as a slave again. Step away from Hartford, daughter, unless you want to die along with him."

"Leave her alone Lansing, she has nothing to do with you and I."

"You're wrong, Hartford, she came between you and my Abigail, causing you to leave my Abby and take up with the likes of her; but, you're right, I really only want you dead."

Jameson tried to convince Delilah to leave, but she would not move, "I told you once before, if you die, I die along with you. I don't want to live without you."

"Isn't that touching, it must be true love, or just plain stupidity. Oh, how rude of me, I didn't introduce you my new friend here, Horace Gravenstein. He's a slave catcher. We met on the trail and I hired him to help me recapture all my runaways. He's an excellent tracker, that's how we finally found you. I told you we would bring back a haul, didn't I Horace?"

"Yes sir, Mister Lansing, this is a bonanza, it surely is," said the burly unshaven shoddily clad Gravenstein.

Horace took a bunch of shackles and chains from a burlap sack that was hanging on his horse and threw them at the workers ordering them, "Put these on, around each ankle your wrists and necks. C'mon, you haven't forgotten how to do this, have you?"

The chains clanged and clinked as they hit the ground reminding everyone of the gruesome past they had all hoped was far behind them.

Jameson, again interceded, "Beau, let them go, they're free, I gave them their papers, you have no right to do this."

"After your dead, nobody will know the difference, so I'm taking them back; the spoils of war and all that."

"You won't make it back to your plantation; there are too many troops and fighting going on all around us."

"That's why I have Gravenstein here, he's a master at avoiding capture and surprising the enemy, aren't you Horace?"

"You can count on me, Mister Lansing, sir. These slaves will be back on your plantation and working again before you know it."

They both shared another repugnant laugh, sure of their plan and its success.

Jameson again made a request, "At least let Nanny go, you always liked her."

"I did until she tried to kill me, now she means nothing to me. Say goodbye to your boyfriend daughter, I'm going to kill him."

"Please Mister Lansing, I'll go with you, just spare his life, please," Delilah pleaded.

"No deal! He would only come after me, he has to die. You know the best part of this Hartford, is that you tried to free all the slaves and now your only child will be a slave, my slave. That is ironic, isn't it?" Beau said laughing.

"Horace, make sure those shackles are secured tightly on those slaves, I don't want any of them escaping."

"Yes sir, Mister Lansing, I'll personally check them" Horace said as he went to secure the locks.

A noise in the brush behind Beau caused him to turn around and witness a wounded survivor of the latest Civil War battle approaching him seeking his assistance.

"Help me, please sir, help me," the stranger in grey pleaded, "I been shot real bad, I'm dying."

Jameson rushed the temporarily distracted Beau, who quickly regained his composure and re-aimed his rifle. Before a shot could be fired Jameson was upon Beau and they tumbled to the ground fighting one another for control. The rifle fell to the side as Beau reached for a Bowie knife he had hidden in his belt. He tried to plunge the sharp blade into Jameson, but Beau was still a little weak from his wounds and Jameson was able to deflect the blade from its intended target. He brought his legs up and pushed Beau away.

The workers all ganged up on the severely outnumbered Horace Gravenstein pummeling him and choking him with his own chains until he could no longer offer any resistance and succumbed to his inevitable fate.

Delilah, witnessing this new dilemma, screamed, "No!" and ran to pick up the discarded pistol.

Lansing would not admit defeat. He brought the knife back up and again swung it at Jameson, who managed to evade yet another attack.

"I hate you, Hartford, I refuse to die unless I take you with me," Beau screamed as he came at his prey one more time and this time managed to slice Jameson's hand.

"Now I got you," he screamed and positioned the blade for a final attempt.

Delilah quickly cocked, aimed, and fired the pistol as Beau was almost completing his murderous task. The bullet could not miss at this close range, and Beau collapsed right on top of Jameson. The blade of the knife plunged into the dirt, right next to Jameson's head. He pushed Lansing's body to the side and looked up at his guardian angel.

"Nice shot," he said.

"You taught me how to shoot," she replied.

Delilah hastened to help Jameson rise to his feet and tore a piece of her dress to bandage his wound. They checked the body and Beau Lansing was not breathing, he was finally dead.

Delilah spit on his face and said, "I'm glad you're dead, and I'm glad I was the one to kill you. You were an evil man who hurt my mother, my people, and everyone I loved and I hate you for it."

She started to sob as years of oppression and bondage came to bear.

"It's over, sweetheart; he can't hurt anyone ever again. You're safe now, we all are."

He held her close as they went over to check on the straggler who inadvertently had saved their lives. He too had passed, and did not know he had lived just long enough to alter the outcome of another battle. They said a prayer for him, helped all the workers unchain themselves and gave Nanny another job, clean and bandage Jameson's sliced hand. They packed their belongings and moved out, not wanting to remain in that location any longer than was necessary.

The weather had been good for the most part, but when a storm approached, they were forced to seek shelter under trees to avoid being drenched. Then they just waited out the rain, wasting more precious time. At night the women slept in the wagons while the men slept on the cold, hard ground, but no one complained; spirits were high. Food was aplenty in the forests, and fish were abundant in the rivers and streams. Forging the rivers proved to be a daunting task, but they somehow managed to overcome each obstacle that was placed in their path. The hope for freedom superseded all else.

All remained quiet, but it was an uneasy peace always wondering if someone was lurking in the shadows, around a tree or crouched behind a bramble bush. They always posted a guard, especially at night when unknown sounds were always louder and more prevalent. Crickets, frogs, owls, bears and other nocturnal creatures broke the peace of the forest and caused an uneasy feeling throughout the camp.

Hours turned into days. Days became weeks, and the weeks added up to well over a month as the little band of nomads travelled northward—unceasing, unstoppable. Dawn was breaking as a whole troop of soldiers loomed ahead. Were they blue or grey? As they neared, Jameson could tell that not only were they union soldiers; they were Negro soldiers. The caravan stopped to allow the soldiers to march past them and to marvel at the sight.

Jameson inquired of the lieutenant, "What state are we in?"

He replied, "Virginia, but a few miles up the road is Maryland." The North!

Daniel said he would like to join the regiment and fight for his people's freedom. Jameson told him he was a free man and could do as he pleased. He jumped off the wagon, waved good-bye to everyone, and joined the blue army. Jameson yelled after him to come to Boston, Massachusetts, after the war and look them up. They would all be waiting for his safe return. Daniel thanked him and said he would do just that. Ozzie wanted to go also, but he was too young, and Sara would not hear of it.

Jameson asked about the train. The lieutenant said it was running but only North, not South. Would it take all of them to Boston? He was told it would if they had the proper fare. Jameson thanked him immensely.

They sped up the horses and kept going all through the night. It seemed they couldn't go fast enough, and then suddenly there it was. They were emboldened as they passed the road sign stating, "Welcome to Maryland." They were free at last. Slavery was illegal in the North. They cheered, yelled, stomped, and praised the Lord for their safe passage and for bringing them out of bondage.

A flock of birds were scared out of their tree and took to the air to escape the clamor below. They hugged each other and thanked Jameson and Delilah for their deliverance. They just couldn't contain their joy at being free at last. The revelry was cut short as Delilah cried out in pain and fell to her knees. She was going into premature labor.

Jameson grabbed her and lifted her onto the back of the wagon. She was moaning and breathing heavily. It appeared as though the rough wagon ride coupled with all the fears and anxieties of the arduous trip, had induced an early labor. Jameson was frantic. They were miles from a doctor and out in the middle of nowhere. He was afraid that Delilah would not be able to withstand another child of hers dying an untimely death.

Nanny stepped in and said, "Let me help. I birthed a few children in my time. I know what to do." She turned to Delilah. "Everything is going to be okay, child."

Delilah was scared, and the sharp pains were getting increasingly stronger.

Nanny took charge and issued orders. "Boil me some water. Get me a clean sheet and blanket."

Everyone obeyed her as if she was a drill sergeant and they were raw recruits.

It was nearly dawn, and the contractions were coming quickly. Jameson felt helpless. He paced back and forth refusing any kind words or any type of consolation. He knew the baby was at least two to three months premature, and the odds of survival were not good. He could do nothing to help except to hold Delilah's hand, offer encouragement, and wipe her brow.

Suddenly Nanny yelled, "It's time."

She told Delilah, "Spread your legs, Lilah, take a deep breath and push, child, push."

Delilah was crying out in the pain of childbirth, sweating, breathing, and pushing.

"You're doing great, child. Give me a big push now."

Every second seemed like an hour as the contractions kept coming closer and closer together and the cries of pain grew louder. Delilah squeezed Jameson's hand so hard he almost yelled out in anguish, but he bit his lip and kept silent as he tried to provide the only thing he could give her—strength.

Nanny again commanded, "Push, child. You've got to keep pushing."

Delilah was screaming. "I can't! It hurts too much. James, help me. I can't push anymore. I have to rest. I want to stop."

"Don't say that. You're going to do it. You have to. I love you too much."

A large contraction caused her to wince in pain and scream louder than ever before. Everyone was becoming concerned. The baby should have come by now. The look on Nanny's face said something must be wrong. Jameson's words of encouragement were falling on deaf ears as Delilah's strength was failing. She could not hold out much longer.

Jameson could not stand the thought of losing her and raised his eyes to heaven, praying for yet another miracle. It was all he could do. Delilah looked as if she was going into shock; her body could not take anymore.

Suddenly, they heard Nanny shout out, "I can see a head! Keep pushing, child. Here comes the baby. Here it comes; one big last push now."

Delilah strained and screamed and with her last ounce of strength pushed harder than ever. The cries of a little baby filled the air as a new life emerged.

"It's a girl," Nanny boasted. "You have a beautiful baby girl."

The baby was carefully wrapped in a blanket and given to Delilah to cuddle. She held on tight, determined not to lose this child.

"She's beautiful, James. Isn't she?" Delilah said with tears of joy.

"She sure is," said Jameson. "And why not, she takes after her mother."

"What shall we name her?" Delilah asked.

"We'll have to give that some serious thought," Jameson said.

"Well, it's dawn, and since this is the dawn of a new life for all of us, we should call her Dawn," Delilah stated.

"Yes, I like it," Jameson affirmed.

Delilah added, "I want to honor my mother's memory also, as if she became free along with us. I want to add her name. How do you like Dawnleah or maybe Dawnalee?"

"That's perfect, darling. Dawnalee Hartford. It fits her perfectly."

"Lee is also your middle name, isn't it, James?"

"Yes, it is. But how did you know that?"

"I saw it on that portrait of you at your home in Boston."

He smiled. "You mean our home in Boston, don't you? We'll have to have a portrait painted of you and Dawnalee when we get home."

"I'd rather have one picture with all three of us in it."

"Then that's what it will be, a picture of us as a new family."

"I'm so happy, James."

They kissed each other and then kissed the little girl, who had surprisingly quieted down and was asleep.

"We'll have to stop here for a while. Lilah needs to rest," Nanny ordered.

They all agreed and made camp for the night. Delilah and Jameson kept little Dawnalee close beside them to protect her from the cold night air. The free men and women each wanted to see the newborn baby and crowded around the exhausted mother. She showed her off proudly. Tomorrow they would try to catch the train, but tonight they celebrated freedom and a new life.

The next morning they proceed north to Baltimore and the train. Delilah was still weak but anxious to get to Boston, as the weather was getting colder, and she feared for little Dawnalee. Jameson wanted everyone to look presentable, so he gave Zeke, Ozzie, and Lewis clothes from his suitcase. Delilah did likewise for Sara and Nanny, who tailored all the outfits to fit each recipient. They washed and cleaned up rather nicely. The men shaved, and the women fixed their hair. Confident they would all be allowed on the train, they made their way to the station.

The city of Baltimore was huge and bustling with well-dressed people from all walks of life. They were excited to be in the outskirts of the capital of the United States.

The train station was very busy. They wondered where all the people could be going. Jameson went to buy the tickets and discovered he was short of cash to buy first-class tickets for everyone. Nanny reached into her secret cache hidden in her bosom and produced a sum of money. It was the same cash Jameson had given her that he had taken from the Wrabble Brothers. Now she was returning it back to him.

At first he protested, but she insisted, saying they were all in this together, and she was not a charity case. He smiled, took the cash, and purchased six first-class tickets. Their luggage was taken aboard. Jameson gave the horses and carriages to a poor-looking gentleman who gratefully accepted them and thanked him for his generosity.

They all entered the train and went to their private cars. It was different here; no one looked unkindly at them or made any snide remarks. Jameson helped Delilah and the baby into their seat and sat down next to her. They could not believe their dream of freedom was finally realized.

In a few minutes, the conductor yelled, "All aboard!" And the train started to chug out of the station.

They all settled back for the trip to Boston.

They could not know what lie ahead for them. Would they be welcomed or would bigotry and fear plague them wherever they went? Only time would tell. They began their journey North with great anticipation, hoping the rest of the world would accept them—not as black and white, but just people who were all the same, just different shades of brown. The train thundered northward.

Chapter 30

HOME

Boston was the largest city any of them had ever seen before. It stretched for miles in all directions, and they were fearful, each in turn wondering about their future. Jameson hailed two cabs and had all their luggage stowed in the back. They stepped on board, and the short ride to Jameson's residence was underway. Delilah and little Dawnalee were resting comfortably, and the baby seemed to enjoy the clip-clop of the horses and the gentle rocking of the coach on the cobblestone roads.

They arrived at the house and were greeted by Millie and Belle, who were glad to see their employer had returned and was still alive. Jameson ushered everyone into the house, carried out the requisite introductions, and asked Belle if she had enough food to prepare a feast to celebrate freedom. She did, and with Nanny's help, a most enjoyable meal followed. They toasted freedom with some red wine and again thanked God and Delilah and Jameson for all their help and support. After dinner they all retired to the bedrooms—the women in one, the men in another, and Jameson, Delilah, and Dawnalee in the third. Finally, a peaceful sleep was forthcoming.

The next morning Nanny was already in the kitchen getting acquainted with her new surroundings when Belle arrived. A battle for kitchen supremacy ensued. Delilah tried to settle the argument with an agreement. They would take turns preparing the meals. It sufficed for the moment, but it was an uneasy peace at best.

Delilah and Jameson hurried to get dressed so they could visit Martha Barrington and show off the baby. They took the short walk across the lawn and up the stairs to the front door. Mrs. Barrington herself answered the door, surprised and happy to see the returned travelers. They hugged and kissed right there on the spot and were enthusiastically ushered into the parlor.

Martha spoke, "Oh, I missed you both so much. I was so worried, what with the war and all... Oh, what do we have here?"

"Martha, I'd like to introduce you to Dawnalee Hartford, my, I mean *our* daughter," Delilah proudly boasted.

"Oh, she is so pretty, my dear. May I hold her?"

"Of course you may, Martha. Here, take her."

Delilah passed the baby to Martha Barrington. She fussed and talked baby talk to the little girl, quite unlike the prim and proper Mrs. Barrington. After Delilah served the perfect tea, they began to relate the unbelievable saga of hope and freedom.

Jameson interrupted the women. "Martha, Delilah and I want to be married, and, of course, we want you there to share the day. Do you think you would be able to help us plan the event? I know very little about such things and—"

Martha politely broke in. "May I be the first to offer my congratulations! I think the world of Delilah and you, Jameson, and I wish you all the happiness in the world. Of course I'll help with the arrangements. What woman doesn't love to plan weddings? We can have the reception right here in my house."

"We don't want to be any trouble," Delilah added.

"It's no trouble, no trouble at all. Then it's all settled. Delilah and I will go shopping today. You'll need a wedding dress, rings, invitations, oh, and we'll have to find a church. Oh, this will be such fun. What date have you decided on?"

"We thought the first Saturday that is available," Delilah stated.

"Oh, that's very ambitious, and there is so much to accomplish. We'd better get started, Delilah, my darling."

"Well, I'll leave you two alone to plan the nuptials. I have to find a job," Jameson said.

"I can help you with that too, Jameson. I have a lot of connections," Martha affirmed.

"Oh, that would be so great. Thank you, Martha!" exclaimed Delilah.

"Thank you, Martha, you are more than kind," Jameson said.

"I'm delighted to help my two best friends," Martha said.

Jameson excused himself and returned to his residence to help his new family acclimate to their new surroundings. Delilah and Martha planned their day: first, the bridal shop, then the jeweler, the printer, and finally the church. It was all so exciting.

The dress shop was most accommodating, showing the two ladies a wide variety of styles and fabrics. They sat on the padded sofa, sipped tea, and anxiously viewed a plethora of dresses carefully shown by the attentive sales staff. Delilah and Martha selected a few gowns and Delilah retired to the changing room. When she emerged, there were *oohs* and *aahs* from Martha and all the sales ladies. Delilah looked beautiful in every dress she slipped on; the full bodied gingham; the flowing hoop skirt; the slender body hugging velvet. But Delilah fell in love with a satin and lace white gown with sequins and pearls sewn around the neck, sleeves, and hem. The headpiece formed a crown, and the veil trailed over her face and down her back all the way to the floor. The dress fit her like it was custom made, just waiting for her to select it.

"You look like an angel, my dear, absolutely beautiful. It's you!" Martha said.

"I can't wait for James to see me in this dress."

"Not until the wedding, my dear. It's bad luck for the groom to see the bride in her gown prior to the wedding day, you know."

Delilah smiled, "I don't believe that…but I'll wait anyway, just in case."

They giggled and told the sales clerk to place it in a box; they would take it with them.

A few doors down the block was the jewelry store. Delilah had never seen so many rings, chains, brooches, bracelets, cameos; and such exquisite gold, silver, and valuable stones. She did not know where to start and relied on selections from Martha and the jeweler.

She tried on many styles, some gaudy, some ornate; but said, "No, they're not quite right."

She pointed at a set of plain gold bands and said, "That one; let me see that one please. Yes, this is all we need. These will do nicely."

Martha said, "Are you sure, Delilah? There are a lot of prettier rings here."

"Oh Martha, love is in your heart, not in a piece of metal that you wear on your finger. These will do just fine."

The jeweler was amazed at how the ring fit her finger perfectly and needed no resizing. She had to guess at Jameson's size, but after holding his hand so much, she instinctively knew the correct measurement for her man's finger. They took the rings and were on their way to the engraver.

They picked out the invitations and the printer, with a little urging from Mrs. Barrington, promised them for tomorrow. There it was in black and white, for all the world to see, etched forever on a piece of paper; Delilah was to be married to Jameson Hartford. It was a dream come true. Delilah was so excited that all the preparations were neatly falling into place.

The church, on the other hand, was not so cooperative. They refused to perform the ceremony, citing a variety of nonsensical reasons. When they were challenged by Martha, the real reason became clear. They would not perform an interracial marriage. Mrs. Barrington protested, saying that God does not discriminate based on skin color and neither should his church. The protest fell on deaf ears; they were still denied. The same reason was given at every place of worship they visited. It seemed that the arm of bigotry knew no borders and extended all the way up North, even as far as Boston. Dejected, they returned home.

After hearing the sad story, Millie and Belle told Delilah that they were sure she would be able to get married in their church. They all quickly set out for the place of worship and were eagerly accepted, no questions asked. The all-black church bore no bias or unfriendly attitude toward the interracial couple but welcomed them with open arms. The wedding date was planned. Everything was set.

Millie asked Delilah if Dawnalee had been baptized. Delilah did not understand the custom, but after Millie explained the tradition, she made plans on the spot to have the child christened that Sunday after services. She asked Nanny and Martha to be twin godmothers. Delilah also wanted to give her baby a baptismal name and did not have to think very long to come up with the perfect second name.

Wedding invitations were sent out to all their friends, old and new, even former acquaintances of Jameson and Abigail, though Delilah was apprehensive of the latter. She acquiesced to Jameson's wishes but hoped he would not be hurt if his one-time friends declined the request.

Jameson had a hard time finding employment. The reasons for refusal were many and varied, but they could all be summed up in one word—bigotry. He was ready to give up when Martha Barrington once again came to the rescue. She convinced him to open his own business and agreed to offer him her financial support. Since his chosen field was financial, he decided to open his own bank but one that catered primarily to the poor and downtrodden, the people that really needed help, especially the black community. They were working and needed a safe, secure place to entrust their hard-earned cash.

He hired primarily Negro personnel, including Zeke, Sarah, and Lewis, instructing them and helping them to become independent. The other financial institutions scoffed at the idea, but one by one their black depositors withdrew all their funds and moved their accounts over to Jameson's bank. When word spread what Jameson and Delilah had done for the one-time slaves, poor people of both colors made it their bank of choice. They came from near and far to open accounts and secure loans that other banks refused to grant them. Jameson was happy not only for his success but for the fact that he was able to employ so many poor people who needed jobs and were grateful for the opportunity to prove themselves. Even young Ozzie managed a part-time job at the bank while attending school during the day.

After services on Sunday, the engaged couple, their child, Nanny, and Mrs. Barrington, along with their friends, were all gathered at the church for the baptism. Jameson wore a dark suit. Delilah wore a tan dress with matching hat and shoes. Dawnalee was clad in a white satin outfit. She cried incessantly as she was dipped into the fountain of water and blessed with oil in the name of the Father, the Son, and the Holy Ghost. The two godmothers promised to raise her in the Christian faith if both parents failed to do so. Delilah told the pastor she wished her daughter to be baptized with the name…Faith.

She proudly stated, "My mother always told me that our people must have faith that one day we will all be free, and faith will keep our spirits high until that day arrives."

A loud amen filled the small church and rose to the rafters, straight up to the heavens and directly to God's ears.

Delilah continued, "And thanks to this special man"—she pointed her finger at Jameson—"things are getting better already."

Jameson was proud but also a little embarrassed. He did not feel as though he was special and thought all men should have felt the way he did and fought for equality.

Delilah added, "My child will not be raised in a world of hate but rather a world of love and tolerance for all people regardless of their skin color."

Another amen rang out loud and clear from all those in attendance, including Jameson and Mrs. Barrington.

Dawnalee quickly quieted down once she was returned to her mother's loving arms, and with the ceremony concluded, they all walked out of church to the sounds of sweet gospel music. Filled with a renewed vigor, they returned solemnly to their homes.

The invitations were returning, and sadly, to no one's surprise, not one of Jameson's or Abigail's former friends accepted the request to attend the wedding. Jameson was not to be dissuaded and was happy that his real friends would be there. Delilah felt bad for her soon-to-be husband and retaliated by requesting Millie to remove Abigail's many portraits that lined the walls and place them in trunks in the attic. This was her home now, and she did not want anyone, particularly Jameson, to be reminded of the former tenant. Millie gladly acquiesced to the wishes of the new lady of the house.

Delilah checked on the sleeping baby and then went into her bedroom. She had one more piece of business to attend to before the wedding. She took a pair of scissors and, looking at herself in the full-length mirror, started to cut her hair. She had not cut it in quite some time, and it had grown long. Although Jameson had not said anything, she remembered how he told her he thought she looked beautiful in short hair and she was going to surprise him.

Piece by piece the lengths of hair fell to the floor, forming a small pile. She took one of the two long mirrors and propped it up on the floor against the bed and then positioned herself in between them so she could also cut the back of her head. She kept cutting and cutting, and soon she was satisfied with the results.

She stood there staring at herself, realizing how different she looked in short hair. She thought it made her look more confident and sure of herself. The door unexpectedly opened, and she was shocked to see Jameson standing there. He stood gazing at her for a moment then grabbed her and kissed her deeply, running his hands through the little wisps of hair. He told her she looked beautiful, and they kissed long and deep. Falling on the bed, they made passionate love to each other for the last time as single people.

The day of the wedding approached rapidly. It was a sunny, crisp autumn day. Leaves of yellow, orange, and red filled the trees and lined the walkways. Everything was set for the big day, and everyone was anxious for the festivities to begin.

Jameson arrived at the church looking sophisticated in his dark suit, complemented with a white ruffle shirt and solid black tie. Zeke was his best man, and Ozzie was the ring bearer, each looking dapper in their new suits as well. The altar was covered with many flowers and candles, while spiritual hymns echoed through the cavernous hall. The men stood patiently together, nervously waiting for the guest of honor to arrive. The pews were lined with all their friends and loved ones. Nanny, dressed in a beautiful auburn gown, was in the first row clutching little Dawnalee.

A hush fell on the crowd as they all turned to witness Delilah enter the church from the rear with Martha Barrington at her side. As she came into view, you could hear whispers emanating from the congregation.

"Isn't she beautiful?"

"How pretty that girl looks."

"She could be a princess."

Jameson's mouth inadvertently dropped open as he stared at his bride to be.

He whispered to Zeke, "She's the most beautiful woman I've ever seen in all my life."

Delilah's elegant white satin gown was covered in beads, pearls, and sequins. It clung to her every curve as she strolled down the aisle. All eyes were transfixed on the stunning woman. Her tiara headdress and long veil tried but could not conceal the happiness that radiated from inside her. Sweet organ music filled the air as she sashayed down the aisle, her hips swinging in rhythm to the soulful sounds. When she approached the altar, Jameson reached out and took her hand.

"Delilah, my love, you look so beautiful."

She beamed a broad smile as a tear ran down her cheek, only this time it was a tear of pure joy. Jameson led her up the altar to the awaiting preacher. Martha sat down next to Nanny.

Jameson and Delilah held hands as the preacher read the vows.

"Do you, Jameson Lee Hartford, take this woman, Delilah, to be your lawfully wedded wife, to love, honor, and cherish in sickness and in health, for richer or poorer, from this day forward until death do you part?"

Jameson looked with love at this beautiful woman before him. They had been through so much together and had almost lost each other so many times. The moment they had waited for had finally arrived. He confidently stated, "I do."

"And do you, Delilah, take this man, Jameson Lee Hartford, to be your lawfully wedded husband, to love, honor, and obey in sickness and in health, for richer or poorer, from this day forward until death do you part?"

Delilah lovingly looked at the man who risked his own life in order to give her a new life because he loved her above all else. She proudly said, "I do."

They each sealed their promises with matching gold bands that they placed on each other's fingers as a symbol of their undying love for one another.

The preacher then loudly proclaimed, "I now pronounce you man and wife. What God has joined together, let no man separate."

Jameson lifted her veil and, amidst tear-filled eyes, kissed her tender lips. "I love you, Mrs. Delilah Hartford."

"I love you too, James." She hesitated and then asked," Say my name again, please."

"Mrs. Delilah Hartford."

"I finally have a last name, a loving husband, and a family. Thank you, James."

"No, thank you, Delilah, for helping me fulfill my dream and for loving me."

They kissed again as the whole assembly applauded. Then Mr. and Mrs. Hartford left the altar and walked proudly, hand in hand, down the aisle and waited at the back of the church to greet all their guests.

As they left the church, a hail storm of rice rained down on the new couple. They entered the waiting coach and were whisked away to the reception at Martha Barrington's.

It was to be a huge gala with plenty to eat and drink. They danced the night away, happy to be in each other's arms and savoring every moment. The hours flew by, and soon the party began to conclude. Jameson and Delilah thanked everyone for attending and for making this day possible. Then they silently slipped out the side door and, hand in hand, ran across the adjoining lawns to their home and safe haven. Jameson paused at the front door, gazed at his beautiful new wife, swept her up into his arms, and carried her across the threshold as she giggled with delight. He continued straight up the stairs and into their bedroom, where they would celebrate their first union as man and wife.

Outside, the war, racial tensions, and bigotry raged on, but in their home and in their world there was only peace and love. It was a long time coming, but through their love and perseverance, they succeeded. They vowed to live happily ever after if the world would only let them.

The Beginning

APPENDIX

Dear Reader,

In order to keep my manuscript safe from being pilfered by unscrupulous agents and publishers while I attempted to get it published, I conceived a devious scheme to secure my authorship without having to copyright it. I cleverly hid twenty-five Beatles song titles within the text of my book. These tiles appear haphazardly throughout the novel.

So, as an added attraction, just for you, my fellow readers, see if you are able to find the titles as you read or re-read the story. The song titles are listed alphabetically on the next two pages so you can mark them off as you find them. However, this is not the order in which they appear in the book. If you give up, the solution is printed on the following page by chapter, page number, and title.

Enjoy!

"A splendid time is guaranteed for all."

—from "Being for the Benefit of Mister Kite"

"And I Love Her"

"Blue Jay Way"

"Dear Prudence"

"Doctor Robert"

"Getting Better"

"Good Morning, Good Morning"

"Good Night"

"Help!"

"Helter Skelter"

"I Feel Fine"

"I Need You"

"I Should Have Known Better"

"It Won't Be Long"

"Let It Be"

"Long, Long, Long"

"Norwegian Wood"

"Not a Second Time"

"Revolution"

"Run for Your Life"

"Something"

"The Night Before"

"Tomorrow Never Knows"

"We Can Work It Out"

"Yes, It Is"

"Yesterday"

BEATLES TITLE SEARCH KEY